Aetherbound
Where Shadows Break

by
J. L. Athey

AETHERBOUND

Where Shadows Break

by

J. L. Athey

Cover design by Rachel Bostwick

Interior formatting by Rachel Bostwick

ISBN: 979-8-9930621-0-5

Printed in USA

First Edition

Dedication

This book is dedicated to my son. As you grow older and begin to go on your own adventures, remember that no matter what happens, daddy will always love you.

TABLE OF CONTENTS

PROLOGUE

They didn't notice when she left.

No one stood at the edge of the village. No one wept or begged her to stay. The house was still dark when she walked past it—just another shadow slipping into morning fog.

One satchel. One knife. Half a loaf of bread. She figured it was more than most got.

The road stretched ahead like a dare.

She didn't look back.

Cass had lived her whole life in that nowhere town, tucked between hills that rolled like bruises and fields that never grew enough. She'd watched her mother die in that village. Watched her father drink himself halfway into the grave trying to forget it. Watched boys grow into bitter men who measured worth by how many teeth they had left after a fight.

She hadn't come from a place where people dreamed. She'd come from a place where people settled.

And she wasn't built for settling.

She remembered the night she made the choice. She'd been standing behind the tavern with scraped knuckles and a bloody lip—again. One of the local sons thought "no" was negotiable. She taught him otherwise.

Her father had said nothing when she came home bruised. Just looked at her like she'd disappointed the air around her.

That night, she packed what she could and slipped out the window.

No grand goodbye. No dramatic farewell. Just mud, mist, and silence.

She told herself it would be better this way. That somewhere out there, the world was waiting for her. A place where she could be more than a name people spat when she passed. Somewhere that gave a damn about cleverness and speed. Somewhere she wouldn't have to fight just to be seen.

Cass wanted to matter.

She didn't want to die in a place that had already buried her.

The first few days on the road were harder than she'd admit. She stole bread. Slept in ditches. Got chased out of a barn by a goat she later tried to stab for dinner. She missed warmth. She missed the way the wind didn't cut through every seam in her coat.

But she never turned back.

Not even when her feet bled. Not even when she got so hungry she licked crumbs off a windowsill.

Because there was something in her chest—tight and quiet and stubborn as hell—that whispered:

You can be more than this.

And she believed it.

Eventually, she made it to the city. And when she saw the guild board for the first time—its paper edges curled from sun and wind, ink bleeding with promises of gold, adventure, and danger—she thought, *this is it*. This is the start of something.

She didn't know yet how hard it would be. How much it would ask of her. That someday, she'd hold a blade in her hand and stare down at something dying and realize there was no going back.

That moment hadn't come yet.

But it was waiting.

Chapter 1

FIRST STEPS, FALSE SMILES

Tarn

T he plaza was crowded, but the crowd gave way. They always did. Steel and a hammer at your side have a way of parting people more surely than words. Sunlight struck my armor and sent whispers following in my wake. Awe. Fear. Curiosity. None of it mattered. I had grown used to being looked at without being seen.

The Adventurer's Guild towered over the square, its white stone walls bright against the sprawl of stalls below. Smoke, sweat, and salt stung the air. Merchants hawked skewers of spiced meat, knives dulled from overuse, charms that hummed faintly with counterfeit magic. The town was a storm of desperation and hunger.

And then came the pull.

Guidance. Not a voice, not a command—just direction. Subtle as breath, steady as a heartbeat. It had never failed me, even when I wished it would.

It led my eyes to the job board. And to her.

She sat in the shadow of the wall, half-hidden by the press of bodies, trying to look like she belonged. Mud streaked her boots, her stockings were torn through. Her shirt clung unevenly to one shoulder, tucked behind pouches that sagged empty. A red ribbon tied back her hair, frayed and faded, the kind of thing you kept long after it stopped being useful.

And she was smiling.

It wasn't joy. It was armor, brittle and false, stretched across hunger. Hunger for coin. For purpose. To matter.

I knew that look. I'd worn it myself.

I stopped in front of her.

"Looking for work?" I asked.

She blinked up, surprise flickering before the grin returned. "That obvious?" Her voice was steady, though her throat worked around the words. "Depends what kind of work you mean."

"I'm heading into the Enchanted Forest. Contracts first—small hunts, monster culls, bandits. When you're ready, we go deeper. There's a dungeon in the heart of it."

Her eyebrows rose, and with them a glint of something sharper than the grin. "Straight to the dangerous part, then. I can move quiet, put a blade where it hurts, and vanish when I need to. Never stepped foot in a dungeon, but... no better way to learn than by surviving it."

"Survival comes before learning," I said.

She tilted her head, as if weighing me. "Fair enough. Cassidy," she said at last. "Cass, if you like. What do I call you? Sir Knight? Or is there a man under all that steel?"

"Tarn."

She tested the name with her tongue, then smirked faintly. "Tarn and Cass. Has a ring to it."

Her body was wiry, her arms nicked with scars, but it was the limp she tried to hide that told me the most. She leaned on her left side wrong.

I should have walked away. She was wounded, untested, desperate. But her mask was too familiar to ignore. To pass her by in shining steel while she rotted in rags would have been no different than turning my back on myself.

"Those wounds will slow us both. Let me heal them."

Her smile faltered. Pride warred with pain before she gave a short, uneven laugh. "Didn't think a stranger would waste magic on me. But... I won't say no."

She lifted her shirt. Purple bruises sprawled across her ribs, cuts raw and shallow. The mask slipped entirely then, her grin falling away.

"All right," she murmured.

I whispered the prayer. Golden light pooled in my palms, spilling into torn flesh. She gasped softly.

"That's... strange," she whispered. "Like warmth in places I'd forgotten I had."

When I finished, she lowered her shirt, watching me differently now. "Better," she said. Then, softer: "Thank you."

"This gear won't keep you alive long," I said, nodding to her rags. "We're stopping at the tailor."

She raised a brow. "First you patch me up, now you're buying me clothes? Careful, Tarn. People might start thinking you're kind."

I didn't answer.

..———..

The walk to the tailor was short. Cass filled the silence with words, as if quiet pressed too close.

"That vendor tried to sell me a luck charm once," she said, pointing to a stall of cloudy gems. "I tripped into a chicken coop five minutes later. Still not sure if that was the charm or just me."

She tossed a copper coin into a fountain as we passed.

"For luck," she said when she caught my look. "Couldn't hurt. Maybe it'll buy me one less scar."

Then she spun once, arms spread, ribbon catching the light for a heartbeat. "I used to dream about this," she said more softly. "Not the hunger. Not the bruises. But walking into a town, finding a partner, stepping into danger like the stories. Makes the pain worth it. Even if I fail tomorrow."

Her grin wavered, but she held it anyway.

I'd seen too many like her chewed apart before they ever had a chance. Most I could pass by, nameless, faceless. But not this one. Not after that look she gave me—grinning through the cracks.

The tailor's shop sat wedged between a blacksmith and a scribe's kiosk, the clamor of hammer and quill cut off by the bell's chime. Warm air greeted us, thick with the scent of cloth and polish.

Cass darted inside first. "Something dark," she said quickly. "Easy to move in. Enough pockets to hide trouble. Nothing that screams 'steal me'."

I scanned the racks. Most of it was showy—good for mercenaries who wanted to look dangerous, not survive it. At last I pulled a moss-green tunic, brown leather pants, a reinforced vest.

"This," I said.

She raised a brow. "Not much for style. But practical keeps you alive, doesn't it?"

"It does."

And it would keep her alive. That mattered more than I wanted to admit. She wasn't my responsibility. Not yet. But the thought of sending her into the forest dressed in rags... no. I'd lost enough people already. I wouldn't watch another fall because I failed to prepare them.

"Then it'll do," she said, disappearing behind the curtain.

Her voice drifted out. "So. Why no party? You don't look like the loner type."

"A story for another time."

A pause.

"My village called me a fool," she said quietly. "I left anyway. Slept in barns. Learned how to vanish when I had to."

The curtain slid back.

She stepped out, the clothes fitting her better than I expected. She looked like she belonged in them.

"This feels right," she said, almost to herself. "Like I was always meant to wear it. Just needed someone to see it."

Then she tugged at the vest, grinning faintly. "Plenty of space for knives. No obvious bloodstains. Perfect."

She caught my forearm suddenly, her grip firmer than I expected.

"We'll make a good team, Tarn. I can feel it."

Her words shouldn't have mattered. She was untested, half-starved, and too quick to smile through the cracks. But something in them settled into place, heavy as a vow. Against my better judgment, I believed her.

The shopkeeper returned. Cass leaned casually against the counter, voice light, eyes alert. Her fingers ghosted across a display, palmed a silver thimble, and slipped it into her vest.

"First loot of the adventure," she whispered to me with a flash of teeth. "Not theft. Just an advance."

I sighed.

She grinned wider. "Come on. Let's go earn something real."

We stepped out into the street. Together.

Chapter 2

BLOOD ON THE LEAVES

Cass

T he town shrank behind us with every step, its noise bleeding away into the hush of the open road. Sunlight spilled through scattered trees, painting the dirt path in broken gold. The air was sharp with pine and damp earth—cleaner, truer—nothing like the stink of sweat, coin, and desperation choking the square.

I walked a little ahead, half to prove I wasn't afraid and half to hide that I was. Every time I glanced back, Tarn was there: plate gleaming, hammer steady at his hip, his eyes never still. Always searching. Always watching. He looked like a man built for war, too calm for someone walking into the unknown.

Me? I'd spent years surviving alleys and rooftops, clawing my way through scraps, convincing myself I was meant for more. Now that I was finally here, stomach twisting with every step, I wondered if the stories had left out the part where your legs wanted to give out before the first mile.

I tried to fill the silence with words. "You know," I said, flashing a grin over my shoulder, "I once saw a man lose to a mimic at cards. Beat him with a royal flush. Should've seen his face when the table grew teeth."

Tarn gave me a single nod, as if I'd just told him the weather was clear.

I blew out a breath. Typical.

Mud sucked at my boot, pulling me off balance. Crouching low, I pointed toward a rabbit chewing clover like it owned the place. "Threat spotted."

The rabbit twitched its ears and bounded away, unimpressed. I slid my dagger back into its sheath with deliberate solemnity. "Crisis averted. Saving our steel for things with sharper teeth."

Nothing from Tarn. His gaze swept the treeline, shield angled just slightly as if danger could leap out at any second. It put a chill in my chest. Not because I doubted him—because he was the sort of man who *expected* trouble with every breath.

The deeper we walked, the quieter it grew. Not peaceful quiet—watchful. Heavy. Like the forest itself was listening.

"So," I said, my voice too loud in the hush, "you've done this before?"

Tarn nodded once. "Years ago. I'll take point. You climb. Stay above me. If something comes, I'll draw them. You flank."

I arched a brow. "Not exactly a jungle panther. More of a rooftop stray. But fine."

He didn't wait for me to agree. He just moved forward, shield lifted, every step purposeful.

I found a thick oak, dug my fingers into the bark, and climbed. Clumsy, maybe, but fast. Leaves brushed my face as I hauled myself up, higher until I could see him below—solid, unshakable, every inch of him deliberate.

"I'll signal if I see anything," I called softly. "Try not to mistake it for me falling."

The words barely left my mouth before the branch cracked beneath me.

The ground hit like a hammer to the ribs. Air ripped from my lungs. I rolled, coughing—and froze.

A goblin stared back at me.

It clutched a stolen chicken, feathers twitching beneath its claws. Its yellow eyes went wide, as startled as mine.

For one stupid second, neither of us moved.

"Wrong nest," I muttered, and threw my dagger. It sailed wide, thunking uselessly into a root.

The goblin shrieked and bolted, feathers scattering.

I pushed to my feet, heart racing. The undergrowth stirred, rustling low. Growls bled from the shadows. Shapes moved—small, fast, too many.

Four of them. Two with bows. One with a cleaver. Another sprinting at me, teeth bared, eager for blood.

"Tarn!"

He was already coming.

The first arrow shattered against his shield with a metallic scream. He didn't flinch. His hammer swung in a clean, perfect arc. The goblin with the cleaver dropped where it stood, skull caved in.

The others shrieked, but Tarn never rushed. He advanced with steady precision, shield shifting, hammer rising again, every step deliberate.

I'd seen fighters scrap in back alleys, all wild swings and rage. This was different. Tarn moved like a man who'd killed too many times to waste motion. Like every strike meant something.

And then I remembered the one sprinting at me.

It slammed into me with a snarl, jagged blade catching the light. I staggered, brought my dagger up just in time. Steel scraped steel, sparks spitting into my eyes. My arms trembled.

I twisted, desperate. *Precision, not power,* I told myself. That's what the stolen manuals always said. I feinted left, slid low, and drove my dagger into its ribs.

Hot blood slicked my hand. The goblin gasped but didn't fall.

Pain lanced through me as an arrow tore across my thigh. I screamed, dropped low, and crawled behind Tarn's shield.

My chest heaved, my hands shaking. But I forced a grin. "New plan. You smash. I'll... stay out of your way."

He didn't answer. He was already chanting, his voice low, deliberate. Light sparked faintly at the edges of his armor, dangerous and restrained.

That was the first time it struck me. Tarn's hammer and shield came first. His magic wasn't a tool—it was something rarer, something costly. Something he wouldn't spend unless it mattered.

The realization set my heart hammering harder than the goblins had.

Light flared. Tarn surged forward, shield raised, hammer drawn back. The goblins shrieked, unnerved by the glow seeping from the seams of his armor, but he didn't falter.

The nearest archer loosed. The arrow shattered against steel, shards spraying harmlessly. Tarn didn't slow. His hammer swung in a brutal arc. Wood splintered, bone cracked. The goblin dropped without a sound.

It should have felt like justice. Instead, it was terrifying.

I pushed myself upright, thigh burning from the arrow's graze, my dagger slick with blood from the one I'd struck. That goblin had already staggered away into the shadows, clutching its wound, leaving a dark trail in the dirt.

The rest fell to Tarn.

Another arrow screamed through the air. His shield snapped up, steel ringing under the impact. He pressed forward without hurry, every step purposeful, every strike final. The second archer shrieked, fumbling its bow. Tarn closed the distance in three strides and brought the hammer down. One clean arc, one body less.

And then silence.

The clearing stank of iron and smoke. My lungs dragged in shallow, uneven breaths. I pressed a hand to my thigh, feeling the sticky warmth where the arrow had grazed me, trying to breathe past the fire in my leg.

Tarn stood in the center of the carnage, shield still lifted, hammer dripping. His gaze moved steadily across the treeline, sharp and relentless, as if the forest itself might try to deceive him. He looked untouched, carved from stone.

I hated that part of me wanted to lean on that steadiness.

Instead, I crouched and forced myself to focus. *Loot the bodies*, I thought. That's what adventurers did, right? Make it practical. Make it routine.

The first pouch I checked held little—knotted twine, a root chewed to the marrow. Another corpse carried a shard of black glass, edges sharp enough to slice skin. Worthless. But one body bore a shortbow across its back. Crude, frayed string, splintered grip—but still a bow.

I tested the pull. Rough, but workable. I slung it over my shoulder. "Rogue and archer now," I muttered. "At this pace I'll be a walking armory."

The words came out bitter. Hollow.

Tarn was kneeling by another corpse, something small and wax-sealed in his hand. A scroll, runes etched deep into its surface. He turned it slowly, unreadable, before slipping it into his pack.

I wanted to ask. I didn't.

I wiped my blade in the grass, but the blood smeared instead of coming clean. The coppery scent clung to my gloves, heavy and wrong.

"You get used to this?" I asked. My voice cracked despite myself.

Tarn shook his head. "No."

The word landed heavier than silence.

I swallowed, throat tight, and turned away. That was when I saw it.

The goblin I'd stabbed earlier slumped at the base of a tree. Its chest still rose and fell in shallow, rattling breaths. Blood stained its side, but not enough to end it. Not yet.

Its eyes found mine.

I froze.

It should have snarled. Should have clawed. But it only watched me. Calm. Aware. Waiting.

The dagger felt like lead in my hand. My pulse pounded in my ears.

"I thought..." My voice was barely a whisper. "I thought it was gone."

Tarn stepped beside me, his shadow stretching long across the ground. He looked at the goblin once, then at me, unreadable.

"Sometimes," he said quietly, "the choice lingers."

The goblin's lips twitched faintly. Not a snarl. Not a plea. Something else. Its gaze didn't waver, even as its chest rattled with every shallow breath.

My knees locked. Every story I'd told myself about being an adventurer cracked under that stare. Monsters weren't supposed to look at you like they understood.

"I can't," I whispered. "Not when it's like this."

I turned to Tarn, begging silently for him to take it away, to finish it for me.

But he didn't. He didn't raise his hammer. He didn't move at all. His hand only settled on my shoulder, heavy and steady as stone.

"Mercy," he said. "Even when it hurts."

My dagger shook in my grip. It should've been simple. Monsters were supposed to be faceless, things you cut down and walked away from. But this one had a face. And it wouldn't stop looking at me.

My throat closed. "I don't know if I can."

Tarn didn't move. His hand stayed on my shoulder, steady as stone. He didn't push. Didn't take the choice. He just stood there, waiting.

The silence pressed in. My heartbeat roared in my ears. I wanted him to end it for me. To take it out of my hands. But he didn't.

The goblin's lips twitched faintly, as if it already knew what had to happen. My stomach turned to lead.

I knelt, knees sinking into the dirt. The dagger felt heavier with every inch I raised it.

"I'm not a killer," I whispered, voice breaking. "This isn't who I am."

Tarn knelt behind me, close but not touching. His voice was low, almost gentle. "Mercy is harder than killing in anger. That's why it matters."

Tears blurred my sight. The goblin blinked once, slow, as if granting me permission.

I lowered the blade.

My lips trembled around the words. "I'm sorry."

The dagger slid home. The goblin exhaled one last breath, soft, almost relieved. Then it was still.

I dropped the blade. Blood seeped across my gloves, warm and slick, filling the cracks in my skin. My breath came ragged, torn from my chest.

Tarn said nothing.

I stumbled back, the weight of it crushing me. I couldn't stop shaking. My throat burned. "Gods... I didn't think it would feel like this. I thought it would be—cleaner."

My chest collapsed under a sob. I pressed a bloodied hand to my face, smearing red across my cheek. "I thought I was ready."

For a moment, Tarn didn't move. He stayed where he was, silent, as if unsure what I needed. Then I moved first.

I reached for him. My hands caught his arm, clung to the weight of his armor.

Only then did he shift. Slow. Careful. He let me lean against him, one arm finally settling around my shoulders. Hesitant at first, but solid once it was there. Not tender. Not romantic. Just... steady.

I buried my face against cold steel and let the sobs come.

Tarn didn't speak. He didn't try to soothe me with hollow words. He just held, letting me tremble and break until the storm inside me began to quiet.

When I finally pulled away, my eyes burned, throat raw. I wiped at my face with a dirty sleeve, leaving streaks of blood and tears.

"Some rogue I am," I muttered hoarsely. "Terrifying, right? Crying in the dirt."

"You're still standing," Tarn said simply.

A bitter laugh tore out of me. "Barely."

"You showed mercy," he said. His voice was flat, but it carried weight. "That makes you stronger than most."

I didn't know if I believed him. But I wanted to.

The silence stretched. The forest, heavy before, felt lighter now—though not forgiving. Just watching again.

We left the clearing. My legs felt leaden. My new bow dug against my shoulder. The blood on my gloves stuck tacky between my fingers. No matter how much I flexed them, the stickiness clung.

Tarn walked a pace behind, shield lowered now, hammer at his side. He didn't look at me. Didn't need to. His presence pressed at my back like a wall.

We walked until the sound of water reached us. A low, steady rush, faint at first, then clearer.

"The river," I whispered, voice raw.

Tarn nodded. "We'll clean up. Rest."

The river wound through a dip in the trees, its surface catching the last scraps of daylight. I crouched by the bank and plunged my hands in. The water ran cold, stinging my skin, turning pink before the current carried it away.

I scrubbed until the ache dulled. But when I pulled my hands back, I swore I could still feel the blood there. Still smell it.

19

Tarn knelt a few feet away, rinsing his hammer and shield with the same methodical care he gave every strike. He didn't look up.

I sat back on my heels, staring at the water. My reflection stared back, blurred, eyes rimmed red, ribbon in my hair gone limp. Not a rogue. Not yet. Just a girl who'd made her first kill and couldn't forget the look in its eyes.

The silence between us wasn't heavy anymore. Just present.

"We keep moving at first light," Tarn said at last.

I nodded. My voice wouldn't come.

As the river whispered on, I knew nothing about the stories I'd told myself was true. This wasn't adventure. This wasn't glory.

This was blood. And mercy. And the kind of weight you couldn't wash away.

Chapter 3

THE WEIGHT OF QUIET THINGS

Cass

The river was colder than I expected. Not the kind of refreshing cold that wakes you up, but the kind that cuts past your skin and settles into your bones. I knelt at the edge, plunging my hands in up to the wrists, scrubbing at blood already half-dried and crusted beneath my fingernails. The cut on my leg throbbed in time with my heartbeat, but it was a quiet kind of pain now. Background noise.

I splashed water on my face next, hoping to wash off something more than dirt. The goblin's eyes still lingered behind mine. I'd never killed before. Not like that. Not with so much... awareness. Mercy, Tarn had said. But mercy didn't feel clean. It didn't feel righteous. It just felt heavy.

Behind me, Tarn moved in his quiet, deliberate way. Armor removed, his boots shifting over dry leaves, tent unrolled, stakes set into the soil. The steady rhythm of someone who had done this all before. Someone who could sleep next to guilt without needing to name it.

I hated him a little for that. And I hated myself more for not being able to.

I breathed deep and let the wind dry my face, watching the current swirl away the evidence of what had transpired. I didn't hear Tarn approach, but I felt him, steady and quiet like always.

When I turned, he held something out.

The scroll—old, but sealed in soft wax and etched with faintly glowing runes.

"This is for you," he said.

I wiped my hands on my trousers before taking it. "You're giving me treasure now? I didn't think we were that close."

"It's a skill scroll. Rare. They imprint on whoever opens them."

"Wait," I turned it over in my hands. "You're giving this to me?"

"You earned it." His eyes met mine, anxious to see what ability scroll would imprint on me.

The seal snapped easily. The parchment unfurled, the runes on it pulsing. For a moment, the symbols twisted like smoke, then surged towards my chest. I gasped as a jolt ran through me—sharp, warm, and then gone.

The words burned behind my eyes:

Shadow Step—Short ranged teleport to a visible shadow. Usable three times daily.

I stumbled back a step, laughing in disbelief. "No way."

Tarn arched an eyebrow.

"I can freaking *teleport*!" I whooped. "To shadows! Okay, only a few times, and only if I can see them, but still!"

I take a few steps forward, wobbling on my injured leg.

"Watch this."

I focus on the shadow of a nearby boulder—and vanish. For a heartbeat, the world twists, then I'm stumbling out of the boulder's shade, giggling like an idiot.

"Holy shit," I gasped, laughing. "You gave me a magic trick."

Tarn smiled faintly. "A useful one."

"I'm gonna be insufferable with this," I warned him, beaming as I made my way back toward the river. "You just handed a rogue the keys to chaos. And you're not even going to lecture me about using it responsibly? Who are you and what have you done with Tarn?"

His smile faded. "You'll need it."

That sobered me fast.

I dropped back to my knees by the water and began scrubbing my vest. "Thanks. For the scroll. And... everything else."

"You've held up well."

I snorted. "That's generous."

"You didn't run."

"I thought about it," I admitted. "That goblin... it looked at me like it understood. Like it forgave me." I squeezed the fabric until my knuckles went white. "I thought I could be someone who made the hard calls. You know? Like in the stories. Stab, loot, move on. But it wasn't like that."

"No," Tarn said softly. "It rarely is."

I wrung out the vest and laid it on a rock to dry. "So what now, oh wise mentor of mine? Is this the part where you suggest I get dinner to distract me from my moral unraveling?"

He handed me the bow. "It might help."

I sighed, taking it. "I swear, if I miss and have to come back with berries, I'm blaming you."

I headed into the woods with the bow in hand, biting my tongue to keep from cursing at the soreness in my leg. The forest was quiet in that heavy way it gets before nightfall– even the birds were beginning to go silent.

I moved slow, keeping low, every step careful. The new bow felt strange in my hands–rough, unfamiliar. I'd never hunted before, not like this. Back home, food came from bartering, stealing, or begging. There were no clean kills, just survival.

The wind shifted, carrying the faintest rustle. I paused behind a tree, heart thumping. A rabbit–a small one–nibbled at a patch of clover not ten paces away.

I crouched lower, steadying the bow, drawing the string back with trembling fingers. "C'mon," I whispered. "Just this once, let me get it right."

I exhaled. Loosed the arrow.

It struck true. The rabbit fell instantly.

I didn't cheer. I didn't move right away. I just stared at it, heart sinking as relief and sorrow tangled in my chest. It was so small.

"Sorry," I murmured. "But I need this."

I picked it up gently, cradling it against my side as I turned back toward camp.

The forest was painted in gold and fire now, the sun sinking low behind the trees. Shadows stretched long across the path as I walked, every step taking me farther from who I used to be.

I stepped into the clearing just as Tarn coaxed the fire into a steady flame, sparks drifting up like fireflies. He didn't look up right away, but I could see the tension in his shoulders relax as I approached.

"Guess who bagged dinner on her first try?" I called, holding the rabbit aloft like a trophy.

Tarn glanced over, then returned to stacking kindling around the growing blaze. "Well done."

"That's it? No applause? No 'wow, Cass, you're amazing, please teach me your ways'?"

He gave the faintest smile. "I was hoping for something bigger."

I scoffed, tossing the rabbit down beside him. "Next time I'll bring you a bear."

He didn't respond, but when our eyes met, something in his expression softened—quiet pride, maybe. Or relief. It made my chest ache a little.

I sat down across from him, the fire warm against my shins. "Told you I could handle myself."

Tarn nodded. "I never said you couldn't."

Tarn took the rabbit without a word, his movements calm, practiced. He cleaned it with efficient strokes of his knife, not hurried, but not hesitant either. The firelight flickered along the blade as he worked, illuminating the ridges of his forearms.

I watched in silence, arms wrapped around my knees. He wasn't squeamish about blood. He didn't flinch. Just cleaned, carved, and skewered the meat on a branch he'd shaved bare a few minutes earlier.

"You've done this before," I said quietly.

Tarn set the spit across the fire, adjusting it with a small tilt of his hand. "Too many times."

The fat began to sizzle, dripping into the flames below. Smoke curled upward in lazy spirals.

"Still," I added, softer now, "you're good at it."

He didn't answer. But he sat beside me after a moment, watching the rabbit turn over the fire like it was the only thing left in the world worth tending.

The fire crackled between us, casting shadows that danced along Tarn's face. He sat with his arms braced on his knees, gaze fixed on the meat turning above the flames like he could out-stare the past.

I shifted closer, not enough to touch, but enough to feel the edge of his warmth. Without his armor on, Tarn seemed less of a walking fortress and more... Human.

"So," I said, trying for lightness, "what's the real story behind you? No vague 'fresh start' crap this time."

His lips twitched, but he didn't look at me.

I leaned in a little. "C'mon, we're sharing a tent tonight. Might as well share some secrets too."

Silence stretched long enough that I thought he might ignore the question altogether. But then he said, quietly, "It's not a story I enjoy telling."

My bravado slipped. "I didn't mean to push."

"You didn't," he said. "You just asked. Most don't."

He didn't speak right away after that. Just watched the fire, like he was waiting for the right part of himself to surface.

The fire crackles between us, but I barely hear it.

My breath catches as Tarn peels off his tunic, revealing a battlefield of scars—some thin and faded, others jagged and angry.

"What the hells did that to you?" I swallow hard, suddenly aware of how small my own scrapes and bruises are in comparison.

Tarn began to speak, his voice full of pain, sorrow, *loss*. "I... I used to be a platinum rank. My party was a part of the Embersworn, the Church of the First Flame's favored hands. Elite. Trusted. We were sent to investigate a tomb. Old, sealed with magic."

He paused. I waited.

"We thought it was a ruin. A resting place. But it wasn't resting."

I didn't interrupt.

"It was something made. Not natural. Not even necromancy. It had bones, but no flesh. Magic coiled through it like veins. We fought it, and we lost."

His voice didn't shake, but it wasn't steady either.

"I watched them die, one by one. I failed them..." his throat caught. "I was the last to fall. But instead of death, I woke up in a cathedral cell. Platinum rank token gone, replaced with a silver one. No explanation. No trial. Just... silence."

My fingers twitch like I want to reach out, but I curl them into fists instead.

"Platinum to silver?" My voice is barely a whisper.

The rabbit forgotten, I scoot closer, eyes tracing the marks. My chest tightens as he continues to tell his tale. About his friends, about trying to start over, about being... *alone.*

Without thinking, I grab his hand. Too tight, like I can anchor him here.

"Listen to me, Tarn. You're *not* losing anyone else. Got it?" My usual bravado gone, replaced by something raw.

"I might be a reckless idiot, but I'm *you're* reckless idiot now. And I don't die easy." I squeeze his fingers, then force a smirk. "Besides, who else is gonna teach me how not to faceplant out of trees?"

Tarn's smile caught me off guard.

"Now you know," he says softly. "I should have died with them, but for some divine reason, I was spared."

Tarn glances down towards my injured leg. "I can't use any more healing magic today, so the best I'll be able to do is bandage that leg until tomorrow. Let's take a look."

For once, my smartass comment dies on my tongue. My cheeks flush crimson as I glance down at my torn trousers. A nervous laugh escapes me.

"Of all the ways I imagined getting you to ask me to take my pants off, field medicine wasn't on the list," I quip weakly, fingers hovering at my waist.

The reality of these stupidly tight leather trousers unbuttoning in front of this giant wall of a man who just bared his soul to me makes my pulse do something concerning.

I bite my lip. "Just, uh, turn around for a second, yeah?"

Once his back is turned, I shimmy out of the ruined pants with the grace of a newborn deer, modesty preserved only by the oversized vest—currently the MVP of the evening.

"Alright, fine," I grumble, flopping onto my bedroll in just my smallclothes and vest. "But if you tell *anyone* about this, I'll deny it to my grave."

Tarn works quickly and efficiently, wrapping the cut on my leg with practiced precision.

"Done." he says, not even sparing a glance at my face.

He continues "I can patch up your vest and trousers for you as well. Head into the tent and pass them out to me through the opening."

I scramble into the tent like a startled cat, tossing them through the flap with more force than necessary

"Y'know, I could help with this," I call through the fabric, sitting cross-legged just inches from where Tarn works. "My stitches are almost straight. Mostly."

The firelight casts his shadow against the tent wall, broad shoulders hunched over in concentration. I trace the movement of his hands with my eyes, inexplicably fascinated. My fingers drum restlessly on my knees.

"Sooo," I drawl, "What's the plan tomorrow? Charge deeper into the murder-forest? Or are we finally gonna admit this was a *terrible* idea and find a nice, goblin-free bakery to pillage instead?"

Outside the needle pauses. I imagine his smirk. "... Silence for now. Enjoy the stars." Tarn says as he pats the ground next to him, indicating he wants me to come out.

For a heartbeat, I hesitate, utterly exposed in nothing but the dark and my own tangled thoughts. Then, with a huff, stretching my tunic down as low as I could before crawling out of the tent.

The night air prickles my bare legs as I plop down beside Tarn, shoulder brushing his. Above us, the stars sprawl endlessly, brighter than any tavern's ceiling.

"...Alright, fine, they're pretty," I mutter, tilting my head back. "Still think a roof's better, though. Less chance of bird shit."

But as a shooting star streaks across the sky, my sarcasm falters. I hug my knees to my chest, suddenly small under the vastness of it all.

"Hey, Tarn?" My voice is uncharacteristically soft. "Whatever's out there... we'll face it. Together. Even if I still fall out of trees."

For a long while we stayed like that, me watching the stars, him watching the fire. The silence didn't feel heavy anymore. Just... steady.

My eyes drifted shut before I realized it. The last thing I felt was the warmth of the flames on my skin and Tarn's presence just behind my shoulder—solid, unmoving, like a wall I could rest against without ever admitting I needed to.

When I stirred later, the fire was banked low and my blanket tucked over me. Tarn's shape sat at the edge of camp, outlined against the embers. Watching the dark. Keeping guard.

And for the first time since leaving town, I let myself believe I might actually survive this.

Chapter 4

BENEATH THE SCALES

Cass

Morning comes too soon. Sunlight filters through the tent fabric as I blink awake, momentarily disoriented. Then, memory. The fight. The goblin. Tarn's scars. Stars.

I bolt upright, vest still hanging open. "Tarn? You better not have stayed up all-"

Peeking outside, I find him exactly where I feared. Slumped against a log, chin to chest, clearly having kept watch until exhaustion claimed him

"Ugh. Typical paladin," I whisper, though my chest does that weird tightening thing again. Grabbing a blanket, I drape it over his shoulders with exaggerated care.

"Rest up, hero. Your turn to be useless." Then quieter, just for me "I'll keep *you* safe this time."

There's a rustle in a nearby bush.

I freeze, daggers in hand, every nerve sharp. I brace myself for claws, fangs, something angry and snarling.

Instead, a small boar stumbles out and snorts at me like I've offended it by existing.

I blink. "This'll do nicely," I chirp, already picturing breakfast.

The boar doesn't stand a chance. After cleaning it I spend a while foraging. Roots, a few herbs, some bird eggs, even a stubborn mushroom or two that *probably* won't kill us. By the time I make it back to camp, the fire from last night is mostly ash and embers, but there's still life in it. I coax a flame back to life and dig through Tarn's pack until I find a battered pan.

Smoke curls upward as I drop strips of boar meat onto the iron. The smell is heavenly.

"You're better at that than you look," comes a low voice behind me.

"Gah!" I nearly fling the pan into the fire, whipping around with wide eyes. Tarn lounges on his bedroll, one eye cracked open, face shadowed with sleep and sunlight.

"Damn it, warn a girl next time! What happened to your armor clanking like a one-man marching band?"

He doesn't answer, but the corner of his mouth lifts, barely.

My cheeks burn. I turn back to the pan and jab at the meat like it insulted me. "And for your information, I'm an excellent cook. Just because I once set water on fire, don't ask, doesn't mean I can't handle breakfast."

I flip a strip with flair and pretend I don't notice the way the firelight softens his features. Sleep-rumpled, quiet... almost normal.

I slide a piece onto a dented tin plate and shove it toward him.

"Eat up," I mutter, not quite meeting his eyes.

"We've got a forest to conquer, and I *refuse* to let you face it on an empty stomach."

Tarn takes the plate without comment, chewing the slightly charred bacon with the solemn dignity of a man facing execution.

I narrow my eyes, hands on hips. "Oh please, it's not that bad. I even remembered to take the shells off the eggs, which were not easy to find by the way!"

I plop down across from him, stealing a piece of bacon off his plate just to annoy him. "Besides, you're one to talk, I've seen your 'rations.' Hardtack that could double as mortar."

The fire pops between us as I scarf down my own cooking, pretending not to notice when he actually finishes the whole plate. Huh. Maybe I didn't poison us.

"Alright, hero," I said, brushing crumbs from my vest as I stood and stretched out my leg. "Time to earn your keep. Heal this thing so I can go back to falling out of trees at full speed."

Tarn looked up, gaze calm and unreadable. "Sit."

I plopped down beside him with a dramatic sigh. "You really know how to charm a girl."

He ignored that, placing a hand just above the wound. The warmth of his magic spread through the muscle, slow and sure. I found myself watching the way his brow creased, how focused he got when he wasn't trying to keep his walls up.

The ache faded, and so did some part of me I hadn't realized was holding tension.

When he finished, I wiggled my toes, stood, and gave the leg a little bounce. "Fully functional again. Better watch your back."

He gave a faint nod, but I caught the way his eyes lingered a moment longer than usual. It made my chest flutter in a way I absolutely refused to examine.

I reached into my sleeve and pulled out the spoon I'd swiped earlier. Held it up between two fingers.

"Also, this is mine now."

Tarn blinked. "...You stole my spoon."

I grinned. "I prefer the term *reassigned without consultation*. You really should label your valuables better."

"You're impossible."

He said it like he meant it. But he wasn't annoyed. Not even close.

"Yeah, yeah," I said, slipping the spoon into one of my belt loops. "Try to keep up, holy man. I'm starting a collection."

I turned away before I could say anything dumber, heading toward the fire with a little too much purpose. Behind me, I could feel him still watching—but, like always, he didn't say a word.

I crouched by the fire, pretending to poke at the embers like I was checking for heat. Really, I just needed something to look at that wasn't him.

The spoon jingled lightly at my hip as I moved. I told myself it was a joke, a bit. A way to needle him. But I hadn't given it back.

Across the clearing, Tarn knelt beside his pack, checking his gear with that same quiet focus he did everything with. He wasn't saying much. He didn't have to. The way he moved—methodical, calm—it did something strange to my chest. Like I could exhale around him. Like I didn't have to be on guard every second.

I shifted my weight, tugged my vest closed even though it didn't really need it.

It wasn't like me to care what someone thought. Not really. But then again, most people didn't look at me the way he did. Like I wasn't just useful—like I was worth keeping alive.

I picked up a twig and started drawing lazy circles in the dirt beside the fire, letting the silence stretch.

He didn't look up, but I could feel it—that quiet awareness he always seemed to carry. Like he'd noticed everything without needing to say it aloud.

I sat there longer than I meant to, stick in hand, lines in the dirt spiraling into shapes I didn't recognize. The camp was nearly packed. Tarn had already strapped his bedroll to his pack and was checking the straps on his armor.

I should've gotten up. Should've helped. But part of me didn't want to break the moment just yet. The air still felt full of something unspoken.

"You always this quiet in the morning?" I asked eventually, eyes still on the ashes.

"Only when there's nothing worth saying," Tarn replied without missing a beat.

I looked up at him. "Wow. That sounded like a backhanded insult and a philosophical proverb at the same time."

He buckled the last strap on his pack. "Take it however you like."

"I usually do." I rose slowly, brushing dirt from my hands.

Tarn slung his pack over one shoulder and gave the camp one last sweep. Always thorough.

I adjusted the strap of my own bag, glanced toward the path ahead—the trees standing tall like sentinels, the forest waiting.

I shifted on my heels, suddenly needing to move. To shake off whatever had settled into my chest during the quiet.

"Race you to the tree line? Loser cooks dinner *and* admits my bacon was perfect." Without waiting for an answer, I bolt, leaping over logs with renewed agility, the morning sun catching the red ribbon in my hair.

I catch Tarn staring as I turn back, just for a second, to flash him a grin. There's something new in his expression, something that makes my pulse skip. I should tease him for it. Should. Instead, I melt into the shadows between the trees, letting my newly unlocked Shadow Step carry me to a high branch.

From this vantage, I watch him approach, all broad shoulders and quiet determination. He thinks I didn't notice, I muse, tracing the outline of his stolen spoon against my palm. But rogues notice everything. When he passes beneath me, I drop noiselessly behind him, pressing the spoon to the back of his neck like a dagger.

"Boo," I whisper in his ear, then dissolve into giggles before he can react.

"C'mon, slowpoke! The forest won't loot itself!" I dart a head again, but my cheeks burn. Because rogues notice everything, including how their own heartbeat stutters at certain looks.

We make our way deeper into the forest, the hush beneath the trees growing heavier with every step. Something prickles along the back of my neck—instinct, not imagination.

I reach out and caught Tarn's arm, tugging him behind a thick tree just as I caught movement through the underbrush.

My voice drops to whisper, low and sharp. "Movement. Ten o'clock. Not goblins this time."

He nods silently, his hand already resting on the hilt of his hammer.

I lean around the trunk and catch a glimpse of it. Scales, the faint cling of talons over damp leaves, the sound of something breathing wrong. Slow, heavy, too wet.

"*Basilisk,*" I mouth, barely turning my head. "Juvenile, I think. See how its crest isn't fully fanned yet?"

Tarn frowned. "Still dangerous. We go together."

I risk another peek and spot what had caught the creature's interest. A pile of old gear, scattered coin, a glint of something shiny. "Looks like it's been collecting," I murmured, eyes narrowing. "Travelers. Probably rich ones."

I tapped his arm lightly. "If I draw its attention, can you circle wide and flank it? We'll pin it."

"No," Tarn said, shaking his head. "I'll take point. You're faster. You sweep the nest. Signal when you're clear."

For a moment, I almost argued. But there was steel in his voice I hadn't heard before. Not just confidence, but experience.

"Alright," I whispered. "Try not to die."

He gave me the faintest flicker of a grin. "You too."

Tarn stepped out from cover, shield raised high.

The basilisk hissed, crest flaring, its eyes glowing faintly with a sickly shimmer. Even juvenile, it radiated wrongness—like the forest itself wanted nothing to do with it. The air stank of damp scales and venom.

Tarn struck the rim of his shield with his hammer. The clang echoed through the trees like a challenge.

The beast lowered its head and lunged, jaws snapping. Tarn braced, shield angled, the impact rattling like thunder through the clearing. The force shoved him back a step, leaves crunching beneath his boots, but he didn't give ground.

I was already moving, darting low, shadows wrapping me like second skin. The nest was scattered coin, scraps of bone, shredded leather packs. I scooped what I could—dagger, pouch, flask—and kept my ears sharp for the rhythm of the fight. Tarn's shield took another blow; his hammer cracked against scales with a hollow thud. Not deep enough. Not yet.

The basilisk's tail lashed, splintering a tree branch overhead. Bark rained down in sharp flecks.

I dove closer to the nest, fingers brushing over something smooth—an emerald, huge, glowing faintly in the dim light. I froze. It wasn't just valuable. It felt... wrong. Heavy in a way gems shouldn't.

I snatched it up just as the basilisk's body twisted, tail slamming through its own hoard. The emerald flew from my grip, vanishing into the undergrowth.

"Dammit!" I hissed, diving after it.

The shadow beneath a bush gave me my chance. I didn't think—I Shadow Stepped.

The world twisted sideways, yanking my stomach out from under me, and I tumbled into the brush, thorns scraping my skin. But the emerald was in my fist.

"Oof—got it!" I wheezed.

The basilisk noticed.

Its head snapped toward me, crest fanning wide. Venom dripped from its jaws, sizzling where it hit the dirt. The ground smoked.

"Shit." My legs tangled in the bush. I yanked, cursed, yanked again. "Tarn!"

The creature surged forward, claws gouging the soil, eyes burning with unnatural focus.

And then golden light flared.

Tarn slammed into place between us, shield braced, hammer raised. The basilisk's strike crashed down, sparks and fire bursting where claw met steel. My ears rang from the impact.

He didn't move. Didn't yield an inch.

I stared up at him, chest heaving, emerald cutting into my palm. "Okay," I whispered, a grin breaking through my panic, "you're officially the coolest."

The basilisk recoiled, tail lashing again. Tarn pressed forward with grim determination, but I could hear the edge in his breathing. That magic he'd spent—it cost him.

I scrambled free of the bush, pressing into his back, dagger ready. "We end this together."

His only answer was a short nod, shoulders tightening.

The basilisk lunged again, jaws gaping. Tarn pivoted, shield angled to deflect the strike, hammer slamming across its snout. Bone cracked, but not enough. The beast shrieked, tail thrashing wild.

I darted to the side, shadows swallowing me in another desperate step. The world twisted, then spat me out beneath its belly. My dagger plunged upward, finding softer flesh. Hot blood sprayed across my arm as the creature convulsed.

It spun, nearly crushing me with its bulk, but Tarn was there, hammer arcing down with brutal precision. The strike cracked through scale and skull alike, a sickening crunch echoing through the clearing.

The basilisk staggered, but it wasn't finished. Its tail whipped down in a desperate last strike.

"Cass!"

I froze. Too slow.

And then Tarn's arm swept around my waist, yanking me backward as the tail slammed into the ground where I'd been. Dirt exploded in a spray of splinters and stone.

I landed against his chest, armor hard and cold, his hand still firm at my side. My pulse skipped, stuttered, then raced too fast.

For one suspended second, I forgot about the fight entirely. About poison, or claws, or anything but the steady weight of him holding me there.

Then he let go, stepping forward as the basilisk gave one last convulsion. His hammer came down with finality, crushing the skull. The body shuddered, then stilled.

Silence fell heavy.

I exhaled, wiping basilisk blood from my cheek with the back of my hand. Then I smirked, because if I didn't, I'd shake. "Teamwork," I said, voice cracking on the word.

The basilisk finally stilled, its massive body sagging into the dirt with a shudder that rattled the ground. Smoke curled from its nostrils, the stench of venom sharp enough to sting my nose.

I pressed a hand to my thigh, forcing my breathing to even out. Every muscle screamed, every nerve still raw with the thought of nearly being crushed.

"Boots," I muttered, voice shaky. "I want boots out of this damn thing. Nobles'll cry with envy."

It was a joke, but my laugh came out thin. Tarn didn't answer, just leaned on his hammer, the glow of his spell still flickering faintly in the seams of his armor. He looked steady, but I'd started to recognize the cost hidden under that calm. His breaths were too measured. His eyes, just for a moment, distant.

I swallowed hard and crouched beside the carcass, wiping my blade on the grass. "Let's see what our friend here's been hoarding."

The nest was a mess, but loot glinted among the shattered bones and shredded leather. I sifted through it—coins, a silver-inlaid dagger, the cracked neck of a potion vial. Then a fang the size of my forearm, jagged and gleaming. I let out a low whistle. "This'll make one hell of a trophy."

And then I saw it.

A key. Small, ornate, half-buried in dirt. I plucked it free, brushing grime off the filigree etched along its stem. The symbol carved into the head caught the sunlight—a star split down the middle.

Tarn's hand shot out, closing over mine before I could tuck it away. His grip was steady, but I felt the tension there. The way his thumb lingered over the etching.

He took it like it might burn him. Calloused thumb traced the engraving, his jaw tightening. His voice was rough, low. "This isn't treasure."

"That's the sigil of the Sons of the Hollow Star," he murmured, voice rough.

I blinked. "You say that like it's supposed to mean something other than 'ominous cult branding.'"

He didn't look at me. "The Sons of the Hollow Star, the ones who razed my village as a child, before the church took me in." His fist closed around the key. The muscles in his forearm trembled.

I froze, the banter gone before I realized it. For once, I didn't make a joke. I just said, quiet but certain, "Then we'll find whatever door this opens. And when we do, Tarn..."

I flexed my still-healing leg, "I'll help you burn down whatever's behind it."

He looked at me then, really looked, like he was trying to measure if I meant it. I held his gaze and didn't blink.

For a heartbeat, I thought he might say something. Instead, he slipped the key into his pack with slow, deliberate care. "You don't know what you're promising."

"No," I said, forcing a grin I didn't quite feel. "But promises make life interesting."

The silence that followed wasn't empty. It was heavy, weighted with the corpse between us, the key tucked into his pack, and the realization that the forest wasn't the only dangerous thing waiting for us.

"We should head back to town."

I exhale sharply, the tension breaking as I sling my pack over one shoulder with exaggerated effort. "Ugh, fine, but only because I deserve a hot meal after carrying your holy deadweight through that fight." I toss him a wink to soften the jab.

As we turn toward town, I fall into step behind him. The emerald weighs between my fingers before I slip it into his pocket, my touch lingering just a heartbeat too long. "Hold onto this, hero. I'd only lose it."

Chapter 5

EMERALD NO MORE

Cass

The clamor of the town square hits me like a thunderclap after two days in the forest. Too many voices, too many smells, too many things not currently trying to kill me. It's... jarring. I adjust the strap of my bulging pack and nudge Tarn with my elbow. "Bet you ten silver the appraisal clerk tries to lowball us," I mutter, eyeing the marble pillars of the Adventurer's Guild like they might collapse on me just for looking poor.

Tarn grunts. "If they value their kneecaps, they won't."

I grin. "Ooh, big talk from Mr. Holy Wrath. What are you gonna do, smite 'em into giving us fair market value?"

He doesn't even bother with a response. We step into the main hall, the warm scent of parchment, sweat, and ambition hits me full in the face. Adventurers bustle between job boards, lounging across mismatched benches, polishing weapons, arguing over loot. It's like walking into a tavern run by accountants and psychopaths. The appraisal counter is near the back, staffed by a woman with half-moon glasses and the permanent look of someone who hates her job *just* enough to be efficient at it.

"Next," she says flatly, without looking up. Tarn steps forward, setting the basilisk fang, a pouch of coins, and a wrapped bundle of scales on the counter.

I follow, dramatically placing the ornate dagger and - very carefully - the emerald. I glance around, then lean in. "Let's keep the shiny green one *off the record*, yeah?" The clerk pauses, her eyes flicking up to mine, then to Tarn, then to the emerald. Her lips press into a thin line. "...Noted." She slides the rest of the haul across a strange square of shimmering crystal and murmurs a few words under her breath. Runes flicker. Numbers dance. "Standard market value for basilisk materials, plus hazard pay for monster class level." She taps a few keys. "Seventy-five silver. Forty-five for the dagger. Coins are unmarked, convertible. Total haul, post-guild fee..." She looks up. "One hundred and one silver, twenty-two copper."

I blink. "Wait, we fought a *basilisk*, and your giving us barely enough to scrape by?"

"The fang is cracked," she replies without inflection. "The scales are juvenile. And you tried to sell me a thimble, a wooden spoon, and three chicken bones."

Tarn just sighs and slids the coins into his pouch, "It's fair."

I frown, "Its highway robbery is what it is."

The clerk raises an eyebrow. "You're welcome to file a complaint with the Arbitration Council."

I nudge Tarn, "Is that a real council or just a broom closet with a nameplate?"

"Both," he replies, deadpan.

"Might as well see what that emerald is worth after all."

The clerk rolls her eyes and taps the rune-inscribed slab of crystal. The emerald sits perfectly still - until she activates the device. The moment the scanning magic touches it, the stone shudders. A low hum fills the air. The vibrant green shifts, sickly at first, then bleeds away entirely, fading into a cool, crystaline blue. Not the warm, foresty shimmer of a normal emerald. No. This is *wrong*, like the reflection of lightning in still water. Everyone nearby stops talking. The clerk goes rigid.

"Oh no," I whisper. "That's bad, isn't it?"

The clerk stares at the now glasslike gem, voice suddenly a lot sharper. "Where did you get this?"

Tarn stiffens beside me, "Is it cursed?"

She doesn't answer. Instead, she grabs a second crystal from under the desk, a darker one. A red rune pulses once, then flares bright. "Aethercore..." She breathes, barely above a whisper.

My mouth goes dry. "Wait wait wait, *what*?!"

The clerk finally looks up at us, really looks. "This is an aethercore. Illegal to own, transport, or sell. Classified under arcane contraband. You didn't find an emerald. You found a disguised powerstone."

"But... it was green a second ago!" I protest, pointing wildly at the gem. "It was just a *shiny rock*! Why does it look like a goddamn soul prism now?!"

Tarn's hand drifts to his hammer. "Is the guild going to confiscate it?"

"We're required to report this to the Academy," she says coolly. "They'll want to examine it. Immediately."

"No," I say without thinking. "I mean, what if we just... *didn't* tell them?" The clerks eyes narrow.

Tarn glances at me. "Cass..."

"It's not like we *knew*! We though it was loot! Shiny, mysterious loot! Like every other shiny, mysterious thing we find in the forest!"

"This isn't just loot," the clerk snaps. "It's a contained Aethercore. These things power warforged constructs. Forbidden Rituals. Whole cities have burned down because of one of these things going unstable."

"Oh," I say weakly. "Cool. Love that."

The clerk sighs and pinches the bridge of her nose. "Just... sit down. The Guild Master will want to speak to you. And I suggest you keep that tongue of yours in check unless you want to answer to the Inquisition."

I shoot Tarn a sideways glance. "Think they'd let me keep my tongue in a jar if they cut it out? Could make a neat souvenir."

He doesn't respond. Just keep staring at the Aethercore like it might explode.

We're only sitting for a minute or two when a heavy-set man in crimson guild robes appears from a side hallway, flanked by two robed assistants. The Guild Master. His expression is unreadable.

"You're the ones who brought in the disguised core?" he asks. No introductions. No ceremony.

Tarn stands. "We didn't know what it was."

"No one ever does," the Guild Master mutters. "And yet here we are, filling out incident forms and praying to the gods that it doesn't resonate with anything else in the building."

He folds his arms. "Legally, I should report this to the Academy. But legally..." His eyes flick to Tarn, lingering on the paladin's sigil. "...your record suggests discretion."

Tarn pulls a few coins from his pouch and slides them onto the table with the same grim efficiency he used to crush the basilisk's skull.

The Guild Master nods once. "For the record, the emerald never existed. The scan was inconclusive. You were cleared of all contraband. Understood?"

"Understood," Tarn says quietly.

The Guild Master turns on his heel. "Don't bring me another one."

I stood up and stretched lazily, "No promises."

Tarn gives me a look. I just shrug.

As we step outside the Guild, the weight of the last hour lifts. Just a little.

"So," I say, nudging him with my elbow. "Since we're not being arrested or melted by arcane containment wards... Boots?"

He exhales. "Boots."

"I knew you'd come around."

The smell hits first—tanned hide, hot glue, singed hair. I wrinkle my nose as we step into the leatherworker's cramped little shop, ducking under a row of drying pelts. A goblin's jawbone dangles above the counter like a cursed

wind chime.

"This is the place?" I whisper to Tarn.

"You said you wanted boots made from the basilisk hide, and this is the best leatherworker I know that works with monster parts," he replies.

"Yeah, I just didn't expect it to smell like something *died* in here."

"It did. Multiple things."

A grizzled dwarf with one eye and two dozen belts strapped across his chest emerges from behind a curtain, squinting at us through a monocle. "You the ones with the basilisk skin?"

Tarn nods and sets the bundle on the counter.

The dwarf peels it open like a gift. "Oho! Juvenile, but decent stretch. You want armor?"

"Boots," I cut in quickly. "Rogue boots. Silent, sexy, and extremely good at not falling out of trees."

He snorts. "Right. The usual."

Tarn clears his throat and, with less enthusiasm, adds, "And durable. She has... a tendency to attract sharp objects."

"I do *not*," I protest, stabbing a finger at him. "The objects just happen to be sharp when they hit me."

The dwarf grunts and starts measuring my feet with a frayed string, muttering about heel width and tendon support. I wiggle my toes dramatically. "Just make 'em snug. I want to feel like I could kick a dragon in the teeth and then steal its hoard while it blinks."

"You pay up front," the dwarf says, ignoring the theatrics.

I glance at Tarn, who reluctantly pulls out the now-pathetically-thin coin pouch.

"You owe me," he mutters under his breath.

"You bribed the Guild Master," I shoot back. "Technically, this is still your fault."

"You owe me."

"I carried that hide half the way back and didn't complain once."

"You complained the entire time."

"Yeah, but I didn't *stop walking*, did I?"

The dwarf ignores us both, already sketching the boot design with surprising precision. "Three days. No refunds. No whining."

As we step out into the sunlight again, I glance down at my scuffed old boots—muddy, torn, and practically begging to be retired.

I grin.

"Tarn, you know what this means?"

He sighs. "What?"

"We didn't die, we didn't get arrested, and I didn't trip over anything important. That calls for a drink. And maybe, if we're feeling reckless... dessert."

Chapter 6

TO STAND ALONE

Cass

The forest road curved like a lazy serpent, mud spitting from the caravan wheels at every lurch. Half a year had passed since that first hunt with Tarn, and the world had changed in ways I hadn't expected. What used to be noise—the clank of harness, the weary gait of horses—now felt like signals. I heard everything, and I couldn't unhear it.

We were escorting a small supply caravan to a remote outpost near the Veiled Ridges. Two wagons. Three donkeys. One driver who wouldn't stop humming. And us. I adjusted my grip on my bow and glanced at the nearest wagon. Stacked crates of food and wrapped bundles of firewood bumped together like impatient children.

"I swear," I muttered, "if I hear that driver sing one more verse about lost love in the snow, I'm going to carve my ears off with the blunt side of my dagger."

Tarn didn't look at me. He was scanning the tree line like usual. "You say that every time we take an escort job."

"Yeah, well. This time I mean it."

His lips twitched into the ghost of a smile.

The trees closed in tighter as we wound deeper into the woods. The air smelled like frost and pine resin. Winter had crept in slowly, nipping at the edges of autumn, and you could feel it even under all the layers. My fingers flexed inside their gloves, still remembering the feel of that emerald. Still remembering how quickly things could go from quiet to chaos.

A low growl snapped me out of the thought.

Tarn stopped mid-stride. I followed his gaze, heart hitching. The forest had gone too quiet.

Even Jasper, the lead donkey, had stopped braying.

"Wolves," Tarn said quietly.

I didn't ask how he knew. I just trusted it. The way birds stopped singing. The way the wind dropped. The silence meant teeth were near.

"Stay close," he said, already lifting his shield.

I readied an arrow.

The first wolf didn't make a sound. It burst from the underbrush like a bolt of fur and fury, heading straight for the front wagon. The driver yelped and scrambled to the far side as the beast leapt. Tarn moved faster, his shield slamming upward with a metallic crunch. The wolf hit it mid-air and tumbled backward, dazed but not down.

Then the rest came.

They emerged from all sides—seven in total, gaunt with hunger and desire gleaming in their eyes. The cold had not been kind to them. I pivoted, letting my first arrow fly. It thudded into a haunch, not fatal, but enough to stagger the target. I was already drawing another.

One wolf came for me, low and fast. I loosed the second arrow—too rushed, it missed. No time. I dropped the bow and grabbed the hilt of my dagger in the same motion, shifting my stance as the wolf closed the distance. My basilisk-hide boots gripped the icy ground with unnatural precision, enchanted traction keeping me grounded as I braced. The wolf lunged. I twisted and drove the blade up into its ribs before it could recover.

Behind me, Tarn's hammer rang out like a temple bell, breaking bone and focus. His shield swept two wolves off their feet in one wide arc. But they kept coming. Snarling. Frothing. A madness in their gaze that didn't feel natural.

"They're desperate," I hissed between strikes.

"Or driven," Tarn grunted, parrying a lunge.

Another wolf lunged for the caravan, snapping at the wagon driver. I raced forward, boots catching a half-buried root. But instead of stumbling, the enchanted traction held fast. I launched off it, springing upward to drive my heel into the wolf's back. It hit the ground with a startled yelp, and I dropped with it, blades flashing.

Blood sprayed my sleeve. I didn't stop to think.

Tarn was surrounded now. Four wolves circled, trying to get past his guard. One managed to clamp its jaws onto his arm, teeth scraping against plate. He growled and brought his hammer down on its skull in a sickening crunch, then shoved another away with his shield. The fourth leapt at his back.

"Nope." I launched the small throwing knife I always kept tucked in my boot—a backup, not much, but enough. It sank into the wolf's flank, buying Tarn the heartbeat he needed to spin and intercept with a killing blow.

One left.

It limped, bloodied and panting, but still braced for another charge.

I stepped forward, raising my daggers. But Tarn held out a hand.

"Let it go," he said.

I hesitated. "You sure?"

His eyes were hard, but his voice was calm. "It's broken. It knows it lost."

We watched in silence as the last wolf limped into the trees, dragging a paw and leaving a thin trail of red behind.

Only when the silence returned did I realize how hard my heart was pounding. My sleeves were slick. My hands trembling just enough to make me notice. I wiped the blade clean on my trousers and let out a shaky breath.

Jasper let out a nervous bray, breaking the stillness.

"Well," I said, trying to force the tension out of my voice, "that was one way to stretch the legs."

Tarn looked at me, one eyebrow raised. "You didn't trip."

"Not once," I said, grinning despite the blood on my collar. "Credit the boots. Or maybe I'm just evolving. Soon I'll be unstoppable. Or at least moderately coordinated."

"Terrifying," he said dryly before turning back to check on the wagons.

The rest of the road passed in a strange quiet. Even the driver seemed to run out of verses. Tarn walked beside the lead wagon, one hand resting lightly on his hammer, gaze ever forward. I followed just behind him, occasionally glancing at the forest shadows, but nothing moved now. The wolves had made their statement, and we'd answered.

By the time the outpost came into view, the sun had already started to sink behind the ridgeline, casting long slashes of gold across the snow-dusted clearing. The place was little more than a fortified lodge tucked between a rise of stone and a half-frozen stream. Smoke curled from the chimney. Guards in mismatched cloaks watched our approach from the low wall, spears tipped with dull iron.

One of them raised a hand in greeting. "You the supply run?"

Tarn nodded. "With a few extra dents, but yes."

The gate creaked open. The wagons rolled in. Jasper brayed his relief.

Inside the walls, the outpost felt warmer than it looked. A few adventurers lounged near the firepit at the center, and someone was already unpacking crates into the cellar below. The commander—an older woman with a scar like a lightning bolt across her cheek—gave us a short nod and less than ten words of thanks. I didn't blame her. This place didn't run on formality.

As the caravan driver was shown to his quarters and the donkeys unhitched, Tarn turned to me.

"You've done enough."

I blinked. "To... unload the carts?"

He shook his head. "To qualify."

It took me a second to catch on. Then my breath caught in my throat. "You mean...?"

"You've fulfilled the contract quota. Met the field experience requirements. Fought things most Bronze-ranks wouldn't even go near." He held my gaze. "You're eligible to take the trial."

Oh. Gods.

A slow, almost childish grin tugged at the corners of my mouth. "Wait, seriously?"

He nodded once. "But."

I squinted. "There's always a but."

"I want to test you first."

The grin faded, but the spark in my chest didn't. "You want to duel me."

"Call it a final check," he said. "To make sure you're ready."

I folded my arms. "Afraid I'll flub it and make you look bad in front of the fancy Bronze-rank examiners?"

His mouth twitched. "Something like that."

I blew out a breath, adrenaline already threading into my limbs again. "Alright. Let's see if you can still keep up."

We found a clearing just outside the outpost walls, ringed by thin trees and blanketed in snow. The cold made my breath mist as I pulled my gloves tight and flexed my fingers. Tarn stood across from me, shield strapped to his arm, hammer resting on one shoulder. The sun had almost fully dipped now, and the sky burned soft orange along the treetops.

"I won't use magic," he said. "And I'll hold back."

"Gee," I said, drawing my daggers, "thanks for the vote of confidence."

"I mean it," he said, more serious now. "Go all out. Treat me like any other opponent."

"Any other opponent doesn't make breakfast and save my life twice a week."

"Then pretend I'm someone else."

I gave him a cocky grin. "Okay. I'll pretend you're that one merchant who tried to charge me double for bandages."

56

"Good. Now focus."

He raised his shield.

And I moved.

I darted in low, feinting left, then spinning right to test his footwork. He blocked the first swipe with ease, turning with me, always just a little faster than I wanted him to be. His movements were tight, practiced. Controlled.

I slipped backward, catching my breath. "So this is what six months of training boils down to, huh?"

"You're doing better," he said. "Your stance is tighter. You don't overcommit."

"You sound surprised."

"I'm impressed."

That threw me off just long enough for him to close the gap.

His shield came in fast—controlled, not meant to hurt, but still enough to knock the breath from my lungs. I rolled, planting my feet as I came up behind him, slashing for his flank. He twisted and caught my wrist in one swift movement, holding it just long enough to make a point.

"Predictable," he said.

I snarled and dropped to a crouch, yanking free and sliding beneath his arm to gain distance again.

This wasn't working. He was too well-defended, too grounded. I couldn't win by dancing around him.

So I stopped dancing.

I went quiet instead. Let the rhythm shift. My boots gripped the packed snow with perfect balance—no slip, no misstep. I inhaled. Waited.

And then—

Shadow Step.

I vanished from his line of sight and reappeared directly behind him, at the edge of his own shadow. His head snapped around in surprise—but I was already there.

My blade kissed the back of his neck—just lightly enough to let him know I could've drawn blood.

We froze.

I met his eyes.

He blinked once. Then slowly straightened and lowered his shield.

"Well," he said, "I wasn't expecting that."

"Didn't think I'd use it against you?"

"Didn't think you could." A breath escaped him, like he'd been holding it. "That was good."

I stepped back, chest heaving. "So... I pass?"

"With flying colors."

Back at the outpost, Tarn crouched by the fire, setting aside his armor piece by piece. I almost didn't notice the bundle in his hands—dark wool, tightly bound with thin twine.

He stood and held it out to me without ceremony.

"For the cold," he said simply.

I took it, letting the fabric unfurl over my arms. It was soft but strong, the deep green of pine forests at dusk. It shimmered faintly—not like light catching metal, but like it was trying to not be seen at all.

"Enchanted thread," he added. "Won't turn you invisible, but if you stay still, it'll help you disappear."

I blinked. "You got me a cloak that helps me sneak better?"

"No," he said. "I got you a cloak that'll keep you alive."

Before I could say anything else, he pulled out a second, smaller bundle and set it in my hands.

The moment I touched it, something in me stilled.

Inside were two daggers—perfect twins. The steel wasn't glossy or flashy, but bright in a way that felt... quiet. Clean. The hilts were wrapped in dusky leather, the pommels etched with a subtle spiral motif that pulled the eye without shouting for attention. Balanced. Elegant. Lethal.

And then I wrapped my fingers around the grips—

Gods.

They didn't feel new.

They felt *mine*.

Like I'd just picked up a part of myself I hadn't known I was missing.

I didn't say anything at first. I couldn't. My throat tightened in a way that wasn't entirely from surprise.

"They're not magical," Tarn said, almost apologetic. "But they're the best I could find. Stronger than standard alloy. Light enough for speed, weighted enough for the kill. They won't fail you."

I looked up at him, still gripping the daggers, afraid to let go in case the feeling slipped away.

"You bought these?" I asked quietly. "With... your cut from the last few jobs?"

He nodded. "You earned these, Cass. Not just for the fights, but for the miles. For sticking through the hard parts and not losing who you are. For growing into someone who deserves more than borrowed blades."

I swallowed hard.

"They feel like they were made for me."

He gave a faint smile. "They were."

Chapter 7

THE SHAPE OF THE TRIAL

Cass

The town gates came into view just as the sun crested the farthest peak, casting long shadows across the frost-laced road. I hadn't realized how tightly I was gripping the strap of my satchel until Tarn slowed beside me and bumped me gently with one armored elbow.

"Relax," he said. "You're not under attack."

"Feels like I am," I muttered. "Just... not with swords."

We passed beneath the weather-worn stone arch that marked the edge of town, the bustle of morning trade already in full swing. My boots scuffed through melting snow, breath misting behind me as we veered toward the adventurer's guildhall.

The guild stood tall and unmoved by the season. Snow clung to the highest reaches of the roof, stubborn and gray-edged, while the heavy doors swung open and shut to let in adventurers, merchants, and more than a few wide-eyed hopefuls.

I stopped at the base of the steps. Tarn paused beside me.

"This is where I stop," he said.

I blinked. "You're not coming in?"

"I'll be there," he said, tilting his head toward a bench tucked beneath the awning. "But the rest is on you."

I stared at the doors a moment longer, half-expecting them to slam shut the second I reached for them. "It's just a test," I said, trying to make myself believe it.

Tarn gave a dry grunt. "A test that decides your future rank. Your career. Whether you get better contracts or get saddled with swamp rats again. You know—just a test."

"You're really bad at pep talks," I said, smirking.

"Good. I'm not here to hold your hand." But something in his expression softened. "I'll be here when you walk back out."

I nodded. The knot in my stomach didn't loosen, but it steadied. I stepped forward and pushed open the doors.

Inside, the guild was a living thing—cloaks cast over chairs, boots stomping slush onto rugs, voices raised over contracts and clinking coin. I made my way to the front desk, where the same sharp-eyed receptionist from six months ago glanced up at me.

"I'm here to take the trial," I said, doing my best not to fidget.

She raised a brow. "Name?"

"Cass. Soon to be bronze rank, field experience logged under Tarn Elros."

She gave a slight nod, then scribbled something into a parchment ledger and reached beneath the counter. A moment later, she handed me a small brass token, etched with looping symbols that shimmered subtly in the lamplight.

"Take this to the right hall. Down the corridor, last door. Give it to the evaluator."

I took the token and made my way down the indicated hallway, passing wooden doors that blurred into shadow at the corners of my vision. At the last door, I paused, hand hovering over the knob.

One step at a time, I told myself.

The room beyond was circular and still. Pale winter light spilled in through a single high window. A raised dais stood in the center, and behind it, a man in parchment-colored robes looked up from a thick sheaf of documents. Middle-aged. Silver threaded through his beard. His eyes flicked over me like I was an inventory to be assessed.

"Cass," he said. "Sit."

I did, handing him the token. He inspected it and set it aside.

"I am Evaluator Meron. Your trial will begin shortly. Before that, a few things to understand." His voice was calm, measured—like this was routine, and I was just another name in a long list. "The test is not standardized. It is shaped for you. By you."

I frowned. "By me?"

He gestured to the far end of the room, where a stone archway stood freestanding like a doorway without walls. Its surface was dull gray, inert.

"This is a scry-gate. It reads your magical imprint, your behavioral markers, and your past experiences—both submitted and unspoken. It pulls from them. What you face inside will be something only you can face. Not Tarn. Not anyone else."

I swallowed. "Right."

Meron stood and approached the gate. He placed a hand on the frame, and pale blue runes flared beneath his touch. The stone hummed softly as arcs of energy rippled up its edges. Tendrils of glowing mist curled toward the center and wove into a shimmering veil.

I stood, pulse kicking faster in my chest.

"What do I have to do?" I asked.

Meron didn't look away from the gate. "Survive. Solve. Adapt. Prove that you are more than a lucky recruit who made it through a few fights."

The words bit more than I expected them to.

"And if I fail?"

"You won't die. Probably. But you will have to wait another year to reapply. You won't be allowed to attempt the same trial again. So if you go through that gate, go through ready."

I took a step closer. Behind the veil, I thought I saw flickers— shadows moving, hints of trees, maybe stonework or ruins. Nothing clear. Just enough to raise every hair on my arms.

I drew my cloak tighter around my shoulders. The one Tarn had given me. The one that would help me disappear, if I needed it.

"I'm ready," I said.

Meron inclined his head. "Then enter."

I took a slow breath, brushed the edge of my hood for reassurance, and stepped into the veil.

The world shimmered as I stepped into the gate.

For a heartbeat, I was nowhere. Weightless. Disconnected. Sound stretched thin like wind through a keyhole. Then, from somewhere within the void, a voice—clear, resonant, and unfamiliar—spoke directly into my mind:

"Your task is simple: Survive. Navigate the path. Face what you carry. The way forward is hidden, but it waits for you all the same."

Before I could ask what any of that meant, the pressure behind my eyes released—like a dam breaking—and gravity reclaimed me.

I landed on solid ground, though the terrain beneath me felt... old. Not ancient in the sense of ruins or dust, but lived in. Saturated with memory.

The sky above was dim and colorless, neither day nor night. Around me stretched a narrow path through an abandoned village, the buildings squat and sagging under time's weight. The air shimmered faintly, like heat distortion, though it was cold enough to see my breath. Frost clung to the crooked eaves, and broken windows stared at me like empty eyes.

Behind me, the portal crackled shut with a whisper of finality.

Then the voice came again. Not loud—almost reverent.

"Face what you carry."

I turned, but there was no one there. No source. Just the sound, buried in the bones of the place.

I drew my new daggers—not from fear, exactly, but to feel something familiar in my hands. Their weight was steady. Grounding.

The village was quiet, but not empty. As I walked, I saw traces of lives long gone. Chairs still tucked beneath tables, a child's wooden toy left by a stoop, a clothesline with frozen shirts stiff in the breeze. But no people. Only the echoes of them.

It felt like I was trespassing inside a memory.

A creak drew my eyes upward. One shutter, half-hinged, swayed in the cold air. I moved past it quickly, boots crunching over brittle leaves. The path narrowed between two collapsed buildings, funneling me toward a small square.

In the center stood a well. Its stone was cracked, the pulley rusted, but the bucket still dangled over the dark. I approached slowly, listening for anything unusual. When I reached the edge and peered down, I saw no water—only reflection.

Not of the sky.

Not of me.

But of *my past*.

The image shimmered like oil on water, then solidified. Me, back in the slums of Harrow's Gate, crouched behind a merchant's stall with blood on my knuckles and my ribs screaming where Father's last shove had landed. I was thirteen. Alone. And furious at everything.

The scene didn't move like a memory—it lived. I watched myself spit on the ground and steal a half-loaf of bread from a passing cart. Watched the younger Cass vanish into the crowd like smoke.

I backed away from the well.

Whatever this place was, it knew me.

I passed an old tavern, its door hanging open. Inside, a fire still burned in the hearth. Warmth spilled out unnaturally—wrong for the cold stillness outside. My steps slowed. Part of me wanted to go in, to sit, to let the illusion tempt me with rest.

But the other part—the smarter part—knew the test had already begun.

I pressed on.

The trail twisted uphill, past the edge of the village. Trees loomed now—crooked and bone-pale, their bark peeling like scabbed skin. It should have been a forest, but the way they leaned in felt theatrical. Deliberate.

The air grew colder.

And the silence changed.

It wasn't quiet like before, it was *expectant*. Waiting.

At the crest of the hill, I found a small clearing. And in the center, sitting on a ruined bench like she'd been waiting forever, was me.

Or rather—

What I had been.

She looked nineteen. Leaner. Wilder. Her old, patched leathers hung off her frame like loose bark. Her hair was shorter, messier. She held a twig loosely in one hand, picking at her nails like I wasn't even worth acknowledging.

I froze.

She didn't look up. Just said, "You got soft."

I didn't answer.

"You let him change you." Her eyes flicked up—sharp, accusing. "You smile too much now. Laugh too easy. Forgot what the world's really like."

I studied her. My past self. Hardened, but hollow. Dangerous, but brittle. She wasn't a test. She was a wound. One I hadn't known was still open.

"That's the point," I said finally. "To remember what the world is like—and choose to be something better anyway."

She smirked. "Sounds like something he'd say."

I took a cautious step forward. She didn't move.

"Are you going to fight me?" I asked.

"Wouldn't be much of a trial if I didn't." She stood, daggers appearing in both hands as if conjured from spite. "But that's not really what this is about, is it?"

"What is it about?"

She tilted her head. "Proving you still deserve to carry the name."

"What name?"

"Mine."

She lunged.

I barely parried the first blow, steel ringing against steel. She fought like I used to—fast, dirty, reckless. Each strike was meant to hurt, not kill. Like she was testing me, not trying to end me.

I blocked a feint and ducked a slash. "You think I'm not you anymore?"

"I think you forgot who made you."

Her words hit harder than her blades.

I slid backward, using the enchanted grip of my boots to keep balance on the slick leaves, and circled warily. "I didn't forget. I just chose to keep going."

She paused, her expression unreadable.

Then she stepped back and lowered her weapons. "Good."

I stared, chest heaving. "That's it?"

"For now," she said, voice suddenly tired. "But there's more to carry. You know that."

The image flickered.

Then she was gone.

Only the wind remained.

The clearing emptied around me, the last echoes of footsteps fading into stillness.

I took a breath—steady, grounding—and pressed forward.

The trees thickened, their trunks growing closer together, their branches forming a tangled ceiling that filtered the dim light into fractured shadows. No birdsong. No wind. Just the soft crunch of frost underfoot and the ever-present feeling that I was being watched.

Not the eerie memory-watch of the trial. No.

This felt real.

The path dipped into a shallow ravine, moss-covered stones jutting like teeth from the ground. Something moved ahead—fast, low to the ground, too quick to identify. I froze. My heart didn't race, not like it used to. But it beat loud enough to make me aware of my ribs.

I knelt and pulled the cloak tighter, drawing the hood up over my head. The fabric shifted in my hands like it understood, its threads cooling slightly, softening to match the earth beneath me. I went still—completely still—and waited.

Footsteps. Slow. Measured.

Not mine.

They came from behind. I risked a glance over my shoulder, careful not to rustle the underbrush. A figure moved between the trees, distant but deliberate. Cloaked. Hooded. I couldn't see the face, but I saw the way they moved. Confident. Searching. Armed.

Whoever they were, they weren't stumbling through a trial of their own. They belonged here. A warden? A hunter? I didn't know.

They didn't speak. Just paused occasionally to scan the trees. The air around them felt colder, heavier. Like the forest exhaled their presence.

I let my breath slow. Let my heartbeat melt into the hush. The cloak didn't make me invisible, but it made me *unimportant*. Forgettable. I was just another patch of leaf-dark earth. Another shadow beneath a twisted tree.

The figure passed within ten paces of me.

I didn't blink.

Didn't breathe.

Their head turned—just slightly—toward where I knelt. A pause. A flicker of attention.

And then they moved on.

Not fooled. Just... not convinced I was worth the effort. Yet.

I stayed motionless long after they were gone, counting heartbeats like a metronome. When I finally shifted, the air felt thinner. Less charged.

I stood slowly and slipped between two trees, changing my course.

This part of the forest sloped upward again. The trees grew denser, almost uniform, as if planted deliberately. Each one looked the same—white bark, black knots, needle-thin branches like skeletal fingers. The path had vanished, replaced by roots and frozen soil.

There was no map. No guidance. Just a voice in my memory:

"Survive. Navigate the path. Face what you carry."

So I kept going.

At the crest of the ridge, I found another clearing, this one ringed by broken monoliths and shattered carvings. A waystone stood half-buried in the center, its runes worn beyond legibility. The wind picked up here, sharp and biting.

And from the far edge of the ring... a whisper.

Low. Male. Not the same voice as the gate.

"I know you're here."

My pulse jumped.

I ducked behind the nearest stone and crouched low, already pulling the cloak around me again. The whisper hadn't come from memory or magic—it was real. Closer. The figure from the forest? Had they circled around?

"I can feel you watching."

No rustle. No crunch of footsteps. Just the voice, drifting through the mist like smoke.

"Don't run. It'll be worse if you run."

I drew one of my daggers, keeping the blade low and angled. Not to fight. To warn. To ward. This wasn't some shadow of my past. This was something hunting me.

But I didn't run.

I went still.

And I waited.

Chapter 8

EMBERS IN THE HALL

Tarn

I watched from the bench beneath the guild's awning as Cass stepped through the doors alone. The morning chill clung to my armor, frost biting through the seams, but I barely felt it. My eyes stayed fixed on the heavy double doors even after they swung shut behind her.

She hadn't looked back.

That was good. She didn't need reassurance anymore.

And yet... I exhaled slowly, steam curling from my lips. I still wanted to give it.

The street buzzed around me with its usual morning clamor— merchants barking about fresh goods, adventurers comparing scars and contracts, horses snorting beside water troughs—but it all blurred beneath the low hum of unease in my chest. I knew Cass would be fine. Better than fine, likely. But that didn't stop the tight coil of worry from winding tighter.

She's ready. You made sure of that.

But readiness didn't mean safety. Not in this world.

With one last glance at the guildhall, I stood and started down the slush-slicked street toward the east quarter—toward the highest building in town, whose spire cut through the gray sky like a blade: the Church of the First Flame.

The church always unsettled me. Too clean. Too still. Its windows never fogged from breath or fire. Its torches never hissed. Every corner seemed scrubbed of humanity, like the sacredness had scoured the warmth away.

I passed through the front arch, nodding tersely to the white-robed attendants in the foyer, and descended the polished stairs into the administrative wing. The lower halls were quieter—oppressively so—and colder still. The walls here were lined not with scripture but with portraits: the saints of flame, the founding martyrs, the Highflame Council.

And the enforcers.

They didn't call them inquisitors here. Not within the church. That title belonged to the Academy. The Church had *Ash Sentinels*—a more righteous title for the same grim function. Executioners in all but name.

And there were far more of them here than usual.

I slowed as I passed one corridor branching off the main hall. Half a dozen Sentinels stood there in silence, armored in ceremonial white, faces hidden behind helmed masks shaped like flame. Their mere presence darkened the hall like a stain.

What are they doing here? This isn't a high-threat zone.

A cold knot began forming in my stomach.

They made me wait—of course. The Archflame never granted immediate audiences unless it was a matter of divine import, and my name hadn't held weight in the church since the day I broke my vows.

The benches in the receiving hall were hard stone, just polished enough to remind you that comfort wasn't the goal. A few other petitioners sat in silence, their eyes lowered or fixed on the mural of the Ascension behind the altar. One woman whispered into a prayer cloth. A man clutched a sealed scroll like it might burn him if he let go.

I folded my arms, closed my eyes, and counted my breaths.

"Didn't expect to see you here."

The voice was familiar. Roughened by age, but unmistakable.

I opened my eyes to find Elias Vorn standing a few feet away, leaning on a walking staff that didn't belong to a man his age. His beard was thicker now, streaked with gray, and his priest's robes were plainer than I remembered—fewer sigils, less trim.

"Elias." I nodded. "You're still in the capital?"

"Still, yes. 'Til they get sick of me." He offered a hand, and I stood to take it. His grip was strong.

He studied me. "You look older."

"You look like you've started losing to stairs."

He snorted. "Still have more spells memorized than you had questions as a novice."

That pulled a smile from me, faint though it was. Elias had been one of the few teachers who treated me like more than a weapon-in-waiting.

"What brings you here?" he asked.

"Trouble. Same as always." I hesitated. "I need to speak to the Archflame."

Elias's expression tightened a fraction. "That's not easy these days. He's... less patient than he used to be."

"I remember." I glanced at the mural again. "But I need him to hear me."

"I can't help you with that," Elias said. "But I can give you some advice."

"Don't start with a heresy charge?"

"Don't start at all unless you're ready to finish it."

I nodded. "Thanks."

He clapped my shoulder once and moved on, leaving behind the faint scent of incense and the echo of older days.

Another thirty minutes passed.

Finally, the heavy doors to the inner sanctum creaked open. A scribe in red beckoned me forward.

"Archflame Vale will see you now."

The sanctum was a tall, vaulted chamber bathed in orange and gold light from suspended braziers. It smelled faintly of myrrh and something hotter beneath it—like burnt cedar. At the far end of the chamber, upon a raised platform flanked by two ever-burning flame fonts, stood Eryndor Vale.

The Archflame was tall, severe, with flowing crimson robes that shimmered faintly with protective runes. His hair was silver, his face smooth with an ageless calm that always unnerved me. The man didn't age. He just calcified.

"Tarn Elros," Eryndor said, his voice smooth as oiled parchment. "I had thought we were done seeing each other."

"Unfortunately, I'm not done trying," I replied evenly, stepping forward. "We need to talk. About the aetherstone. And about the key we recovered from the basilisk den."

Eryndor inclined his head slightly, expression unreadable. "I was briefed on the report. You suspect the Sons of the Hollow Star."

"I don't suspect. I know. That key had their sigil. The emerald wasn't just enchanted—it was cloaked to mimic a different artifact entirely. Cass watched it change when exposed to diagnostic magic. It was an Aethercore."

"And yet it was inert."

"Not for long. We both know what these stones are capable of."

He stepped down from the dais with a slow grace, his hands clasped before him. "The Church appreciates your vigilance. But you've been warned before, Tarn. Your history with the Sons makes your judgment... clouded."

"My history with them is why you should be listening. You think it's coincidence that they keep appearing near places under church protection?"

"You were relieved of your station for a reason. Your personal vendettas—"

"This isn't personal," I snapped. "This is the second time we've seen evidence that they're experimenting with Aethercores. And this time, it was practically on your doorstep."

Eryndor studied me, silent. Then he moved past me, toward the windows that overlooked the inner courtyard. "The First Flame teaches restraint. Control. You lost both."

My jaw tightened. "The First Flame teaches truth. And you're ignoring it."

That earned me a glance. Cold. Sharp.

"I've entertained this conversation," the Archflame said. "But if you're implying corruption in this church, I advise you to step very carefully, Elros."

"I'm not implying anything," I said flatly. "I'm warning you. If you keep ignoring the signs, more people will die. The Sons aren't working alone anymore."

He returned to his platform. "You've had your audience."

I didn't bow. Didn't speak. I turned and left the sanctum, boots echoing harshly across the stone.

As I reached the upper hall, one of the Sentinels shifted slightly. Just enough for me to know it was deliberate.

I met the hidden eyes of the mask and didn't flinch.

Let them watch.

Archflame's Sanctum

The moment the chamber doors closed behind Tarn, Eryndor exhaled slowly and turned toward the flickering braziers that lined the sanctum. The flame never wavered. It never dimmed. How enviable, that constancy.

"Elros," he murmured, more to the fire than to himself. "Still as persistent as ever."

A whisper stirred the air behind him, subtle as the shifting of ash. Eryndor didn't turn. He didn't need to.

"You said he wouldn't come sniffing," came a voice from the shadows near the far wall—fluid and dry, like silk over rusted nails.

"I said he would be manageable," Eryndor replied, calmly. "I underestimated his sense of purpose. That was my error."

A figure stepped into the brazier's light, his robe unmarked but finely tailored. No symbols, no rank—nothing that would draw attention. And that was precisely the point. The mark of the Sons of the Hollow Star was not worn on the chest. It was worn in deeds.

"And now?" the man asked.

Eryndor finally turned. "Now, I ask whether your people have already moved."

The man's smile didn't reach his eyes. "You assume we waited for your permission."

"I assume nothing." Eryndor stepped down from the platform, robes trailing behind him like coals in motion. "You said you had contingencies."

"We do." The man clasped his hands behind his back. "Examiner Meron has already been... compensated. He shaped the girl's trial according to our parameters."

"And?"

"And one of ours entered after her." His voice dropped, almost reverent. "She won't walk back out."

Eryndor let that sit in silence for a moment. "If she does?"

"She won't," the man repeated, tone flat. "But if she does... she'll be broken enough to pose no further threat. We're not foolish enough to underestimate her."

"She's more like him than she knows," Eryndor said softly, eyes returning to the flame. "That should worry you."

"It does," the man said, smiling again. "Which is why we've sent someone very... convincing."

Eryndor turned back to him. "And Tarn?"

"We're watching him. Closely. But he's too public to move against directly."

"I'm not asking for his removal," Eryndor said. "He's still useful. In time, he may even serve us better than he knows."

The man's smile thinned. "You want him diverted."

"Tempered," Eryndor corrected. "Let him chase ghosts. Feed him just enough truth to keep him believing he's in control. The more noise he makes, the easier it is for us to work in the quiet."

The man gave a slow nod. "We can manage that. And when the time comes?"

Eryndor's gaze lingered on the ever-burning flame. "When the time comes, he'll kneel—or break on his own convictions."

The man inclined his head. "As you wish, Archflame."

Without another word, he turned and disappeared once more into the shadows from which he came—gone as if he'd never been there at all.

Eryndor stood alone once more in the heatless glow of the flame, and for the first time in years, he felt the edge of something ancient curl through his gut.

Doubt.

Chapter 9

TRIAL BY SHADOWS

Cass

The cold stone at my back did little to slow the frantic hammer of my heart. I crouched low, breath held, the silence pressing in around me like a vice. Shadows stretched long across the ruined clearing, fractured light spilling through the broken canopy overhead. My fingers clenched around my dagger's hilt—slick with sweat and fear.

He was out there. Not a beast. Not a phantom. A man. And that made it worse.

His voice had been calm when he spoke. Too calm. It didn't match the wildness of the trial or the dread coiling in my gut. It hadn't sounded like part of the test. It had sounded real.

I peeked around the edge of the crumbled stone. He stood not far off, scanning the ruin with slow, deliberate precision. Black leather armor. Close-cropped dark hair. No emblem. No guild crest. Just a lean frame coiled with intent.

He hadn't drawn a weapon. Didn't need to.

I eased forward, inching away from the shattered wall, staying low. My boots made no sound—gods bless whatever enchantments still clung to them—but silence was no guarantee of safety. Not against someone like him.

A blur of motion. Pain exploded behind my ear.

I hit the ground hard, breath torn from my lungs. My dagger skittered out of reach. I rolled on instinct, barely avoiding the follow-up blow meant to crush my ribs. My vision spun, stars dancing at the edges of my sight.

"How—?" I gasped.

He didn't answer. He moved like smoke—silent, practiced, merciless. I kicked out blindly, catching his ankle, but he absorbed it with barely a flinch. In the same motion, he grabbed my arm and hauled me upright like I weighed nothing.

I struck with my offhand—sloppy, desperate. My knife grazed his side. He grunted. First sound he'd made.

Then he threw me. Hard.

I hit the ruin wall with a crunch. My shoulder screamed. I staggered as he lunged again. I dropped, letting his fist crash into the stone where my head had been.

No way this was part of the trial. This wasn't a test. This was an execution.

My shoulder ached from the last throw, and my lungs burned, but I kept my grip on the wall. I had to. He was circling again, and I didn't know from where.

I pivoted, catching movement out of the corner of my eye—just in time. His hand sliced through the air where my throat had been a heartbeat earlier. Open-handed, fast, and brutal. I ducked under the strike, twisted on one knee, and slashed upward with my dagger.

He blocked it with his forearm. Sparks flew as metal kissed metal—his vambrace was enchanted, clearly. He retaliated with a low, sweeping kick. I jumped over it, barely, then slammed the heel of my boot into his chest to force distance.

It didn't work.

He caught my ankle mid-kick and *twisted*. I cried out, pain flaring up my leg, and slammed hard against the ground, the wind knocked clean from me.

He came in fast—fist aimed for my stomach. I moved to block—

Too late.

Steel flashed. I hadn't seen him draw it—hadn't even known he carried one. But the blade was there, small and curved, and it sliced a line of fire across my upper arm before I could react.

I screamed, staggered back, clutching the wound. Not deep, but gods, it bled fast.

"You're persistent," he said softly, almost like it was a compliment.

"You're losing," I spat.

He grinned. "Am I?"

"Come on, Cass," I whispered to myself. "Think."

My arm burned like it had been dipped in flame. Every time I moved it, the pain flared sharper, but I couldn't stop. Not now.

He pressed forward, relentless. Each strike came faster than the last—jabs, slashes, kicks meant to break my rhythm. I couldn't think. Could barely keep up. My world narrowed to footsteps and instinct.

Steel rang as I deflected another blow, the impact jarring up my wrist and into my bones. I ducked under his next swing and drove my shoulder into his gut, buying myself inches. Not enough.

He pivoted with me—his elbow slammed into my ribs. Something cracked. I gasped and dropped to one knee, seeing white behind my eyes.

A boot came at my face. I rolled aside, breath ragged, dragging myself upright with sheer spite.

"You're slowing," he murmured. "Doesn't suit you."

"Neither does talking," I spat, then hurled a handful of dirt at his eyes.

He snarled—not blinded, but distracted. I rushed him, slashing at his thigh. The blade tore leather, and blood followed. Not deep. Not enough.

He retaliated with a palm to my face—an open-handed strike that rocked my skull back and sent me stumbling.

I landed hard against a fallen pillar, the impact rattling my teeth. Blood dripped into my eye. I wiped it away with a shaking hand, heart hammering like a war drum.

He was walking toward me now. Not rushing. Just walking. Like he knew it was over.

Like he was done playing.

I needed something. Anything.

My fingers brushed the edge of my belt pouch.

Then I remembered the flare stone Tarn had given me months ago.

I reached in to check, still there.

I palmed it, heart stuttering.

One shot.

Make it count.

I shifted my weight, hiding the stone. He was still approaching, slowly, blade held low, like he didn't see me as a threat anymore.

Let him believe that.

My vision swam from the blow to my head, and my ribs throbbed with every breath. My arm felt slick and hot with blood. But I had one shot—and it had to be perfect.

He raised the blade.

I flinched backward, exaggerating it.

He smirked.

And I hurled the flare stone into the ground between us.

Light exploded.

White, blinding, searing through the clearing like lightning trapped in glass. He shouted, staggering back, one arm raised too late to block it. I lunged through the bloom of brilliance, blinking against the afterimage, driving my dagger for his side.

He twisted at the last second. My blade caught the edge of his coat instead of flesh.

He elbowed me in the jaw. I reeled—but didn't fall.

We clashed again—steel and speed and fury. I didn't give him a second to recover. Slashes. Feints. Dodges. I aimed high, then swept low. He stumbled—but his footwork saved him.

I pressed harder. My blade kissed his cheek, drawing a line of blood.

"You're bleeding," I rasped, chest heaving.

"So are you," he growled.

We locked eyes—both of us panting now.

Then he surged forward. Too fast.

He slammed me back into the ruin wall. The blade scraped across my collarbone. I screamed and dropped my dagger.

His hand clamped around my throat.

My feet left the ground.

He bared his teeth. "It's over."

I clawed at his wrist, vision tunneling.

No.

Not yet.

Not like this.

My fingers scrambled for anything—rock, shard, gods, something—

And closed around my boot knife.

I drove it up with everything I had.

The knife punched into his side.

He gasped—sharp, guttural—and dropped me.

I hit the ground hard, coughing, blinking away stars as air flooded back into my lungs. He staggered backward, blood dripping from his side, hand clutching the wound.

I didn't wait. Couldn't. I scooped up my main blade and pushed to my feet, legs trembling under me. Every muscle screamed, but I shoved the pain aside.

He was still standing.

Still watching me.

Still smiling.

"You're full of surprises," he said, voice thinner now, tinged with something that might've been admiration—or contempt.

I didn't answer. I couldn't waste breath.

He darted forward again, slower now but no less precise. I met him with steel, our blades clashing in bursts of sparks. He struck high, then low. I twisted, deflected. My arm burned with each parry, but I held fast.

He spun—aiming a heel toward my head.

I ducked and slashed across his ribs. Another cut.

He hissed and punched me in the stomach, but I absorbed it, dropping to one knee, sweeping at his legs. He leapt over, landing light.

Too light. Too perfect.

I faked a stumble and spat blood in his face.

He recoiled, cursing, just enough for me to close in again.

Slash. Feint. Thrust.

I caught his wrist, twisted, and for a moment—just a moment—he lost his grip on the dagger. It clattered to the stones between us.

We both dove.

I reached first.

But not for the blade.

My fingers found his shadow—cast long across the ground by the burning flare stone.

And I *stepped.*

The world twisted. Cold. Silent. Weightless.

I emerged in his blind spot, behind him.

His knife missed air.

I drove mine home.

Time stopped.

His body stiffened, breath caught. Blood bloomed. He turned, confused, as if the rules had just changed on him.

"You weren't supposed to win," he rasped, blood spilling from his lips. "They said... it'd be easy."

He collapsed, motionless.

I staggered back, chest heaving, my whole body trembling from the effort. Blood trickled from a dozen scrapes and the searing cut on my arm. My lungs burned. My knees nearly buckled.

But I was alive.

The flare stone guttered out behind me, plunging the ruins into cold shadow. For a moment, I just stood there—blade still clutched tight in one shaking hand—staring at the crumpled figure on the ground. The man who'd tried to kill me.

Not test me.

Not scare me.

Kill me.

That truth pressed down harder than anything else.

I wasn't just fighting phantoms in this place. Someone had sent him. Someone wanted me dead.

And I'd survived.

I wiped the blood from my lip with the back of my hand and took a shuddering breath. My heart still raced. My limbs ached. But I wasn't done yet.

The path wasn't over.

Past the assassin's body, the shattered wall crumbled into a slope of uneven stones leading downward. Faintly, beyond it, I saw light—pale and steady. Not firelight. Not illusion. Something real.

I followed it.

The descent led me into a chamber unlike the rest. Smooth walls instead of ruins. A single pedestal rose from the center, carved from obsidian and veined with silver runes that pulsed softly with light. Atop it sat a puzzle: nine interlocked rings etched with stars, each rotating freely on its axis.

Above the pedestal, inscribed in old tongue:

Only one truth leads forward. All else must align.

A test of the mind. Not the blade.

I stepped forward. My hands shook as I touched the rings. They moved easily—too easily.

I'd just survived an assassin. And now I had to solve... this?

The fear that rose next wasn't the sharp panic of battle. It was deeper. Heavier.

What if I wasn't enough?

My fingers hovered over the spinning rings, the metal cold beneath my touch. The stars etched into them shimmered faintly, but there were no instructions. No guidance. Just that inscription echoing in my head.

I stared at the rings, heart still thudding in my ears. I couldn't tell if the pounding was from adrenaline or fear now. Probably both.

I wasn't a scholar. I wasn't a priestess or a mage or anything trained for this kind of thing. I fought, I survived. That was who I was.

But was that enough?

The stars rotated as I twisted one ring, and the others shifted with it—interconnected. Move one, and three others turned. I grimaced. Of course it wouldn't be simple.

I tried again, slowly, carefully, tracing the paths as best I could. I made a few moves, aligning crescent constellations in a pattern that looked vaguely familiar.

And then... nothing.

The runes dimmed, then flickered like dying coals.

Wrong.

I hissed through my teeth and stepped back. My whole body ached. Blood soaked through a bandage as I hastily wrapped it around my arm. My legs felt like they'd fold any second. And now this?

I clenched my fists. "Come on, Cass," I muttered. "You made it this far."

But the voice that answered wasn't mine. It was softer. Crueler.

You only made it this far because someone else gave you a chance.
Tarn. The guild. You're not special. Just lucky.

I looked down at my hands as a storm began to brew in the background. They trembled.

What if that voice was right?

What if this wasn't a trial I was meant to survive?

I'd killed a man. I'd fought with everything I had—and still nearly died. And now the trial wanted more. It wanted my mind. My heart.

What if everything I had left... wasn't enough?

I sank to my knees.

Not from weakness. Not entirely. Just... to stop moving for a second. To breathe.

The rings loomed in front of me, carved with symbols I barely understood. But as I sat there, chest rising and falling in slow, shallow breaths, I let my gaze blur. Not trying to solve the puzzle. Just... seeing it.

The crescents, the stars, the shifting constellations... they weren't random.

They weren't maps. Not celestial ones, at least.

They were moments.

Tiny fragments of things I remembered. Not places in the sky—but pieces of my life.

The broken ring on the left bore a trio of interlinked stars—exactly like the sigil on the locket my mother once wore.

The upper band was etched with a crooked line that looked like a river bending east—the same shape as the map Tarn had shown me before our first job.

And the center...

The center was a half-buried crescent moon.

I'd seen it once before. Long ago. In a book my brother had kept hidden under floorboards when we were young—old stories about the night goddess, the patron of secrets and shadow.

She'd been called the Keeper of Burdens.

The words returned to me then, cold and sharp and true:

Face what you carry.

It wasn't about the puzzle. It was about me.

All of this—the fight, the wounds, the puzzle—was never meant to test just my strength or wit. It was about whether I could carry the weight of what came next. The blood. The choices. The fear.

The guilt.

I reached out again. This time, I didn't think like a thief or a fighter. I thought like a girl who still remembered what it meant to lose things. Who carried them, even when they hurt.

My fingers turned the rings. Once, twice.

The stars aligned—not in the sky, but in the memory.

The crescent moon locked into place.

And the stone pulsed with light.

The light swelled, steady and silent, casting shadows across the ruin. It wasn't harsh or blinding—just full. Complete.

As the brilliance faded, my eyes adjusted—and that was when I saw it.

The pedestal was smaller than I expected—stone worn smooth by time and weather, its top just barely wide enough to hold the crescent-shaped pendant that waited there like a sliver of captured moonlight. Even with the storm still flashing behind me, the gem nestled within it gleamed—blue as twilight, deep as memory. A sapphire.

I stepped closer, blood still slick on my arm and leg, breath hitching with each ragged pull of my chest. My reflection shimmered faintly on the pendant's curved surface, framed by filth and bruises. I looked wrecked. I felt wrecked.

But I'd made it.

"Is this it?" I asked the empty air, half-expecting the voice from the gate to answer again.

It didn't. The silence that followed wasn't cruel. It wasn't indifferent. Just... still.

I reached out, hand trembling, and lifted the pendant.

The moment my fingers closed around it, warmth surged through my palm. Not heat. Not fire. Something gentler. Something older. Like moonlight on water. Like the hush after a long cry.

The sapphire pulsed once with soft blue light—and I knew.

This was what I'd come for. Not the fight. Not the survival. For this.

I slipped the chain over my head, let the pendant settle against my collarbone. It was light. But the weight of it—of what it meant—sank into me like truth.

The storm behind me faded.

Wind hushed.

The broken world stilled.

A sound—soft, like a bell struck in a dream—rippled through the glade. The stone floor beneath me shimmered, and in its center, the outline of a door began to glow. A portal, just like the one I'd stepped through to enter the trial.

My trial was over.

But I was not the same girl who had stepped through that gate. Not anymore.

Chapter 10

SPRING'S ECHO

Cass

The frost had finally lifted.

Two months had passed since the trial. Since the pain. Since Tarn carried me out of the trial chamber, my cloak clinging to his armor like a second skin, my breath shallow and uneven.

Now, spring sunlight streamed through the warped windowpanes of our shared room at the inn. It chased away the chill that had clung to my bones like memory. Outside, children's laughter echoed through the narrow streets. The scent of early blossoms floated in on a breeze that stirred the curtains like a sigh.

I lay sprawled across the rumpled bedroll near the hearth, a half-eaten apple in one hand and an empty teacup in the other. My body still ached on occasion—a dull throb in my ribs, a twinge in my side—but for the first time in weeks, I felt whole.

And safe.

I traced the rim of the teacup with my thumb, thinking about the last few months.

Tarn had barely left my side. When the fever struck, it was his voice that called me back. When I screamed in my sleep, it was his hand that grounded me, steady and patient. He never asked for thanks. Never made me feel like a burden. He simply was—a solid, steady presence in the haze of pain and recovery.

We'd developed a rhythm. Quiet mornings with bitter tea and half-burnt toast. Long afternoons where he taught me how to shift my stance, how to read a blade's weight by sound alone. Evenings where we shared stories beneath oil-lamp light, trading barbs and laughter like currency.

There were no confessions. No promises.

But he always looked at me like I was worth waiting for.

I smiled faintly and pushed myself to my feet. The inn creaked around me, familiar now. Our room was still cramped—one bed, one trunk, a shared table littered with scraps of parchment and half-finished gear repairs—but it had become something like home.

Tarn had gone out earlier to run errands. Something about restocking supplies and checking on a job board posting. I stayed behind, for once not because I had to—but because I wanted to do something in return.

He had cleaned my blood off my gear more times than I cared to count.

I sat cross-legged on the floor now, his armor splayed out before me like a puzzle. Dented, scratched, and heavy with use, it was still somehow pristine—worn, but not neglected. Just like him.

I exhaled through my nose and picked up a cloth.

"This is stupid," I muttered to no one in particular. "You're not a housemaid."

But I kept cleaning anyway.

My fingers moved in practiced circles, rubbing oil into the joints and wiping grime from the ridges of the chestplate. The silence was strange. I hadn't spent many mornings without Tarn over the past couple months. When my wounds kept me bedridden, he'd been the one bringing soup. Reading aloud. Watching over me when nightmares came.

He never made me feel weak, even when I was.

So when I spotted a scuffed patch just beneath the shoulder brace, I grabbed a small pick to dig the grime from the crevices. The steel creaked faintly as I pried under the edge of the plate—and something small fluttered loose, catching on my wrist.

A slip of waxed paper.

I blinked and pulled it out, expecting a note or old receipt. Instead, it was a photograph—worn at the edges, faded but intact. Four people, standing close together with the kind of ease that only comes from trust. There were names written on the back.

Tarn stood in the middle, arms folded but smiling. Not his usual smile, either. This one was softer. Almost shy.

To his left stood a man with a braided beard and arms like tree trunks—Brannick, I guessed. A classic fighter's stance. A big grin, half-cocked like he was about to elbow someone in the ribs.

To Tarn's right was a woman in soft robes, her hair woven in intricate loops over her shoulders. Her expression was serene. Selara, likely. The priestess.

And then there was her—a woman draped over Tarn's shoulders with easy intimacy. Laina. Her smile was wide, eyes crinkled at the corners as she leaned into him like gravity didn't apply. Tarn had his arm around her waist without even seeming to think about it.

I stared at the image for a long time. My grip tightened.

I hadn't known. Not really.

Laina wasn't just a friend. Wasn't just a comrade. She was someone important. Intimate. Maybe the most important person in his life before all this.

Something hot and unwelcome stirred in my gut.

I set the photo down gently, then stood and crossed the room to pour myself a glass of water. I wasn't angry. Not exactly. Tarn had a past—of course he did. It wasn't like I expected him to be some kind of chaste knight waiting in a tower for me.

Still... I felt stupid for how much it stung.

Maybe it was the way Tarn had carried me when I couldn't walk. The way he smiled when he thought I wasn't looking. The nights he sat up beside me when I couldn't sleep. I didn't know what we were, but it had started to feel like something real. Like something that mattered.

And suddenly, I wasn't sure anymore.

The door creaked downstairs—boots on wood, laughter from the street drifting in.

I blinked hard and stuffed the photo back under the armor. My hand lingered there a second too long.

I didn't hear Tarn return. It wasn't him.

A knock came at the doorframe instead, and when I turned, a tall figure stood leaning in the open doorway with a crooked grin.

"Well, well," the man said. "Still breathing, I see."

I blinked at him. "...Vaelen?"

The boyish charm was unmistakable. A little taller than I remembered, a little broader in the shoulders, but the same lazy smile tugged at his lips. He hadn't changed much since the last time we'd seen each other. I hadn't expected to feel a lump in my throat.

I stepped forward without thinking and slugged him in the arm.

"Ow," he said with a grin. "Still violent, then."

"You disappeared."

"I wrote."

"Once."

"Twice."

I rolled my eyes, but I didn't pull away when he wrapped me in a warm hug. It wasn't romantic—not anymore. But it was familiar.

As we broke apart, something squirmed near his hip. His bag rustled—and suddenly a small weasel-like creature poked its head out, blinking up at me through tiny round spectacles.

"Don't touch the tail," the creature said. "It's sensitive."

I jerked back with a yelp. "By the stars—what the hell is that?!"

The weasel sniffed. "Eliza, thank you very much."

Vaelen smirked. "Animist. She's my partner now."

Eliza yawned and stretched inside the satchel. "And by partner, he means babysitter."

I stared, then laughed—sharp, bright, and a little breathless. I hadn't realized how tightly my chest had felt until it broke.

Eliza yawned again, her tiny jaw stretching unnaturally wide, and then she glanced up at Vaelen with a sigh.

"Well, if we're going to play catch-up like a bunch of sentimental softies, I'm shifting before we go downstairs. I refuse to eat crumbs off your shoulder again."

She gave a flick of her tail and hopped down from Vaelen's satchel. A faint shimmer danced across her fur as her form rippled—one moment a sleek weasel, the next a short woman with flowing chestnut hair and the same round spectacles perched on her nose.

She straightened her robes with a practiced tug and adjusted her sleeves like she hadn't just been curled up in a leather bag.

"Much better," she said, and offered me a hand. "Eliza. Animist. Scholar. Magic prodigy. Tired of being underestimated."

I shook her hand, still blinking. "That... was impressive."

She beamed. "I know."

Vaelen rolled his eyes. "Come on. I'm starving, and I haven't had food that wasn't smoked jerky or trail bread in three weeks."

I followed them out the door and down the creaking staircase into the tavern below. It was midmorning, just past the rush. A few late drinkers slumped over their mugs in the corner, but the fire was still going strong, and the smell of roasted meat and warm bread hit me like a spell.

We found an empty table near the back. Vaelen flopped down without ceremony and flagged down the innkeeper with a wave that was all charm and zero manners.

"Something hot, something filling, and something that won't make us regret it," he called. "And a round of whatever passes for beer in this place."

I slid into the seat across from him. Eliza sat between us, still smoothing her robes like she hadn't just transformed in front of me with barely a blink.

"So," I said, leaning my arms on the table, "you gonna tell me where the hell you've been?"

Vaelen tilted his chair back, balancing it on two legs like he always used to. "Here. There. The coast. A few mage duels in Hallowmere. Almost got married in Westdrake."

I raised a brow. "*Almost?*"

"She turned out to be cursed. Kept turning into a goose during thunderstorms."

Eliza didn't even flinch. "True story."

I blinked. "You're serious."

"She bit him," Eliza added.

"She *hissed* at me," Vaelen corrected, eyes wide. "I still have a scar."

Despite myself, I laughed. It felt good. Familiar. Like peeling back the years one dumb story at a time.

"So what really happened?" I asked, softer now. "After everything with my father... you just left."

Vaelen's smile faded just a little. "Yeah. I did."

He let the chair drop forward with a thud and leaned on his elbows.

"I wanted to stay. You know that, right? But your father wasn't exactly subtle about what he'd do if I did. I was two weeks from being arrested or 'going missing.' And you were too proud to let me fight for you."

I swallowed. That part still stung.

"I didn't want you getting dragged into my family's mess," I said. "I thought—"

"You thought you were protecting me," he finished. "I know. But you never asked if I *wanted* to be protected."

He didn't sound angry. Just tired.

I looked away.

A barmaid arrived with three plates—steaming stew, dark bread, and mugs of frothy ale that sloshed dangerously close to the rim. The moment she left, Vaelen dug in like a starving wolf.

Eliza took a single bite and chewed thoughtfully. "This is decent," she said, pleasantly surprised.

"Best meal I've had in a week," Vaelen mumbled through a mouthful of meat and potatoes. "Don't suppose you've got room for two more upstairs?"

"You didn't book a room?" I asked.

He grinned. "Wasn't sure you'd be happy to see me. Figured I'd sleep in the stables if I had to."

I shook my head. "Tarn won't care. Just try not to charm the innkeeper's daughter this time."

"No promises."

We ate in a lull of silence after that—comfortable, mostly. I kept stealing glances at Vaelen, trying to reconcile the version of him at this table with the memory I'd carried for years. He was older, sure. A little more rugged. But the grin was the same. The way he talked with his hands, the lazy sarcasm—still there. Still *him*.

And yet... I wasn't the same girl he'd known, either.

"You've changed," he said, catching me mid-thought.

I smirked. "You saying I used to be soft?"

"I'm saying you used to pretend to be hard. Now I think you really are."

"Eliza," I said, turning to her, "is he always this flattering?"

"Only when he's trying to apologize without saying it directly," she said.

"I *never* apologize directly," Vaelen muttered.

I leaned back, nursing my drink. My emotions still churned under the surface—the photo upstairs, the ache in my chest, the questions I wasn't ready to ask—but for now, sitting here, with old friends and a warm meal...

It didn't feel so heavy.

Chapter 11

CROSSCURRENTS

Cass

The tavern door creaked open behind us just as I finished laughing at something Eliza said—something ridiculous about a noblewoman and a miscast glamour spell. I was still smiling, the warmth of it lingering in my chest, when the air shifted.

I didn't even have to turn around.

Tarn's presence was unmistakable. Quiet. Solid. Like the gravity in the room had suddenly changed direction. My breath hitched before I could stop it, a strange pressure curling in my chest. I felt like I'd been caught doing something I shouldn't—like a teenager caught sneaking sweets, only the guilt ran deeper, stranger. I wasn't doing anything wrong. And yet... the moment I sensed him there, I sat up straighter, my smile fading just a little.

Something unspoken tugged at the edge of my thoughts.

Was I nervous? Or just guilty?

No. Not guilty. Not really. Just... seen.

And somehow, that was worse.

I looked over my shoulder and met his eyes as he stepped inside, arms full with a satchel and a small bundle wrapped in oilcloth. His gaze flicked to me, to Vaelen, to Eliza, and back again. The pause between those glances said more than any words could.

"Tarn," I said, standing.

Vaelen stood too, smooth as ever. "You must be the paladin," he said, offering his hand across the table. "Vaelen Rime. Old friend. Former bad influence. Current swordsman extraordinaire."

Tarn took his time setting the bundle down before shaking his hand. "Tarn."

Just his name. No title. No smile.

I winced internally.

"They just got into town," I said, trying to break the tension. "We ran into each other upstairs."

Eliza gave a polite nod. "Hello."

There was a long moment before Tarn sat down, his eyes lingering on Vaelen longer than I liked. He didn't say anything, but I knew him well enough by now to read the shift in his posture—subtle, but unmistakably alert. Like he was trying to size up a potential threat.

Something about the way Tarn looked at Vaelen made my throat tighten. It wasn't anger exactly—it was that paladin calm of his, stretched taut like a wire. I couldn't tell if he was being cautious or protective. Or if he just didn't like the way Vaelen's smile lingered a little too long on me.

Vaelen, of course, didn't seem bothered in the slightest. He leaned back in his chair like he owned the whole damn inn.

"So," he said after a sip of his drink, "this the one who pulled you out of that death trap you called a trial?"

I tensed, unsure how Tarn would react, but he just gave a short nod.

"He saved my life," I said, a little sharper than intended.

Vaelen raised a brow at that, then smiled and leaned back in his chair. "Looks like I owe you one, then."

Tarn's eyes didn't leave him. "That depends. You planning to stick around long enough to be useful?"

"Only if Cass wants me here," Vaelen replied easily.

My breath caught just for a second. The way he said it—like my opinion was all that mattered—sent a flutter of emotion through me I couldn't quite name. Was it comfort? Guilt? Or maybe the weight of being seen so clearly by two men who knew different versions of me. I glanced at Tarn, half-hoping he hadn't noticed the warmth that crept into my cheeks. "But from what I've heard, the road ahead's getting ugly. And I'm not the run-away-from-a-fight type."

"Eliza's not bad in a scrap, either," I added, glancing toward her. "She nearly turned a drunk into a squirrel last time we traveled together."

"I was aiming for a stoat," Eliza corrected with a shrug.

Vaelen chuckled. "Besides—Cass and I make a good team. Always did."

That landed. I saw it in Tarn's jaw, the slight tightening that meant he was biting down on something he wouldn't say.

"Used to drive her father mad," Vaelen continued, flashing me a grin.

I felt a flicker of something cold at the mention of him—my father. We hadn't spoken in years, not since I walked out and chose my own path. His disapproval still lingered like a phantom bruise, more memory than wound, but it ached all the same. Back then, I thought leaving would mean freedom. All it really did was make the silence louder.

Vaelen had been one of the few people who made that silence bearable—who reminded me I wasn't completely alone.

"We'd sneak out the back gate at night," he went on, still smiling, "raid the old manor's wine cellar, teach each other spells we weren't supposed to know. You remember the fireworks over the temple square?"

I laughed. "You nearly set your eyebrows on fire."

"You threw the bottle that exploded."

Tarn didn't laugh.

He reached for his mug, calm and composed, but I caught the tightness in his grip. He wasn't angry. Not exactly. But something protective flared behind his eyes—and maybe something else, too.

Jealousy?

I wasn't sure. But I knew Tarn well enough now to recognize the warning signs. He was trying to stay composed. Still, his eyes never left Vaelen.

There was a charged silence at the table. I could feel the weight of two very different histories pressing down between them. One written in years of friendship and flirtation, the other forged in fire and bloodshed and quiet nights spent in shared silence.

"So," Vaelen said, breaking the tension with a lopsided grin, "Cass mentioned you two have been traveling together a while now. Must be nice having someone who can actually cook. She once burned soup."

"It was stale broth," I muttered, but the heat in my cheeks betrayed me.

Eliza smiled faintly. "This is already my favorite table in the building."

"You're an Arcblade," Tarn said suddenly.

Vaelen tilted his head. "And you're observant."

"Lightning affinity."

"You catch that from the boots, or are you just good at reading people?"

I glanced down. Static shimmered faintly across the trim of his boots—just enough to notice if you were looking.

"Both."

The grin that spread across Vaelen's face was pure challenge. "Wouldn't mind showing off. Haven't had a real spar in weeks."

I blinked. "Wait, seriously?"

Eliza sighed and reached for her drink. "Every time we visit a new town. It's like a compulsion."

Tarn stood. "Courtyard, then."

Vaelen rose in one smooth motion. "After you."

I followed them out, a tangle of nerves knotting in my chest. Something about this felt more personal than it should have.

More than a spar.

More like a warning.

The late morning light painted the courtyard in soft gold as we stepped outside. Birds chirped from the crooked shingles overhead, and somewhere nearby, a blacksmith's hammer rang out like a slow heartbeat. But even with the quiet, something buzzed beneath the surface—tension and static and expectation.

The courtyard behind the inn was wide enough for a duel, though uneven. Patches of moss crept through cracked stone. A crooked bench leaned against the fence, and I found myself settling there, trying not to look too invested as Tarn and Vaelen squared off.

Vaelen loosened his coat and rolled his shoulders. "Ground rules?"

Tarn said nothing. Just stepped forward, his stance relaxed but centered.

Eliza took a spot beside me, her arms folded as she watched. "Five seconds in and they're already posturing."

I nodded, but my throat was dry.

Vaelen unsheathed his sword in one fluid motion. The runes etched along the spine pulsed with blue light, like thunderclouds trapped in metal. He whispered a word I didn't catch. Lightning flared to life along the blade.

Tarn hadn't drawn anything. No hammer. No shield. He just waited.

Vaelen moved first.

He surged forward with a speed that would've startled anyone who hadn't seen him fight before. I had. It still startled me.

The sword came down in a clean arc, lightning trailing behind it like a comet. Tarn didn't block. He sidestepped, pivoted, and let the blow crash into the stone where he'd just been standing. Sparks scattered. Stone chipped.

Then Tarn struck.

A single palm to Vaelen's side—not flashy, not brutal. Just precise. But it threw him off balance all the same. Vaelen rolled, coming up on one knee, laughing.

"I see you don't believe in warm-ups."

Tarn didn't answer.

Lightning crackled in Vaelen's gauntlet as he swung again, the force of the magic sending a ripple through the air. He feinted, ducked, twisted the angle. Tarn parried with a gauntlet, catching the blade and pushing it wide. The impact snapped through the air like a crack of thunder.

They broke apart again, circling. Vaelen's coat fluttered with each movement, his sword crackling brighter with each breath. Tarn stood firm, expression unreadable, not a hair out of place.

"He's testing him," Eliza murmured beside me. "Seeing what kind of warrior he is."

I swallowed. "He doesn't trust him."

"He doesn't trust easily," she said. "But he's not trying to humiliate him. If he were, he'd have ended this already."

Vaelen lunged again, faster now. The tip of his sword arced toward Tarn's shoulder, but Tarn dipped low and let the strike glance off his bracer. Then, with barely a shift in weight, he swept Vaelen's legs out from under him.

Vaelen hit the ground hard, sparks skittering across the stone. He stayed down a beat longer than necessary, then groaned and rolled to his back.

"Well," he said, staring at the sky, "that answers that."

Tarn offered a hand.

Vaelen took it.

"I've seen enough," Tarn said.

The tension eased a little.

"You're good," Tarn added. "But you rely too much on flair. You waste energy with every step."

Vaelen grinned as he stood. "That's the point. The flair distracts them from what really matters."

"Not me."

"No," he said. "Not you."

I stood too, brushing my palms on my thighs. "So does this mean—?"

"If you trust him," Tarn said without turning to me, "that's enough."

The words struck deeper than I expected. After everything—after the way he'd studied Vaelen like a blade poised to cut, after the stiffness in his shoulders whenever our past came up—I'd thought he might protest. Or at least hesitate. But instead, he gave me the choice.

He trusted *me*.

And yet, the absence of him saying he trusted *Vaelen* lingered like a splinter. Was that caution? Doubt? Or something quieter—something more personal? I didn't know. But I felt the shift inside myself, a flicker of guilt tangled with gratitude, made heavier by the weight of things left unsaid.

I wasn't sure if I wanted to thank him or ask what it meant that he hadn't said he trusted *Vaelen* himself.

Eliza stepped forward. "And me?"

Tarn gave her a rare nod. "You're welcome."

She raised an eyebrow. "Just like that?"

"I've seen the way you watch people. You miss nothing. We'll need that."

Her expression didn't change, but something in her shoulders relaxed. Just a little.

I looked between them, my heart still unsettled. This was my old life and my new one colliding. Vaelen, with his charm and mischief and half-masked grief. Tarn, with his gravity and fire and silence.

And me, standing in between, unsure which way I was leaning.

The sun was higher by the time we gathered our things and stepped back into the street. A breeze caught the edge of my cloak as I fell into step beside Tarn, Vaelen and Eliza walking just ahead, already bickering over who had the worst travel habits.

"You're the one who insists on bringing five changes of clothes," Eliza said, arms folded.

"It's called being prepared," Vaelen replied. "Sorry not all of us can look effortlessly put together while crawling out of a swamp."

Eliza rolled her eyes. "Magic. Learn it sometime."

I smiled at the banter, but my thoughts were still tangled around the look Tarn had given me back in the courtyard. Not judgmental. Not cold. Just... watching. Weighing. Like he saw something I hadn't realized I was revealing.

"You okay with this?" I asked him quietly.

He didn't look at me, but his voice was sure. "I trust you."

That should've been comforting. It wasn't.

I kept walking, matching his pace. I wanted to say something else. Ask him about the photo. Ask if he still thought about her. But the words stuck in my throat.

Instead, I asked, "You think this will work?"

He glanced sideways. "Vaelen has skill. Eliza has sharp instincts. That matters. The road ahead isn't safe."

I nodded. "You didn't answer the question."

"If they stay true," he said after a moment, "it will."

Ahead of us, Vaelen spun on his heel and walked backwards, his hands tucked behind his head.

"You two always this serious?" he called.

"Only when you're talking," I shot back.

He grinned. "That's the Cass I remember."

We reached the adventurer's guild just as the square began to fill. Merchants called out prices, kids darted between stalls, and the faint clang of steel from the nearby smithy rang steady as a heartbeat.

The guild doors loomed ahead. Inside waited missions, ranks, rules, and expectations.

Outside, we were just four travelers. Inside, we'd be something more.

Vaelen stepped up beside me as we reached the entrance.

"Whatever happens," he said under his breath, "I've got your back."

I glanced at Tarn. He was watching the door, expression unreadable.

I took a breath.

Then I stepped forward.

Together, we crossed the threshold.

Chapter 12

EMBERS AND ECHOS

Cass

The Adventurer's Guild doors shut behind us with a solid *thunk*, the familiar scent of parchment, sweat, and firewood greeting us like a half-forgotten memory. I felt the weight of the city slip from my shoulders—replaced almost immediately by the stiff weight of expectations. This was the first time the four of us entered as a group. Not just me and Tarn anymore.

The room buzzed with activity. Teams of adventurers huddled around posted notices and scarred tables. Some were laughing, others shouting, and a few just sat quietly nursing bruises and ale.

Tarn walked ahead without hesitation. Vaelen and Eliza flanked me, drawing curious glances. Vaelen always turned heads with his confident stride and travel-worn armor, but Eliza—with her unreadable eyes and long coat still dusted with road grit—drew more than a few wary looks.

We approached the main desk where a lean half-elf man I vaguely recognized was sorting mission scrolls.

Tarn cleared his throat.

The clerk looked up, blinked, then gave a cautious smile. "Ah, Tarn. Cass. And... newcomers?"

Tarn nodded. "They'll be registering under my sponsorship."

The clerk's eyes widened slightly but said nothing. He reached beneath the counter, pulled out a pair of crystal tokens and pushed them toward Eliza and Vaelen. "Standard provisional marks," he explained. "You'll be officially listed as a party now that you have enough members—have you decided on a name?"

Tarn didn't answer.

I glanced at him. He didn't even flinch.

Vaelen leaned on the counter. "No need for a name. We'll make one for ourselves on the road."

Eliza took her token with two fingers and turned it thoughtfully in the light. "These things track everything?"

"Combat stats, kill counts, spell imprints," the clerk said with a shrug. "Nothing exact, but enough to know who ran and who stood their ground."

Vaelen slipped his into his pocket with a grin. "Guess we'll have to make sure ours look good."

The clerk scribbled something into his logbook, then nodded toward me. "Cass, you're Bronze now, correct?"

I nodded. "Got the mark last week."

"You'll be listed as team lead."

Vaelen raised an eyebrow. "No offense, but shouldn't Tarn be the one leading? He's Silver, and she just made Bronze."

The clerk didn't even glance up. "Tarn's registered as an independent Silver. Rank trials are solo by design, and while he passed his alone, it also means he's not part of any official team charter. Unless he petitions to transfer out of independent status—which takes council approval—he can't serve as team lead. Cass is the only ranked member eligible under the standard advancement rules."

Vaelen leaned back. "Right. Because gods forbid anything in this place makes sense."

Tarn just gave a small nod, like he'd already read the fine print.

And just like that, the weight of responsibility landed squarely on my shoulders.

Me. In charge.

It shouldn't have been a big deal—just a name on a form—but the knot forming in my stomach said otherwise. Tarn might trust me. The guild might have stamped it without hesitation. But I wasn't sure I trusted myself. What if I messed up? What if someone got hurt because I wasn't fast enough, smart enough... enough?

I forced myself to breathe, to stand a little straighter. I could handle this. I had to.

After that, it was a blur of forms, stamps, guild crests, and one too many ink smudges. We were given a quest to start—standard courier work to a nearby supply depot two days east, along the same route we'd eventually need to travel to reach the dungeon frontier.

Low risk. High exposure.

Perfect trial run.

By the time we stepped back into the sunlit square, I felt like my head was full of parchment and my nerves were stretched thin from pretending everything felt normal.

The four of us paused at the top of the guild steps. I looked at each of them in turn.

Tarn. Always calm. Always heavy.

Vaelen. Grinning like this was all some grand game.

Eliza. Quiet, but already watching everything.

And me, standing at the center, the crescent moon pendant at my collar cool against my skin.

"So," I said, hitching my bag a little higher. "Shall we?"

Tarn gave a nod. "The sooner we start, the sooner we get answers."

We left the city behind in silence.

The road stretched ahead, wide and rutted from caravan wheels, flanked by tall grass and lazy summer wind. Tarn walked ahead of us, his boots leaving steady imprints in the dust. I found myself walking between Vaelen and Eliza again, like some awkward link between two halves of a puzzle that didn't quite fit.

We were traveling light. Two days out, one night camping, then back. Enough time to see how well we worked together before the dungeon trip. And maybe enough time for me to get my head on straight.

But that seemed less likely the longer we walked.

I still hadn't talked to Tarn about the picture.

He hadn't brought it up, and I hadn't found the words. I didn't know if I *wanted* to know more about her—the woman in the photo. The one with her arm around him like it was the most natural thing in the world. The one whose absence still haunted his eyes when he didn't realize I was looking.

I rubbed the edge of the pendant through my cloak, the crescent shape smooth beneath my fingers.

"You all right?" Eliza's voice came soft beside me.

I blinked. "Yeah. Just thinking."

She looked at me for a moment, then reached into her bag. "Something I wanted to ask you about."

I glanced over as she pulled out a small satchel and carefully opened it. Inside was a folded piece of parchment, some chalk, and a vial of silvery dust.

Eliza nodded toward the pendant. "That from the trial? I don't remember seeing you wear it before."

My hand went to my chest protectively. "You want to test it?"

"Just a basic resonance check," she said. "No spells, no damage. I'll do it here, in the open."

I hesitated... then nodded and slipped it off.

She moved to a nearby rock and knelt, drawing a quick circle in the dust with a practiced hand. It wasn't fancy—just a set of containment runes and a focus glyph—but it still made my stomach twist to see the pendant placed inside it like evidence at a crime scene.

Eliza sprinkled a bit of the silvery dust, then whispered a few words under her breath.

The pendant pulsed.

Just once.

But the air shifted with it. A breath of something older than wind, a feeling like someone had just whispered behind my ear.

Vaelen shivered. "Okay, *definitely* not normal."

Eliza sat back on her heels. "It's not harmful. Not inherently. But it's old. Ancient. And it's tied to something... hidden. Buried. Whatever this thing is, it doesn't want to be found."

Tarn, who had been watching in silence, finally spoke. "Keep it close. And don't let anyone else see it. Especially not anyone from the Church."

My stomach flipped. "Why?"

"I've seen that symbol before," he said, eyes still locked on the pendant. "And if I'm right... there are people who would kill to possess it. Or to destroy it."

The pendant was back around my neck by the time we got moving again, its weight more noticeable now that I knew it wasn't just decorative. It felt heavier somehow—like it knew it had secrets and was daring me to ask the wrong questions.

We left the testing site behind and pressed east along the trade road. The chatter from earlier had faded into a more thoughtful quiet. I caught Eliza glancing at me every now and then, like she wasn't quite done with her curiosity, but she kept whatever thoughts she had to herself. For now.

Eventually, she shifted again—literally this time. With a shimmer of magic and a quiet puff of displaced air, her figure collapsed inward and shrank until a sleek little weasel scrambled up onto my shoulder like it was the most natural thing in the world.

I tensed at first, but didn't shrug her off. It wasn't unwelcome—just new.

"You know," Vaelen said, not even looking back, "every time she does that, I wonder if she's going to pick something weird, like a pigeon or a crab."

The weasel on my shoulder squeaked indignantly and flicked her tail.

"I'm just saying," he added, grinning over his shoulder, "she could have at least picked something useful. Like a dire wolf. Or a hawk with laser eyes."

"Pretty sure those don't exist," I muttered.

"Not with that attitude."

The levity helped. A little. But it didn't completely chase away the lingering chill from the pendant's pulse. Or the heaviness sitting low in my gut.

I was team lead. I was supposed to be setting the tone. Guiding us. Watching the terrain, making the calls. And instead I was letting myself spiral into weird pendant mysteries and emotional confusion.

Get it together, Cass.

I adjusted my pack and forced myself to focus on the surroundings. The trail was still broad and clear, but the hills were starting to swell around us, and the trees were thickening. Shadows lengthened quicker out here. Easy for bandits to find cover. Or worse.

We stopped near a creek when the sun was high. Tarn gestured to a clearing with some half-buried stone markers—an old waystation, maybe—and we settled in to eat and rest. Vaelen took point, checking the perimeter while Tarn knelt at the creek to refill canteens.

I sat on a fallen log, biting into some dried fruit from my pouch, when the weasel on my shoulder twisted and dropped down to the grass. She shimmered mid-hop and stretched upward into her human form again, coat rumpled, boots dusty, glasses a little crooked.

"Still watching me?" I asked.

Eliza didn't blink. "You're wearing something dangerous and carrying unresolved emotions about two different men. That's not a safe combination."

I nearly choked. "That bluntness is new."

She shrugged and sat beside me, legs crossed. "I'm direct when it matters. You've been watching Tarn since this morning. You didn't say anything when he mentioned the Church and that pendant. And you still haven't asked him about that picture in your pocket."

My jaw clenched. "I didn't know I had a personal spy."

"I'm not spying. I'm reading the terrain."

I didn't answer. I didn't know how to.

After a long moment, Eliza spoke again—softer this time.

"I know what it feels like," she said. "Seeing someone you care about haunted by someone who's not around anymore."

I looked at her. "You lost someone?"

She didn't answer right away. Then she looked at the pendant hanging around my neck. "We all carry something. Some ghosts are just heavier than others."

We sat there a while longer, letting the quiet settle. I didn't push for details. And she didn't ask anything else.

Eventually, Tarn returned with the filled waterskins and gave us both a small nod.

"We move in ten."

Eliza stood and gave me a final glance before shifting again. This time, she chose badger form—bulkier, broader, claws meant for digging and defense. A combat-ready shape.

I couldn't help but feel like the transformation was a statement.

Vaelen came back with a handful of wildberries and offered them around like we were on a picnic. "Still alive. No signs of trouble. Unless you count that overly aggressive squirrel I had to negotiate with for trail rights."

Tarn didn't respond. He was already tightening the straps on his gear.

We packed up and headed out again.

The afternoon dragged long. Heat shimmered off the road and the air felt thick with something unspoken. We were traveling light, but I felt every step in my shoulders.

Near dusk, we finally spotted the rise of buildings in the distance—small ones, mostly wooden, clustered near a narrow pass flanked by red stone cliffs.

The supply outpost.

Two guards nodded as we approached, one of them barely looking up from a ledger. The other took our guild token, checked the seal, and waved us through with barely a grunt.

We delivered the packet to the depot clerk, who paid us in stamped paper and a half-hearted thanks. Routine. Mundane. Almost boring.

But maybe that was the point.

We set up camp just outside the settlement—on a hill with a view of the stars and a cool wind cutting through the heat.

As the fire crackled to life, I found myself staring up at the darkening sky, one hand wrapped around the crescent at my collar.

The others were talking, laughing even.

But I sat quietly.

Still wearing that damn pendant.

Still wondering what it meant to be in charge of a team that didn't quite feel like mine.

And still thinking about a photograph I wasn't supposed to have seen.

The fire crackled low, casting long shadows across our little camp. Vaelen was already half asleep, boots off and stretched out beside the logs like he owned the whole hill. Eliza had shifted again—this time into her compact weasel form—curled near the fire with her nose tucked under her tail. Tarn, as always, sat slightly apart. Awake. Still. Watching the stars like he expected them to rearrange themselves into answers.

I sat beside him. Not close enough to touch. Not far enough to pretend I didn't want to.

Neither of us spoke for a while. Just the quiet hum of insects and the rhythmic rustle of trees in the wind. I should have been tired, but my thoughts wouldn't settle. They spun circles inside me, tangled knots of what-if and why-now and why-her.

Tarn finally broke the silence. "You're still thinking about what Eliza found."

I glanced at him. The firelight caught the edge of his jaw, highlighting the tension there.

My fingers moved unconsciously to the pendant. I didn't answer.

"I meant what I said," he continued. "Keep it close. And don't let anyone else see it. Especially not anyone tied to the Church."

I turned toward him, the question slipping free before I could stop it. "You said you recognized it. That you've seen the symbol before. Where?"

He didn't respond right away. His gaze was fixed on the flames.

"I saw something like it once," he said finally. "On a document I wasn't supposed to read. Years ago. It was in the archives beneath the Citadel—sealed records, buried under layers of classification.

But the crescent was there, carved into the wax of a forgotten scroll."

"And?" I pressed.

"And the title on that scroll was 'Aetherbound.'" He looked at me now. "It was marked for incineration. Scheduled for destruction under the direct order of the Flame Council. I didn't stay long enough to see if they followed through."

The name hit like a stone dropped in water. "Aetherbound."

He nodded. "It's not a name the Church uses openly. Not anymore. Whatever it was, they buried it for a reason. And if your pendant carries that same mark..."

He didn't finish the sentence. He didn't need to.

I shivered, clutching the pendant tighter.

Tarn's voice lowered. "You didn't choose that thing. It chose you. And I don't think it's done with you yet."

The words sank in deep, leaving a strange hollow in my chest. I wanted to laugh, or cry, or maybe just sleep for a week. But the weight of it all was too sharp to ignore.

"You think I'm in danger?"

"I think we all are," he said. "But you especially. That pendant isn't just some relic. It's a key. And you're already being followed."

I stiffened. "What?"

"I didn't say anything before," he added, his tone like steel drawn slowly from a sheath, "but when we left the city, I saw someone trailing too close. A woman in pale robes. Didn't follow us long. Just long enough to make sure we saw her."

"Do you think she was with the Church?"

"I think she wanted us to wonder."

Chapter 13

CHOSEN, NOT ASKED

Cass

The next morning broke slow and warm, with dew clinging to the grass and birdsong threading through the trees. We'd left the outpost behind before the sun finished stretching across the sky, following the ridgeline east where the map said the forest would begin to thicken. The road had grown quieter, more narrow, its stones breaking apart beneath years of wagon ruts and careless boots.

It felt like the world was watching, waiting for something to shift.

I adjusted the strap on my pack and quickened my pace to catch up with Vaelen. "How much farther, you think?"

"Couple more hours at this pace," he said. "Near the foothills, just past the bend. We'll know we're close when we start smelling burnt stew and soaked leather."

Tarn walked at the front, his silhouette calm and unreadable as ever. Eliza trailed just behind him in owl form, wings beating soundlessly above the trail. I envied her sometimes—how easily she could pull away from it all and see things from a hundred feet higher. Detached. Free.

Vaelen nudged me with his elbow. "You've been quiet this morning. Brooding? Or planning?"

"Can't I do both?" I muttered, though the edge softened into a smirk.

"You've changed," he said, looking at me more seriously than I expected. "Not in a bad way. Just... I remember how you used to flinch if someone tried to hand you a sword."

"Technically, I still do. That's why I carry daggers."

He laughed, but I could see the curiosity behind it. Not judgment. Not pity. Just... interest.

"You ever miss the way it was?" he asked.

I didn't answer right away. Instead, I pulled the crescent pendant from beneath my shirt and traced its edge with my thumb.

"Sometimes," I said. "But I don't think I could go back, even if I wanted to."

He watched me for a beat, then tossed his pack to the ground as we reached a flat clearing by the side of the road.

"Let's see what you've learned."

I blinked. "Now?"

Vaelen grinned. "You're not the only one itching to stretch their legs. You've been dodging the subject since the last town. I've heard rumors, Cass. Heard you got scary."

I raised a brow. "Scary?"

"You know. A little ghost-footed. Little blink-and-you're-behind-me." He mimed a dramatic backstab. "Shadow Step, right?"

I couldn't help the grin. "Maybe."

He drew his sword, the hum of his Arcblade flickering with electricity along the edge. "Then come on. Show me."

I glanced toward Tarn, who had paused further down the trail. He wasn't looking directly at us, but I knew he was listening. Watching.

"All right," I said, tossing my cloak aside. "First to three."

Vaelen's eyes lit up. "Magic?"

"All in."

We circled, boots sliding over the mossy earth, dust curling beneath us in lazy spirals. The moment slowed, stretched—until the first crackle of Vaelen's Arcblade lit the air and he lunged.

I twisted sideways, calling on the pulse of shadow inside me. The world snapped like a rubber band—space folding, light bending—and I stepped through his strike, reappearing behind him in a blink.

He barely caught the motion, pivoting with a shout and swinging wide. I ducked low and kicked out, catching his knee and sending him stumbling. He recovered fast, lightning flaring up his blade as he brought it down hard.

This time, I met him.

Steel screamed. My daggers sparked against his sword, the impact driving a tremor up my arms. I gritted my teeth, leaned into it, then vanished again.

His blade cut empty air as my pommel struck him between the shoulder blades.

"Two-nil," I said from behind him, breath short.

"Not bad," he called, spinning to face me. "But I'm just getting started."

He surged forward, faster now. Sparks burst beneath his boots as he accelerated, a trail of light blooming from his blade. I countered with twin arcs of silver, my body moving faster than it ever had in training—faster than even I expected.

We danced like that, striking and vanishing, testing and pressing, the clearing alive with magic and grit. Eliza had landed somewhere above in the branches, watching with quiet calculation. Tarn leaned back against a tree, arms crossed but his eyes sharp, following every move.

I was sweating, panting, but grinning all the same. I wasn't flinching anymore. I wasn't guessing.

I was holding my own.

And it felt damn good.

We moved faster now—Vaelen with arcs of crackling energy, me with flickers of shadow. Every strike met resistance, every dodge left the air humming. He was stronger. I was quicker. And both of us knew how to make the other work for every inch.

I ducked under a slash that buzzed so close it singed a strand of hair. My boots skidded across the dirt as I twisted back, lashing out with one dagger low and the other high. He parried both with a grunt, sending a ripple of force down my arms.

"You've been holding out," he said, breathless but smiling.

I smirked, eyes narrowing. "So have you."

He surged again—this time with a burst of speed that left afterimages behind him. His blade carved glowing sigils in the air, pure lightning coiled into each strike. I backed off, step by step, until my foot caught a raised root.

He saw the stumble and went for the finishing blow.

I vanished.

Shadow wrapped around me like a second skin, and I appeared behind him mid-lunge. My knee hit his back hard enough to knock the wind from his lungs, and both daggers found the curve of his collar in a clean, practiced motion.

"Three," I said, panting.

He froze. Then slowly raised his hands in surrender.

"Well," he muttered, laughing through the breath he'd lost. "That's cheating."

"Nope." I grinned, flipping one of the daggers in my hand. "That's training."

He turned, eyes wide with surprise—but not at the win. At me. "You've really changed."

"Thanks," I said, lowering my blades. "I think."

He gave a low whistle, wiping sweat from his brow. "You've come a long way. I always knew you had it in you, but seeing it? That's something else."

We stood there a moment, sweat-streaked and smiling in the dappled shade. A breeze rolled in, cool and fragrant with pine. The sound of Tarn's slow clapping broke the quiet.

"Well done," he said, stepping into the clearing. "Both of you."

Eliza glided down from the trees, touching down with barely a rustle before shifting back. She adjusted her glasses, her expression unreadable.

"You're fast," she said to me. "Not just physically. You adapt. That'll matter in the dungeon."

"I'm not as good as Tarn," I replied, still catching my breath.

Tarn shrugged. "That wasn't the point. You didn't hesitate. That's what matters."

Vaelen offered me a water skin. "If that's just a taste of what's coming, I'm not sure if I should be excited or terrified."

I drank, heart still thudding in my chest. "Little of both, maybe."

We lingered a bit longer in the clearing, letting the tension ease off our shoulders. Vaelen collapsed against a rock with a dramatic groan, Eliza returned to her weasel form and curled up in my lap, and Tarn... well, Tarn stayed close, watching the treeline with that same silent vigilance he always wore like a second cloak.

Eventually, he spoke. "We should keep moving."

We packed up and hit the trail again, the mood lighter now—charged, but not tense. I walked beside Tarn this time, and for a few quiet minutes, neither of us said a word.

"You didn't flinch," he said eventually.

I glanced up at him. "During the fight?"

He nodded. "You didn't hold back."

"I couldn't afford to. Vaelen's good."

"You're better than you think."

The words settled into me like warm coals, low and steady. I didn't respond. Not aloud. But something about the way he said it made my chest tighten.

We kept walking as the sun dipped lower, shadows lengthening across the trail like spilled ink. The road bent gently around a rocky outcrop where wildflowers clung to cracks in the stone. It should've felt peaceful. Instead, my thoughts twisted tighter with every step.

I walked beside Tarn again—close, but not quite close enough to brush arms. The others trailed behind; Eliza had returned to owl form, gliding low along the treetops, while Vaelen hummed tunelessly under his breath as he kicked at loose stones.

Tarn hadn't said much since the spar. Just watched. Waited. Let the silence speak for him, as he always did.

I broke first.

"You said it chose me." I didn't look at him, just kept my gaze fixed ahead. "Back in camp. When we were talking about the pendant."

"I did." His voice was calm. Measured.

I reached under my cloak and pulled the crescent moon free from where it rested against my collarbone. It didn't glow. Didn't stir. But it felt heavier now, like it was listening.

"And you meant it?" I asked.

He didn't hesitate. "I don't think it would've appeared during your trial if it wasn't meant for you."

I thumbed the edge of it, careful not to cut myself on the sharp curve. "It's just a pendant."

"It's not," he said quietly. "And you know that."

I stopped walking. The others were still a ways behind—far enough not to hear. Tarn halted beside me.

"You told me not to show it to anyone from the Church," I said. "That it was dangerous."

He nodded. "It is. Because of what it's tied to."

I turned to face him. "Then why let me keep it?"

He met my eyes without flinching. "Because taking it away wouldn't change the fact that it chose you. And I don't think we can afford to ignore what that means."

Something in his voice caught at me—like he'd thought about that a lot longer than he was letting on.

I lowered my hand slowly. "You said you saw the symbol once. On a scroll called *Aetherbound*."

"I did," he confirmed. "And I wasn't supposed to. The records were sealed beneath the Citadel—meant for incineration. Whatever *Aetherbound* was, the Church didn't want anyone to remember it."

"But you did."

His jaw tensed slightly. "I remember everything they wanted me to forget."

I swallowed the sudden ache in my throat. "Do you think this has something to do with them? The ones following us?"

"I think it's all connected. The Church. The Sons. That emerald we found. And now this."

A breeze passed between us, tugging at the edges of my cloak. I looked down again at the pendant. It still didn't shine. Still didn't move. But something in it *felt* alive, like a heartbeat just beneath the surface.

"I didn't ask for any of this," I said again, more quietly this time.

"I know."

That same word again—but this time, he said it differently. Not as a dismissal. Not as comfort. Just truth. A quiet acceptance of everything I couldn't say.

I started walking again, slower now.

"Do you think it'll do something?" I asked. "The pendant, I mean."

"I think it already has," Tarn said. "It brought questions no one else dared to ask. And you're the one holding them now."

"That's not comforting."

"It wasn't meant to be."

We walked in silence a while longer. The road had narrowed again, winding upward into low ridges. The forest loomed taller to the north, and though the map said we were still a few hours from the camp, I could feel it. Something ahead was shifting. Waiting.

Vaelen jogged up behind us and slowed to match pace. "You two always this dramatic, or should I be worried?"

"Eliza would've said the same thing," I muttered.

"She did," Vaelen said, with a pointed glance up at the owl circling above.

I offered a tired smile. "We're fine."

"You look like someone handed you a prophecy wrapped in a threat."

"Something like that."

Vaelen didn't press. Just walked with us a while, letting the silence stretch comfortably.

Eventually he broke it with a low whistle. "You know, back when we were kids, you never shut up. Now I feel like I need a permit to hear your thoughts."

"I've learned to pick my moments."

"I liked it better when you talked too much."

I shot him a side-eye. "Still do."

"Fair."

Ahead, the trail began to slope gently downward into a shallow ravine. Tarn paused, scanning the terrain, then motioned for us to stop.

"We camp near the canyon mouth," he said. "Half a mile from here. Keep sharp. Last time I passed through this region, we saw signs of bandit movement."

Vaelen's hand drifted to his sword. "Got it."

The sun was near the horizon now, casting long shadows across the trees. The air had grown still—not in that peaceful way, but in the way that made you feel like something was watching. Not an enemy. Not exactly. Just... expectation.

I reached up and touched the crescent moon again.

Aetherbound.

Whatever it was, it had waited long enough.

We followed the path down into the shallow ravine, boots crunching against old gravel and broken leaves. The road narrowed where the stone walls pressed in—less a canyon and more a forgotten scar carved by time and runoff. Vaelen walked ahead now, blade sheathed but hands loose and ready. Tarn kept his pace slow but watchful, always scanning the edges.

Eliza remained above, a gray owl against the copper sky, wings wide and gliding just beneath the last stretch of cloud. Her silhouette passed across the ridge like a signal, silent and sharp.

It wasn't long before the scent of campfire smoke hit—dry wood and boiled stew, mixed with the unmistakable tang of leather, oil, and too many bodies in one place. Vaelen had been right. You smelled the camp before you saw it.

We crested the bend, and there it was.

The adventurer camp sprawled across the plateau ahead like a temporary city—tents of varying sizes scattered around communal fires, makeshift pavilions flying guild banners, training dummies hammered into the dirt beside crates of potion flasks and sharpened tools. A dozen caravans had parked along the southern edge, wheels removed, forming a rough perimeter. Beyond them, half-shrouded by mist and trees, loomed the dark entrance of the Enchanted Forest's dungeon.

I'd never seen it before. Not up close.

Even from here, the trees near it didn't look real. The trunks were too wide. The shadows between the leaves too deep. Colors shimmered faintly where they shouldn't—purples and greens rippling beneath the boughs like refracted light underwater. It didn't feel natural.

It felt alive.

We stopped at the ridge, letting the view sink in. Eliza landed beside us in owl form, shifting back with a shimmer and a soft breath. She didn't speak. None of us did.

Finally, Tarn broke the silence. "We'll check in with the camp overseer, then set up on the outer ring. Keep close tomorrow. The dungeon briefing happens at first light."

I nodded, pulse quickening. This was it. The last breath before everything changed again.

Vaelen tilted his head toward the woods. "That place doesn't like us."

"Good," Eliza said quietly. "Then we'll know where we stand."

I smiled faintly, one hand brushing the pendant at my neck.

The dungeon waited.

Chapter 14

WHΛT WΛITS BEYOND

Cass

T he camp buzzed with the low hum of preparation—sharpened steel against whetstone, muffled orders, the clatter of boots over hardened dirt. By the time we reached the registration post, the sun had dipped behind the ridgeline, casting long shadows that bled into the edges of the tents. Fires dotted the sprawl like stars drawn down to earth, their smoke rising in lazy curls toward the dusky sky.

We were waved through by a guard with tired eyes and a clipboard, his tabard marked with the Guild's official crest. No one asked questions. No one looked twice.

I supposed that was what happened in places like this—when the danger beyond the trees made everyone's business their own.

Tarn led us past rows of mismatched tents and makeshift lean-tos, scanning for open ground. Eliza trotted at his heels in badger form, fur bristling with each unfamiliar scent, while Vaelen kept pace beside me, gaze flicking across the camp's many corners.

"You get the sense nobody here sleeps with both eyes closed?" he muttered.

"Feels more like no one sleeps at all," I replied, stepping around a pair of arguing dwarves and a merchant cart stacked high with bundles of enchanted rope.

We found a patch of flattened grass near the outer ring—close enough to the briefing tent, but far enough from the noise to sleep. It wasn't glamorous, but it would do. I dropped my pack, rolled my shoulders, and looked toward the forest's edge.

Even from here, the dungeon entrance loomed. Not like a doorway, not really. More like the treeline itself had formed a threshold, arching inward as if swallowing the path whole. The shadows between those trees didn't move with the breeze. They lingered. They waited.

I didn't like how it made my skin feel—like a storm was crawling beneath it, just out of reach.

Tarn knelt beside the firepit and began laying stones into a neat ring. "We'll keep shifts tonight," he said without looking up. "Don't trust these outer camps. Too many strangers. Too many stories."

"Think we're in one now," Vaelen said, setting down his sword and grabbing a flint.

"Exactly," Tarn replied.

I let out a breath and dropped to the ground beside Eliza, who had shifted back into her human form and now sat cross-legged, nose buried in a folded map. "You see anything interesting on there?" I asked.

Her eyes didn't leave the parchment. "Only that this dungeon wasn't here six months ago."

I blinked. "What?"

"It doesn't match any of the official cartography logs," she continued, fingers tapping an empty quadrant labeled Enchanted Forest - Southern Reach. "The Guild issued a scouting expedition back then, but the only thing they found was dense woods. Then the mana readings spiked."

Tarn's voice cut in. "Which means something made it appear."

"Or something woke it up," Eliza said quietly.

We sat with that for a moment—each of us staring at the trees like they might offer an answer. They didn't.

When the fire was lit and camp was finally set, Tarn took first watch. Eliza curled up on her bedroll, glasses tucked into her satchel. Vaelen stretched out nearby, arms behind his head, humming again—some old tune I half-remembered from our childhood, back when things were simpler.

I lay back and pulled my cloak tighter, the pendant cold against my collarbone. The crescent moon didn't pulse. Didn't glow. But it felt heavier than usual, like the silence around us was pressing into it.

I didn't sleep much.

When morning came, it came hard and gray, with clouds blotting out the early light. Someone sounded a bell across the camp and voices began to rise, groggy and low. Tarn woke us with a soft shake and a nod toward the briefing pavilion—a wide canvas tent ringed with chairs and a long table at the center. Adventurers were already gathering, weapons slung across backs, cloaks wrapped tight against the mist.

I took a seat near the back, flanked by Eliza and Vaelen. Tarn stood just behind us, arms crossed, helm hanging from one hand.

The man who stepped into the center of the tent wore dark blue robes with silver inlays and a clasp bearing the Guildmaster's seal. He was tall, pale, with thin lines across his face like old calligraphy—marks of age and too many years dealing with death.

"I'm Master Veylan," he said, voice carrying easily through the tent. "Appointed liaison between the Guild Council and this expedition. You've all been briefed on your entry assignments. You know the risks. But there's something else you need to hear before you step foot inside."

The crowd shifted. Boots scuffed. Someone coughed.

Veylan turned, and for a moment his eyes met mine. Cold. Clear. Measured.

"There have been sightings," he said. "Things that don't match any known dungeon class. Patterns that don't repeat. Rooms that shift."

Vaelen muttered, "Great."

"Elves from the northern outposts reported visual hallucinations. One team vanished for three days—came back with no memory of having entered at all. Another... didn't come back."

A murmur rippled through the room.

"Eliza," I whispered, "is that normal?"

"Not unless the dungeon's sentient," she replied under her breath.

Tarn stiffened behind us. He said nothing, but I could feel it—something had just clicked in him.

Veylan raised his voice again. "If you sense changes in time, memory, or direction, retreat immediately. Do not split your party. Do not attempt to record arcane readings alone. And above all—do not touch any objects that seem to resist identification."

I swallowed.

We all did.

The air felt different after that—heavier, somehow. Not with fear, exactly. But with knowing. The kind of knowing that only comes when you realize you've already stepped too far to turn back.

"We begin at noon," Veylan said. "Good luck."

The crowd dispersed slowly, boots crunching gravel as adventurers murmured among themselves. Some looked shaken. Others just annoyed. But none of them looked surprised.

Tarn led us back to our camp without a word. I kept glancing over my shoulder, half-expecting someone to be following us— Veylan, maybe, or one of the other higher-ranked parties. But the path stayed empty, save for shifting mist and the occasional muttered curse from nearby tents.

Once we reached our little patch of ground, Eliza immediately dropped into weasel form and dove into Vaelen's pack. He didn't flinch. Just sighed.

"She stress-naps in there," he said. "It's a thing."

"She's not wrong to be stressed," I muttered, settling onto my bedroll and letting the cloak pool around me. "That briefing was... a lot."

Vaelen knelt to check the straps on his boots. "You think they're exaggerating?"

"No," Tarn said quietly. He stood with his back to us, eyes fixed on the treeline again. "They wouldn't mention memory loss if it hadn't already caused casualties."

I looked up. "You've seen something like this before?"

"Not exactly." He turned to face us. "But the pattern fits. Magical anomalies. Shifting terrain. Things resisting identification. That kind of instability doesn't come from a normal dungeon. Either something inside is manipulating it... or something outside is."

That was worse, somehow.

"I don't suppose there's a good chance we'll go in, find some goblins, and be home by supper?" Vaelen asked, only half-joking.

Eliza poked her head out of his pack. "You're the worst liar I've ever met."

"Optimist," he corrected with a grin.

She sniffed and disappeared again, rustling through his gear.

I tilted my head back and stared at the sky. The clouds had started to break—just a little—but the light that filtered through felt wrong. Like it didn't quite belong to the same world we'd woken up in.

"I don't like going in blind," I said softly.

"You're not," Tarn replied. "Not entirely."

I glanced at him, brow raised. "You mean the pendant?"

He gave a small nod. "Whatever its purpose is... it's connected to all of this. That much is clear."

"Eliza's been researching it whenever she gets the chance," I added. "But so far, nothing matches. Not in any of the recorded relics she's seen."

"I doubt it will," Tarn said. "If the Church sealed the Aetherbound scrolls away, then anything related to them would've been erased from public record."

"Which means we're carrying something no one else has seen in centuries." I reached up to touch the crescent again. Still cold. Still quiet.

Vaelen looked between us. "And we're about to walk into a dungeon that changes its layout, eats time, and makes people forget who they are. What could possibly go wrong?"

This time, none of us laughed.

Later that morning, after a quiet breakfast of dried meat and weak tea, Tarn sent us to scout the nearby pavilions. "See what the others know," he said. "Rumors, formations, anything odd from the last few runs. Just listen."

He didn't come with us. Said he wanted to check the weapon supplies and get eyes on the perimeter. I didn't ask more than that. We all knew he preferred moving in the background.

Vaelen and I took the southern quadrant—rows of temporary shelters lined with supply crates, old weapons, and adventurers with faces worn thin by sleepless nights. Most ignored us. A few nodded in greeting. One woman in black lacquered armor sharpened a spear that had clearly seen better days.

"Rough go?" Vaelen asked, jerking his chin toward the splintered shaft.

She didn't look up. "Lost two of my team in there yesterday. Found their packs near the entrance this morning. No blood. Just... gone."

I felt the chill snake up my spine.

"What happened?"

She stopped sharpening. Her voice was flat. "We walked through a doorway and came out somewhere else. Should've been a straight hallway. Instead, it was the same room we'd started in. Over and over again. Like the dungeon forgot we were there."

"Or like it wanted you to stay," Vaelen muttered.

The woman nodded once, as if that was the part she hadn't wanted to say aloud.

We thanked her and moved on.

At the next fire, a pair of dwarves shared a flask of something sharp-smelling while bickering about time loss. "I swear we were inside for ten minutes," one of them said. "Came back and it'd been four hours. The sun moved!"

"And your bloody beard didn't!" the other snapped. "You're just old and slow."

I took mental notes. Time distortion, loops, vanishing people, arcane anomalies.

And none of them seemed surprised anymore.

When we returned to camp, Tarn was already there—checking the edge on his hammer with slow, deliberate strokes. Eliza sat nearby in human form again, scribbling notes across a fresh parchment with ink-stained fingers.

"I think I've got a theory," she said the moment we dropped down beside her.

Tarn looked up.

"Go on," I said.

"This dungeon isn't new," Eliza said, tapping her page. "It's not a dungeon at all. It's something older. Maybe older than the Guild. It didn't just appear—it woke up. The forest wasn't hiding it. It was it."

Vaelen raised a brow. "You think the dungeon is the forest?"

She nodded. "At least partially. Or maybe they share something deeper. It would explain why nothing about it matches conventional mapping—why it doesn't follow rules. Normal dungeons follow a template. This one feels... organic. Alive."

Tarn didn't blink. "Then we tread carefully."

The noon bell sounded.

We stood.

Weapons checked. Cloaks fastened. No speeches. No last-minute prayers.

Just motion.

Together, we made our way through the thinning crowd toward the path that led beyond the camp. The trees ahead loomed impossibly tall, their canopies stitched into a patchwork sky. The air grew cooler the closer we came—quiet, like a held breath.

The mouth of the dungeon yawned ahead, a wide arch framed by twisted roots and pale moss. Beyond it, only shadow.

Vaelen rested a hand on his hilt. "You all ready for this?"

"No," I said honestly. "But I'm going anyway."

Tarn stepped past the threshold first. Eliza followed, her form already shifting.

Then Vaelen.

Then me.

The forest swallowed us whole.

Chapter 15

IN THE SHADOWS OF FLAME

Eryndor Vale

The candlelight flickered against the stone walls of the sanctum, throwing long shadows across the polished marble floor. Incense curled in the air—sandalwood and ash—masking the deeper, acrid scent of something alchemical that clung to the robes of the visitors seated across from me. Even here, buried beneath the Cathedral in a room no acolyte could enter, their presence soured the air.

The sigil of the First Flame burned above us on a golden disc, but none of us looked up at it. Not even me.

I leaned back in my chair, hands folded atop the carved armrests. "You failed."

Across the table, the man in the silver half-mask didn't flinch. His voice was even, sharp as glass. "She was more resourceful than anticipated."

"That girl was barely more than a street rat a year ago," I snapped. "You sent an assassin into a conjured trial meant to test character and resolve. And she *walked out*."

"She's grown," the masked man said, as though it were a compliment. "And you were the one who insisted on subtlety. We followed your orders."

I waved a hand dismissively. "Don't play semantics with me, Hollow Star. If you had done your job, we wouldn't be having this meeting."

The other figure, robed in deep plum and wearing a veil of rune-stitched silk, finally spoke. Her voice was soft but precise. "The charm she carries—do you know what it is?"

My gaze narrowed. "No. But I intend to find out."

"It activated during the trial," she continued. "Only for a moment. The aether in it is... unique. Stabilized. Old."

"Then we're back where we started," I said. "With too many variables."

I stood, walking to the tall arched window that overlooked the lower cloister. From here, you couldn't see the forest. Couldn't see the dungeon blooming like a rot beneath the horizon. But I *felt* it—like a heat building behind the eyes. Like a storm that refused to break.

"She's with Tarn now," I muttered. "That makes her dangerous."

"She's still young," the man in the mask said. "Unrefined."

"She's learning," I countered. "And we've both seen what happens when Tarn decides to *care* about someone."

They didn't respond. They didn't need to. We all remembered Laina.

I turned to face them. "Tarn's judgment is compromised. I could see it on his face when he brought the emerald to me. He's still trying to be a hero."

"And what are you trying to be, Archflame?" the masked man asked.

I smiled. "A survivor."

He gave a humorless chuckle. "Then you'll be pleased to hear we've brought the next phase."

A shiver ran up my spine. "You're releasing it?"

"In the dungeon," the woman confirmed. "It will serve as both bait and data. Its behavioral pattern will adapt to the magic density of the environment. If the girl's pendant activates again, it will register."

"And Tarn?"

"If he gets in the way, he'll be dealt with." The masked man tilted his head. "He's expendable, isn't he?"

My lips thinned. I looked down at the small flame burning in the lantern beside my chair—a sacred ember drawn from the original pyre beneath the capital. I had been trained to see fire as purity. As judgment. But fire could consume anything, if it was hungry enough.

"Tarn is a relic," I said at last. "And like all relics, he's dangerous when cornered."

"Then perhaps it's time to test what burns hotter—his loyalty to the Church... or his feelings for her."

The veiled woman inclined her head. "Our people are watching. They've followed them since they left the outpost. The girl wears the crescent— she keeps it hidden but, it responds to her nonetheless. She does not yet understand it. That may change."

I returned to my seat, steepling my fingers. "You said the experiment is ready?"

"The prototype is unlike the others," the veiled woman said, her voice low with something bordering on reverence. "We built it from the essence of a Phaseling—a planar aberration that should never have survived this realm."

She paused, letting the weight of that sink in.

"It doesn't simply hunt. It reflects. When engaged, it mimics the form, stance, and tactics of its opponent—like fighting a version of yourself twisted through shadow. Its presence disrupts mana threads, blurs time, and alters memory recall. In its wake, even truth feels suspect."

The masked man added, "We call it *Mirror Stalker*. It doesn't kill for sustenance. It kills to become.

"And its temperament?"

The woman's voice was almost reverent. "Violent. Inquisitive. It learns quickly. Hunts in silence. Leaves no trace."

"Good," I said. "Let it loose in the forest before dawn. Make sure it reaches the heart of the dungeon. Let it tear into anything that gets too close to the truth."

The masked man stood, smoothing his robe. "And if Tarn or the girl interferes?"

I met his gaze. "Then burn them both. Quietly."

There was a moment of silence. Then, wordlessly, the two emissaries of the Sons turned and left through the shadowed arch at the back of the room, leaving only the scent of scorched metal and old secrets behind.

I remained seated long after they'd gone.

Outside, the bells of the cloister began to toll the coming of midnight.

Beneath my robes, I drew a folded letter from my sleeve. A report, penned in cipher, detailing Tarn's latest movements. His hesitation. The sparring matches. The pendant. Her.

I stared at the final line.

"They trust each other now."

I crushed the paper in one fist, letting the flames from the lantern lick up the edge. It caught quickly, curling black as it vanished into ash.

"Trust," I murmured, eyes on the flame. "Let's see how far it carries you."

The embers in the lantern hissed as the last curl of parchment burned away.

I stood slowly, brushing ash from my robes, and crossed the chamber to the far wall where the stone was darker—untouched by torchlight or time. With a soft whisper of magic, I placed my palm to the cold surface. The runes etched into the stone pulsed once, then parted like threads unweaving.

Beyond lay a narrow passage, lit only by dim flame sconces that flickered like dying stars. Few knew of this corridor. Fewer still had reason to walk it.

At its end, I entered a smaller chamber—no sigils, no relics. Just a simple altar of black stone and a steel case atop it, sealed with six chains and a glyph that hadn't been used since before the last Purge.

I approached slowly.

Inside the case was an Aethercore—raw, unstable, pulsing with fractures of violet light. Not a relic, but something far worse: a forbidden core taken from a ruin sealed by the Founding Flame itself. Our alchemists had broken laws older than the kingdom refining it. Reforging it. Twisting it into something that could think, adapt... and hunger.

The Mirror Stalker had been born from this core. Aether-infused. Rewritten. It should never have existed.

And yet, here it was. Purpose-built. Engineered for destruction.

I placed my hand atop the case. Felt the low thrum of malevolent energy pulse against my skin like a second heartbeat.

"This is the cost," I said aloud, to no one. "Not of power. But of keeping order."

A soft scrape echoed from behind me.

I turned.

A young priest stood in the doorway, robes half-fastened, breath catching as he realized where he'd wandered. His candle trembled in his grasp.

"Forgive me, Archflame," he stammered, bowing low. "I—I was delivering the incense records. I didn't mean to—"

"You didn't see this room," I said, my voice calm but heavy.

He nodded quickly. Too quickly. "Of course. Of course, I didn't. I'll—I'll go."

"Wait."

He froze.

I stepped forward, each footfall slow, deliberate. "You're loyal to the Flame, aren't you, acolyte?"

He swallowed hard. "Yes, Archflame. Always."

"Then remember this: sometimes, the fire doesn't illuminate. It cauterizes. Understand?"

He hesitated.

Then: "Yes, Archflame."

"Good."

From the darkness behind the altar, a figure stepped forth—silent, cloaked in deep gray armor etched with smoldering runes. An Ash Sentinel, faceless behind a hood of burnished steel. The candle in the acolyte's hand flickered as he turned.

He didn't scream. There wasn't time.

A glint of motion. A soft sound—like air being cut—and the boy crumpled to the floor, blood already seeping into the ancient stone. The Sentinel offered no salute, no words. Just returned to the shadows from which he came.

I didn't look away.

"Faith is obedience," I murmured. "But loyalty without restraint is a liability."

I turned my gaze back to the sealed case, its chains still humming faintly with restrained power. Outside, the wind howled against the chapel's spires, and the bells began to toll the hour.

Dawn was coming.

And soon, so would the fire.

Chapter 16

INTO THE SHIFTING DARK

Cass

The forest swallowed us whole.

The air shifted the moment we crossed the threshold—colder, heavier, as if we'd stepped underwater. Light filtered through the canopy in fractured beams, but it didn't behave the way sunlight should. It bent, wavered, and shimmered faintly with hues I'd never seen before, purples and greens sliding under the edges like oil on water.

The trees themselves loomed impossibly high, their trunks smooth instead of rough, ridged like stone worn down by centuries. Vines dangled like ropes, swaying though the air was perfectly still. Somewhere in the distance, water dripped in a rhythm too steady to be natural.

My fingers brushed the crescent moon at my collar. Cold. Silent. But it felt heavier than before—like it had grown roots straight into my chest.

"Stay close," Tarn said from the front. His voice carried farther than it should have, echoing off trunks and vines that swallowed sound. "Don't trust the paths. Dungeons like this... they shift."

Eliza padded just behind him in human form, her glasses catching fractured light as her gaze darted constantly. "Mana density's unstable," she murmured, fingertips grazing the nearest tree. "It spikes, then plummets. Like the whole place is breathing."

Vaelen drew his Arcblade but kept it low at his side. The edge hummed faintly, electricity prickling in the stale air. "Can't say I'm surprised. This place doesn't exactly scream normal."

"Nothing about this is normal," I muttered.

We followed a path too neat to be wild. Roots curled around it like veins around a wound, and moss grew in deliberate spirals. The deeper we went, the quieter the camp behind us became. By the time I risked a glance back, there was no ridge. No tents. No firelight. Only more forest.

I swallowed hard. "Anyone else feel like we've been walking longer than we have?"

"Time distortion," Eliza said, though her voice was quieter now. "Could just be perception. Could be worse."

Tarn halted and raised a hand. We froze.

The forest seemed to hold its breath. Then came a rustle—low, deliberate. Not wind. Not an animal.

My hands tightened around my daggers, every nerve screaming for action.

Then it stopped.

The vines stilled. The shadows returned to their unnatural places.

Tarn's eyes narrowed, scanning the treeline. He lowered his hand but didn't relax. "Eyes sharp. This place watches."

We moved again, slower, boots crunching over dirt too smooth to be natural. The air smelled faintly of wet stone now, even though we hadn't seen any yet.

The change came gradually. At first it was subtle—the trees grew closer together, their branches arching overhead until the canopy knitted tight. Then the ground shifted underfoot, dirt giving way to packed stone paved with slabs I didn't recognize. Moss still clung to it, but the symmetry was too precise. Too deliberate.

"This isn't just forest anymore," I murmured.

"Transition zone," Eliza said, crouching to brush her fingers over the stone. "The dungeon's outer shell."

Vaelen gave a low whistle. "So we're officially inside."

We stopped in a clearing ringed with ancient stone markers half-buried in moss. Tarn crouched to examine one, brushing dirt away. Faded lines etched into it revealed a crescent curve. My stomach twisted when I realized it matched the pendant resting against my chest.

Eliza crouched beside him. "These weren't made by the Guild."

"No," Tarn said quietly. "Older."

I reached down, tracing the faint groove. The stone was warm beneath my fingers, like it had been waiting.

Vaelen shifted uncomfortably, scanning the treeline. "So remind me—why are we walking deeper into the place covered in mystery runes and time-warping trees?"

"Because that's the job," Tarn answered flatly.

I tried for a smirk, but it didn't quite land. Not when I could feel the shadows bending around us like they wanted to listen.

We pushed on, and the world shifted again. The trunks grew even wider, merging into stone columns. The air smelled stronger of wet granite and faint ash, and the ground sloped downward into a corridor flanked by arching roots hardened into black stone.

I slowed, breath catching. "This... this wasn't here before."

"It was," Eliza corrected softly, eyes narrowing as she ran a hand over the wall. "We just weren't allowed to see it yet."

The silence pressed tighter now, broken only by the faint sound of dripping water somewhere ahead. The corridor bent sharply left, vanishing into shadow.

Tarn's voice was steady. "Stay close. This is where it truly begins."

I tightened my grip on my daggers. The crescent against my chest felt like it was pulsing again.

And for the first time since we entered, I wondered if it was warning me.

The corridor bent sharply, and with it, the air grew heavier. Damp stone replaced the smell of moss and earth, and faint carvings appeared along the walls—patterns too worn to make out, their grooves glowing faintly with mana. They flickered when we passed, as though reacting to our presence.

"Anyone else think those are watching us?" Vaelen muttered, one hand brushing the carvings as we walked.

"They're resonant," Eliza said, adjusting her glasses. "Old warding glyphs, maybe. Whatever they were meant to hold back, it wasn't human."

"Comforting," Vaelen deadpanned.

I kept my eyes forward, not trusting the walls. My pendant was cold again, but heavier.

The corridor opened into a vast chamber. The ceiling arched so high it vanished into shadow, supported by pillars carved from root and stone alike. Patches of bioluminescent moss lit the space in eerie green, just enough to show the floor's geometric pattern—circles within circles, broken only by the narrow path leading forward.

We paused at the threshold.

Eliza crouched, brushing a fingertip across the floor. "It's a focus array," she murmured. "Mana channels. This whole room is designed to shift energy."

"Toward what?" I asked.

She didn't answer.

Tarn stepped past her, boots striking the stone with a sound that seemed too loud. He tested the floor with the weight of his hammer, eyes scanning the pillars. "It's stable enough. But don't touch the moss."

"Why not?" Vaelen asked.

Tarn pointed at the nearest patch. It pulsed faintly, and a second later, the moss recoiled as though offended by the attention.

"Because it notices," Tarn said simply.

My throat tightened. Great. Living moss. Just what we needed.

We moved carefully, single file, along the narrow path. Every step echoed. My heart beat faster with each one, and the walls seemed to lean inward, like the chamber itself was waiting for us to slip.

Halfway across, the air shifted. Not a sound, not a movement—just a feeling, like a hand brushing the back of my neck.

I froze.

"What is it?" Tarn asked quietly, noticing.

I shook my head. "I don't know. Just—felt something."

Eliza's eyes narrowed. She reached into her satchel, scattering a pinch of silvery dust ahead of us. For a moment, nothing. Then the dust spiraled unnaturally upward, forming faint shapes in the air—doorways, staircases, paths that weren't really there.

"Illusions," she whispered. "The room's layered. If we step wrong, we might not land where we think."

Vaelen gave a low whistle. "So basically, don't trip."

I tightened my grip on my daggers. "Thanks for the encouragement."

We pressed forward. Tarn led, steady as a mountain, Eliza's murmured wards shimmering faintly behind him. Vaelen followed, sword humming softly with static. I brought up the rear, every muscle wound tight.

By the time we reached the far arch, my palms were slick with sweat.

The corridor beyond was narrower, the stone walls etched deeper now. Some of the carvings looked like crescent moons. Others... I couldn't identify.

My pendant grew colder.

"Question," Vaelen said softly as we walked. "If this place can shift paths, what happens if it decides to close behind us?"

"Then we find another way out," Tarn replied without hesitation.

"And if there isn't one?"

"Then we make one."

The confidence in his voice should've been comforting. Instead, it only reminded me how serious he was.

We walked for what felt like hours, though it couldn't have been more than thirty minutes. The walls closed tighter, the floor sloping down into another chamber—smaller, circular, with no visible exits except the one we entered.

At the center stood a pedestal, waist-high, its surface cracked but glowing faintly with the same green light as the moss.

Eliza's breath caught. "It's a trigger point."

"Trap?" I asked.

"Or a test," she murmured. "Depends on who built it."

Vaelen circled it warily, sword at the ready. "Looks harmless enough."

"Which means it's not," I muttered.

Tarn studied it for a long moment, then turned to us. "Stay sharp. If this is what I think it is, the dungeon wants to separate us."

The word sank cold into my stomach. Separate.

I didn't like the sound of that.

The pedestal pulsed once. A faint vibration rippled through the stone beneath our boots.

Vaelen stepped back. "I don't like that."

"No one does," Eliza said flatly, already drawing another warding circle in the dust with a piece of chalk. "But I think we tripped it just by walking in."

Tarn raised his hammer, eyes on the faint glow bleeding up the pedestal's cracks. "Cass. Eliza. Stay behind me."

The light brightened, seeping across the floor like veins of molten glass. The circular pattern beneath us came alive, lines flaring one by one until the entire room hummed with a low, resonant thrum. My pendant grew cold enough to sting, the crescent digging into my skin through the cloak.

"Definitely not harmless," I whispered.

The glow reached the outer edge of the chamber, and with a sound like stone grinding against stone, the walls themselves began to shift. Doorways appeared where there had been none. Shadows stretched wrong, bending away from the light instead of toward it.

"Multiple exits," Eliza breathed, eyes darting. "It's forcing a choice."

"Or forcing a split," Tarn corrected.

The ground shuddered violently. I stumbled, catching myself on Tarn's arm. He didn't move, steady as ever, but his jaw tightened.

"We need to move," Vaelen barked, pointing to a newly formed archway across the chamber. "Pick one before the whole place caves in!"

Tarn shook his head. "No. That's what it wants."

Another tremor. The pedestal cracked down the middle, spilling green light like liquid. The air grew heavy, thick with a pressure that made it hard to breathe.

Eliza swore under her breath. "Too late."

The floor split.

A jagged line of blinding light ripped between us, faster than I could react. Tarn shoved me hard, sending me stumbling toward Eliza just as the fissure widened into a gaping chasm.

"Tarn!" I screamed.

"Stay together!" His voice cut through the roar as the floor gave way. "Cass, don't let go!"

Eliza grabbed my arm, yanking me back as the stone beneath Tarn and Vaelen crumbled away. They fell back into the opposite side, the ground solidifying between us like a closing wound.

I slammed against the wall, chest heaving, Eliza's grip iron-tight on my wrist. The light faded, leaving only the echo of the pedestal's hum and the sound of distant grinding stone.

The chamber was still again. But we were cut off.

I pressed both hands to the wall where the fissure had sealed, panic clawing up my throat. "Tarn!"

No answer.

"Eliza—" My voice cracked. "We have to—"

"We can't," she said firmly, though her own face was pale. "It sealed. And if we try to force it, we could trigger another collapse."

My throat tightened. The pendant against my chest was like ice, silent but heavy, as though it knew exactly what had just happened.

I slid down to my knees, hands trembling against the unyielding wall.

Eliza crouched beside me, her hand steady on my shoulder. "They're alive. The dungeon doesn't kill this way. It tests."

"Tests what?" I asked, my voice shaking.

Her gaze flicked to the sealed stone, then back to me. "How badly we want to get back."

I looked down at the crescent, my pulse hammering in my ears.

"Then we're going to pass," I whispered.

Chapter 17

FRACTURED PATHS

Tarn

The world snapped sideways.

Stone groaned like a living thing, and in the blink of an eye, the path behind us collapsed into a wall of shifting slate.

Dust choked the air, and Vaelen coughed beside me, swinging his arm to clear it. The echo of Cass's voice cut off mid-shout, leaving only the low rumble of settling rock.

"Cass!" I shouted, but the sound bounced uselessly off the jagged surface.

I pressed my palms against the wall—cold, seamless, as though it had always been here. No cracks. No give. Just stone that hadn't existed a breath ago.

Vaelen slammed his fist into it. "Damn it! Cass! Eliza!" His voice carried nothing back but our own panic. He leaned his forehead against the rock and swore again, quieter this time. "They're gone."

"They're not gone." My voice came out sharper than I intended. "They're somewhere else. The dungeon split us."

He stepped back, brushing dust from his hair. "You sound awfully sure of that."

"I've seen this kind of magic before," I said, scanning the new corridor stretching ahead. The air felt different here—thick, as if the dungeon itself was watching. "Shifting mazes. Illusory walls. Designed to test, to isolate."

"And you'd know, wouldn't you?" He smirked without humor. "Guess the Church taught you more than hymnals."

I ignored the jab. "The priority is regrouping. We find the exit to this passage. It'll lead us back to them."

He exhaled, long and slow. "Right. Lead the way, paladin."

The corridor stretched into shadow, lit only by faint glyphs carved into the walls. They pulsed with a dull silver glow, like veins carrying some kind of lifeblood through the stone. I raised a hand to one of them, but stopped short. The magic in it thrummed too steady. Too calculated.

"Don't touch," I warned.

"Wouldn't dream of it." Vaelen adjusted his grip on his sword. The faint crackle of residual lightning danced along the blade's edge, casting fleeting light across the walls. "So... what now? Walk until something decides to eat us?"

I didn't answer right away. The floor underfoot was smooth—too smooth. Not worn by time or boots, but etched as part of the dungeon's design. A trial, then. It wanted us here.

"Eyes open," I said. "And stay close."

For a while, the only sounds were our boots and the occasional drip of unseen water. The corridor bent downward, narrowing until we had to walk single file. My shield brushed the walls more than once, the runes sparking faintly at the contact. Each time, the air pressed closer, heavier, until even Vaelen's usual grin faltered.

"Feels like walking into a coffin," he muttered.

"That's the idea," I replied.

At last, the tunnel opened into a chamber. Circular, high-ceilinged, with a dais in the center. On it sat a pedestal carved of black stone, a silver bracelet resting atop like an offering. Around the walls, four doorways waited, each marked with a different glyph—sun, flame, eye, and sword.

Vaelen gave a low whistle. "That looks suspicious as hell."

"It's a trial," I said, stepping forward. The runes in the floor converged at the pedestal, faintly glowing beneath the bracelet.

Vaelen leaned on his sword. "Let me guess. Take the shiny trinket, and we either get blessed or roasted alive."

"More likely, both." I scanned the glyphs. "These doors won't open until we choose correctly. And the bracelet is the key."

He cocked a brow. "You're awfully calm about it."

I met his gaze. "Because panic gets people killed."

For a moment, he just watched me. Then his expression shifted—lighter, almost teasing. "Speaking of panic, can I ask you something? About Cass."

My jaw tightened, but I kept my tone even. "What about her?"

"You care about her." He said it flat, no question in his tone. "More than you'd admit to anyone else."

I stayed silent.

He smirked faintly. "Relax, I'm not about to compete with you. Whatever Cass and I were... that was years ago. We were kids. She's grown past that, and so have I. These days, she feels more like a little sister."

Relief sparked in my chest before I could stop it. Dangerous relief.

Vaelen leaned a little closer. "But you... you watch her like you're waiting for the world to try and take her away."

I forced my eyes back to the pedestal. "She's strong enough to stand on her own."

"That wasn't a denial," he said softly.

I ignored him, focusing instead on the glyphs. But his words had already settled under my skin.

The bracelet gleamed faintly, catching the silver glow from the runes. Whatever it was, the dungeon wanted us to have it.

"Help me check for traps," I said, pushing forward.

He grinned. "Finally, something I'm good at."

We approached the dais together, his Arcblade humming low, my shield raised. As I stepped onto the runes, the glyphs along the walls flared brighter.

The dungeon had been waiting.

Cass

The wall slammed shut behind us.

I spun, dagger in hand, breath sharp in my chest. The corridor that had been there a heartbeat ago was gone—swallowed by solid stone as if it had never existed. No Tarn. No Vaelen.

Just me and Eliza.

"No—" My palm slapped the wall, fingers scraping for any seam. Nothing. "Tarn!"

The stone didn't echo. It absorbed the sound, leaving only silence thick enough to choke on.

"They're alive," Eliza said, calm but firm. She pushed her glasses higher up her nose, though they were already straight. "The dungeon split us."

I turned toward her. "And you say that like it's not a problem?"

"It's a problem," she admitted, brushing dust from her coat. "But not the kind we solve by screaming at walls."

My hand trembled against the stone. I forced it down, shoved the dagger back into its sheath, and turned to face the corridor ahead. It sloped downward, the ceiling pressing lower with each step, lined with faint veins of violet light that pulsed like something alive.

Eliza shifted into weasel form with a shimmer of magic, scampering ahead before reemerging as herself again a dozen feet down. "No traps yet," she reported.

"Yet," I muttered, following.

The corridor opened into a wide, half-collapsed chamber. Jagged roots pushed through the ceiling like skeletal fingers, dripping with condensation. The air was damp, smelling faintly of iron. In the center of the room, a pool of water reflected the violet glow from the walls.

I froze. The surface rippled.

"Something's in there," I whispered.

Eliza's hand brushed mine, steady and grounding. "Stay behind me."

She shifted again—this time into her badger form, heavier, claws digging into the stone as she padded closer to the pool. The ripple grew, spreading outward, until a figure rose from the water.

No—not a figure.

A beast.

Its body was a warped echo of a wolf, but its hide shimmered translucent, half-formed like glass catching moonlight. Where its eyes should have been, two hollow voids burned faint violet.

The pool shuddered as a second form began to rise.

"Eliza—"

"I see them," she growled, her voice low and strange in this form.

I drew both daggers, the weight familiar, the shadows around me whispering like old friends. The first wolf lunged, its body splashing but leaving no droplets behind. My blade caught its shoulder—and passed half through it, like cutting fog.

Pain lanced up my arm, sharp and cold.

"They're altered," Eliza barked, raking her claws through the creature's side. "Not physical!"

"Could've mentioned that sooner," I snapped, vanishing in a burst of shadow. I reappeared behind the second wolf, slashing across its back. This time, the strike landed true, its form shattering into fragments of light before reforming with a guttural snarl.

"Not enough," Eliza said, claws scraping sparks as she held one at bay. "We need to destabilize them!"

I gritted my teeth. "How?"

"Focus on their cores," she panted, nodding toward the faint glow pulsing inside their chests. "The aether threads holding them together."

The wolf in front of me snapped its jaws, teeth clamping shut a breath from my throat. I ducked, slid low, and drove a dagger into the glow at its center. For a moment, the shadows around me surged—then the creature fractured with a sound like breaking glass, dissolving into mist.

The second lunged at Eliza. I blinked behind it, both daggers sinking into its core as her claws tore through its throat. Together, we brought it down.

The silence that followed was worse than the fight.

Both of us stood panting, the pool calm again, the faint violet glow seeping back into the stone.

I wiped my blade on my cloak, my hands still trembling. "That wasn't... normal."

"Nothing in here is going to be," Eliza said, shifting back into human form. She pushed her glasses up, though her hands were shaking too. "And that wasn't the worst of it."

I frowned. "What do you mean?"

She glanced toward the far end of the chamber. My gaze followed—and I froze.

There, just beyond the rippling shadows, something stood.

Not wolf. Not man.

A shape, tall and distorted, its edges blurring as though reality itself refused to hold it still. It didn't move. Didn't breathe. Just watched.

Then it vanished.

My stomach turned to ice. "Did you see—"

"I saw," Eliza said quickly. Her voice was steady, but her eyes were wide. "And we keep moving before it decides to come back."

We crossed the chamber, careful not to look back at the pool.

For a while, the silence stretched, broken only by the drip of water and the echo of our footsteps. I didn't realize how tight my grip was on the daggers until Eliza spoke again.

"Cass."

I glanced at her. She wasn't looking at me—just ahead, glasses catching the faint glow of the runes. "You and Tarn. How do you feel about him?"

My chest tightened. "What?"

"You heard me," she said evenly. "It's obvious you two are close. More than close."

I faltered. The words tangled in my throat. "I... don't know."

"Don't lie," she said softly. "Not to me. And not to yourself."

I opened my mouth, then shut it again. I'd thought about it— too many times to count. In the quiet moments. In the way his eyes lingered when he thought I wasn't looking. In the way my chest always tightened when he put himself between me and danger.

"I've thought about it," I admitted finally. My voice was raw. "But I haven't... let myself."

"Why not?"

"Because..." I swallowed hard. "Because it's easier to pretend I don't know."

We walked in silence for a while longer. Then I turned it back on her. "And you? You and Vaelen?"

That got a faint smile. "Partners. Nothing more. He does enough woman-chasing on his own time to keep himself busy. I'm not interested in being another one of his stories."

Despite myself, I huffed a laugh. "Sounds about right."

She glanced at me finally, something soft in her gaze. "But you... you should stop pretending."

I didn't answer. Couldn't.

Because I already knew she was right.

Tarn

The runes flared so brightly I had to narrow my eyes against the silver light. The doors around the chamber rumbled as if the stone itself was waking.

Vaelen muttered under his breath, "Knew it was too easy."

"Stay sharp." I kept my shield raised, my eyes fixed on the bracelet. "The dungeon doesn't hand out gifts without a cost."

The first glyph ignited—the sun. Its doorway blazed open, flooding the chamber with light so harsh it painted shadows across the walls. A figure stepped through, and my blood ran cold.

It was me.

Or close enough. The armor was the same, though blackened at the edges. The hammer it carried was my own, but etched with runes that pulsed a dark, unnatural violet.

"Mirror test," I said, voice tight. "It's going to make us fight ourselves."

"Not both of us, apparently," Vaelen muttered, tightening his grip on his Arcblade. "Guess you're up first."

The doppelganger lunged. I barely had time to raise my shield before the hammer crashed into it with the weight of a landslide. The force rattled my bones.

"Not going to lie," Vaelen called, circling the edge of the dais, "this is really uncomfortable to watch."

"Then don't," I gritted out, shoving back hard.

The thing moved like me—too much like me. Every feint, every pivot, it mirrored perfectly. My hammer strikes met theirs with bone-jarring precision, sparks spraying as steel clashed. Sweat ran down my spine.

Vaelen darted in once, blade crackling, but the doppelganger's head snapped toward him instantly. It swung wide, forcing him to retreat.

"Yeah, okay," he said, backing off. "Definitely just you."

"It's reading me," I said, breath sharp. "Learning my moves as I make them."

"Then stop doing what you'd normally do."

I risked a glance at him. He was grinning—the madman actually looked entertained.

"You're insane," I muttered.

"Works for me."

The doppelganger swung again, and this time I let it connect, angling my shield at the last second to redirect the blow. It stumbled a half-step, just enough for me to slam the rim of my shield into its side and drive my hammer low.

The impact cracked its knee with a sound like splitting stone. It hissed—my voice, warped—and staggered back.

"Nice!" Vaelen shouted. "Again!"

I pressed the advantage, feinting high and swinging low. The doppelganger tried to mimic, but the damaged leg faltered. My hammer slammed into its chest, and it shattered into motes of silver light that drifted upward and faded.

The glyph above the sun doorway dimmed.

I lowered my shield slowly, breath ragged. "One down."

"Three to go." Vaelen pointed his blade toward the flame glyph, which was already flickering brighter. "You ready?"

The flame doorway burst open, heat rolling across the chamber. This time, it wasn't a mirror. Shapes of fire coalesced—humanoid, faceless, each carrying weapons of molten steel.

I muttered a prayer under my breath and raised my hammer again.

Vaelen smirked, lightning running up his blade. "Don't worry. I've got this dance partner."

We moved together, striking and countering. His blade carved arcs of lightning through flame, dispersing the creatures before they could reform, while I smashed the ground with shockwaves that doused their fire. One tried to slip past, but Vaelen intercepted it, grinning like he'd been waiting for this.

"You fight like you're carrying the world on your shoulders," he called between strikes. "Maybe let someone else take a turn."

"This isn't a game," I growled, slamming a creature into ash.

"Never said it was. But you don't have to carry it alone."

His words hit harder than they should have. I didn't answer, just kept fighting until the last of the flame-born dissipated.

When the glyph dimmed, the bracelet on the pedestal pulsed faintly, as if acknowledging our progress.

"Halfway," Vaelen said, wiping sweat from his brow.

I met his eyes. "Stay focused."

The third doorway—the eye—flared open. A wave of pressure slammed into my mind, and suddenly the chamber wasn't stone and glyphs. It was the battlefield from years ago. The one I'd tried not to see again.

I froze.

Vaelen's hand clamped onto my shoulder. "It's an illusion. Fight it."

The screams echoed. The smell of blood hit my nose like it was yesterday. I saw her—Laina—reaching for me as the monster descended.

"Tarn." Vaelen's voice cut through, sharp. "Look at me."

I forced my gaze away from the vision, locking on his. His eyes were steady, grounding me.

"It's not real," he said firmly. "She's not here. Cass is."

The illusion wavered. I gritted my teeth and drove my hammer into the floor. Light erupted, shattering the vision into shards of silver.

The glyph dimmed. Only one remained.

The sword.

The doorway opened, and standing there was... Cass.

Not real—I knew instantly. But perfect. Her daggers gleamed, her cloak trailing shadows. She smiled—not the smile I knew, but something sharper. Predatory.

"You'll fail her," it whispered, though her lips didn't move.

Vaelen muttered, "Oh, that's dirty."

I raised my hammer, heart pounding.

The false Cass lunged.

Cass

The corridor twisted downward, walls tightening until every step felt like walking into the throat of something alive. The violet veins in the stone pulsed harder now, throwing faint light over our faces.

Eliza slowed, crouching near a half-buried alcove in the wall. She brushed dust away and pried something free—a sealed scroll case, dark wax glinting faintly.

She studied it for half a breath, then shoved it into my hands. "Yours."

I blinked. "What? You don't even know what it is."

"You'll need it more than me," she said firmly, pushing her glasses up. "If that thing we saw comes back, you'll want every edge you can get."

My fingers hesitated over the seal. "Eliza—"

"Cass," she cut in. "Use it."

The wax broke under my thumb. The scroll unfurled with a whisper that sounded more like breath than parchment, glyphs spilling into the air like smoke before searing into my skin.

I bit back a gasp as the knowledge settled inside me—unwelcome, undeniable. A blackened chain flickered to life along my arm, coiling once before vanishing again, leaving a phantom weight.

Umbral Chain.

The name whispered in my mind, sharp and heavy.

"It worked," I said, voice low.

Eliza gave a single nod. "Good. Because we're not alone."

The growl came before I could ask. Low, rolling, rattling through the chamber as two shapes slunk from the shadows. Wolves—like the others—but wronger this time, their forms splitting and reforming as though reality itself couldn't hold them still. Their hollow violet eyes burned brighter than before.

They lunged in unison.

I vanished in a flicker of shadow, reappearing behind the first. My dagger found its chest, but this time I called the chain. It snapped into being, black and sparking, lashing around the creature's core. The glow inside flared, convulsed—and shattered like brittle glass.

Eliza met the second head-on in badger form, claws raking sparks as she held it back. "Core!" she barked.

I blinked behind it, chain coiling tight as my blades struck. The glow burst, and the creature dissolved into mist with a sound like breaking stone.

The chamber fell silent.

Eliza shifted back, breath coming fast. "Efficient," she said, though her eyes lingered on the fading chain.

I forced a thin smile. "Guess I finally earned the scary rumors."

She smirked faintly but didn't reply. Instead, she turned to the far wall.

That was when I noticed—there were no doors. No corridors. Just smooth stone all around us.

My stomach knotted. "It's a dead end."

"Not for long," Eliza murmured, scanning the runes. "Dungeons don't waste effort without purpose. It's waiting on something."

I swallowed, the pendant at my chest cold against my skin. Waiting. Watching. Testing.

We stood in the violet glow, the silence pressing tighter than any wall, knowing this wasn't the end.

Just the pause before whatever came next.

··———◆——··

Tarn

The false Cass moved like the real one—quick, precise, shadows curling around her strikes. My shield rang as her daggers slammed against it, faster than I'd braced for. The smirk on her face wasn't Cass's, though. Too cold. Too cruel.

"She doesn't need you," the doppelganger hissed, circling. "She never did. You're just waiting to fail her, like you failed the others."

My grip tightened on the hammer. "You're not her."

It flickered—her, then not her, its features warping between Cass's face and a shadowy blur. "Aren't I?"

Vaelen's voice cut through from the edge of the dais. "Don't listen. It's just playing with you."

The false Cass darted forward, a blur of steel and shadow. I blocked high, but she slipped low, a dagger carving across the rim of my armor. Sparks flared. My chest burned.

I swung back hard, aiming for center mass, but she vanished in a swirl of darkness—appearing behind me in an instant.

"Shadow Step," I muttered.

Her daggers scraped along my shield as I spun, hammer arcing wide. She caught it on crossed blades, the force rattling us both. For a heartbeat, our eyes locked—hers empty, void-black.

"You'll watch her die."

Rage flared. I shoved forward, breaking the lock, and slammed my shield into her chest. She stumbled, shadows fraying.

"Not again," I growled.

She lunged once more, blades aimed for my throat. I feinted left, then let the hammer fall right, a downward arc fueled with everything I had left. The strike connected.

The false Cass shattered into silver motes, dissolving into the air.

Silence dropped heavy in the chamber.

Vaelen exhaled, lowering his sword. "Well. That was horrifying."

I didn't answer. My chest heaved, sweat dripping into my collar.

The last glyph dimmed. The bracelet on the pedestal pulsed, brighter than before. I stepped forward and lifted it. Up close, the silver gleamed with faint etchings—lines that shifted if I looked too long. Power thrummed against my palm.

"What do you think it does?" Vaelen asked.

"Doesn't matter." I slipped it into my gauntlet, hiding the glow. "For now, it's a luck charm."

He snorted. "That's vague enough to be worrying."

Before I could answer, the chamber groaned. The wall opposite us split, stone drawing back in a slow reveal.

Beyond, I saw them.

Cass, standing with daggers still in hand, Eliza beside her, her glasses catching the glow. Relief hit me so hard my knees nearly gave.

"Took you long enough," Cass said, her voice steady but her eyes betraying the fear she'd been holding back.

Vaelen grinned, striding forward. "Told you we'd find you."

Eliza muttered, "Barely."

The runes in the walls pulsed brighter now that we were whole. Then, as though the dungeon itself was satisfied, a new seam split in the far wall—an exit, leading deeper into shadow.

I moved to Cass's side, close enough to feel the brush of her cloak.

"Together," I said quietly.

She nodded, the faintest smile tugging at her lips. "Together."

We stepped through the threshold as one.

And the dungeon closed behind us.

Chapter 18

SHADOWS IN GLASS

Cass

T he moment we crossed the threshold, the stone sealed behind us with a grinding finality that made my skin crawl.

No going back. Not that I'd expected otherwise.

The air here was different—colder, heavier, as if the stone itself remembered every step we'd taken to get here and was waiting to see what we'd do next. The corridor ahead sloped downward. The runes along the walls shifted from cool silver to a deeper violet, their glow crawling over Tarn's armor in broken bands, skating along Vaelen's Arcblade, and catching for an instant on the glass of Eliza's spectacles.

"Feels different down here," Vaelen murmured. "Like it's watching us closer."

"It is," Eliza said without looking away from the carvings. "It's funnelling us."

"Toward what?" Tarn asked, voice low.

I didn't answer. I already knew. The shape Eliza and I had seen earlier hadn't just been lurking. It had been leading.

The walls narrowed until Tarn's shield kissed one side and Vaelen's shoulder rubbed the other. Every few steps, my fingers found the hilts of my daggers just to make sure they were still there. The new magic—the chain—rested at the edge of thought like a coiled animal waiting for a hand signal.

The corridor spat us into a wide antechamber paved in black stone polished to a mirror sheen. The ceiling soared into shadow so thick it might as well have been a night sky with the stars scraped out. Runes circled the floor beneath our feet—clean lines, deliberate spacing. The kind of pattern you didn't step into unless you were forced.

"Not a fan of the floor," Vaelen said, eyeing his reflection. "Feels like it's staring back."

"That's because it is," Eliza said quietly.

Silence pooled. Then—just as the knot in my shoulders started to loosen—the runes flared to life.

The chamber's reflection rippled. Our mirrored selves blurred, distended, peeled up from the floor as if the dark stone had turned liquid and decided to stand.

The thing we'd glimpsed before stepped free of our inverted world and into this one.

Up close, it was worse. Far worse.

Its shape was human the same way a doll is human— proportions just a fraction off, arms a touch too long, fingers tapering into talons that leaked flecks of cold silver. Its surface wasn't skin so much as a warped reflection of everything around it. When it turned its head toward me, my own face glinted back in broken shards.

No voice. No hint of breath or heat. Just a jerky tilt, like it was cataloging us.

Vaelen swore under his breath. "That's not going to die easy."

It didn't give us time to decide how. One moment it stood across the chamber; the next it was on Tarn, talons raking across his shield in a screech that set my teeth on edge. The force shoved him back two steps; his boots skidded on the glassy floor.

"Fast," Tarn barked.

I cut to the flank. Shadows slid at my heels. My dagger flashed toward its ribs, but the creature twisted with impossible economy; steel squealed uselessly along its reflective hide. It flicked an arm at me almost lazily. Cold rushed up my shoulder, not ice—absence—stealing warmth the way a tide empties a bay.

"Cass!" Tarn snapped.

"I'm fine." I rolled, shook feeling back into my arm, and rose low.

Eliza surged past me in badger form, stocky weight slamming into the thing's legs. Claws threw sparks on glass-flesh. It staggered, and Vaelen pounced—Arcblade lit with a humming corona as he carved a diagonal cut across its chest.

The wound rippled shut.

"It heals," Vaelen said, already fading back.

"Then we hit it harder," Tarn growled. He met its counter with the rim of his shield, pivoted, and brought the hammer down. The blow split a spiderweb of cracks across the floor and stamped a jagged fracture through its torso. For an instant, silver light flickered under its reflective shell.

The core. Like the wolves.

The thought didn't so much occur as arrive. The chain answered. Heat licked up my forearm as links of shadow coalesced—blacker than black, edges swallowing the violet glow around them.

"Center mass!" I shouted. "There's something in it."

Its head snapped toward me. It slid sideways—literally—into its own reflection. Movement skimmed under the floor like a darker stain racing just beneath the surface, arrowing straight for me.

"Cass—move!" Tarn.

I braced. The thing erupted from the mirrored flagstones in front of me, talons spearing for my throat—

—and met the chain.

It bit with a sound like stone cracking in winter. Links cinched tight across its chest. The reflection inside it buckled, buckled again, as if the chain was pulling its image out of alignment.

"Now!" I yelled.

Tarn didn't need the prompt. His hammer fell like a verdict, smashing into the bound glow beneath its chest. Light burst. Fractures shot through the creature's body, each vein bleeding silver that leaked and froze like run-off in shadow.

It shuddered. The vibration clawed through the floor, up my legs, into my jaw. The chain seared hot. For a heartbeat, I thought it would snap.

The creature tore free.

I reeled as the links recoiled into me and vanished. It staggered, fissures still glowing across its frame. Still moving. Still hunting.

Vaelen flashed a humorless grin. "Round two."

It blurred—and became three. Distorted copies slid apart, fanning to our flanks. They moved together like a single thought spread across three bodies.

"Which is real?" Eliza demanded, back to back with me now, human again, hands raised.

"All of them," I said, though I had no idea. My pulse thudded hard enough to hurt. The rules here were its rules. It set the angles, the speed, the reflections.

The three copies moved as one—perfect sync, perfect timing, every step calculated to box us in.

The one on Tarn hit first, talons raining down in a blur that rang against his shield like drumbeats. He absorbed the blows, pivoted his stance, and shoved forward with the force of a battering ram.

Light flared at the edges of his armor—gold and white, sharp enough to cut through the violet haze of the room. The runes etched into his gauntlet came alive as he slammed his palm into the creature's chest.

"Lux Invictus!"

The words rolled like thunder. A flash of holy light burst from his hand, the kind that left a shadow burned into your vision. The copy staggered back, the silver in its body shuddering as if the light was searing it from within.

But it didn't fall.

Vaelen met his own with a rising slash that split it from hip to shoulder—only for the wound to ripple closed before he could pull his blade free. "Getting real tired of that trick!" he shouted, twisting away as talons raked the air where his throat had been.

The third one was mine.

It came at me low, sliding across the mirrored floor like a smear of oil. I stepped sideways, shadows pulling me into a flicker-step, and reappeared behind it. My dagger drove for the glow in its chest—only for its torso to twist in a way that no human spine should, catching my wrist mid-strike.

The cold bled into me instantly, numbing from fingers to shoulder. My grip faltered.

The chain surged in my mind before I could think. Links snapped into place around its arm, wrenching it back and breaking its hold on me. The pull sent cracks lacing its forearm; silver light dripped from them like liquid moonlight.

I yanked hard. Tarn saw the opening. He stepped past me, his hammer already lit from within—runic lines burning like molten gold.

The strike landed dead center. The copy burst into silver motes that scattered across the floor like shattered glass.

And then it reformed.

From the other two.

The fragments bled toward them, pulling up through their legs and knitting into their bodies. The cracks in both copies sealed, and they seemed... heavier. Denser.

Eliza swore under her breath. "It's consolidating strength."

"Means it's getting tired," Vaelen countered, teeth bared in something between a grin and a grimace.

"Or it's getting desperate," Tarn said. His voice was steady, but the set of his jaw told me he didn't believe it was that simple.

The two remaining copies didn't waste time. One barreled into Tarn with a full-bodied slam that rattled his armor; the other streaked for Eliza, claws aimed for her throat. She twisted away in human form, then shifted mid-spin into a weasel to slip under its legs. Her hands came up glowing with some crude, earthbound magic as she returned to human, slamming her palm to the mirrored floor.

The surface buckled under the creature's feet, throwing off its balance. I took the moment, Shadow Stepping into its flank and letting the chain burst from its own shadow. It coiled up its torso, locking it in place long enough for Vaelen to plant a lightning-charged strike through its midsection.

The hit left a deep fracture, the glow inside flickering like a dying flame.

Tarn didn't waste it. He shoved the other copy off him with a golden shockwave that radiated from his shield. The burst sent hairline cracks through the mirrored floor itself.

The violet runes in the walls dimmed for a moment.

The thing noticed.

Both copies froze mid-motion—then dove, not at us, but at the floor. They melted into the reflection in unison, silver bodies vanishing beneath the surface.

"Eyes!" Tarn barked.

The chamber erupted in movement beneath us. Shadows darted through the mirrored depths, impossible to track for more than a heartbeat. Every time I thought I knew where they'd surface, they veered away, streaking toward a different angle.

They came up together, one in front of Tarn, the other behind him. Perfect pincer.

I didn't think. The chain roared to life, not from my hands but from the reflection beneath Tarn's boots. It shot upward, wrapping his legs and yanking him down just enough for the first swipe to pass over his head. Tarn's eyes flicked toward me for a fraction of a second—surprised—but then the hammer was already moving.

He twisted from his crouch, bringing the head of it up in an arc wreathed in holy flame. The strike connected with the nearest copy's jaw, splintering its head into a spray of silver shards that evaporated before they hit the ground.

The other one raked his backplate. Sparks and golden light flared where talons met enchanted steel. Tarn hissed in pain but shoved back hard, and Vaelen was there in a blink, carving a crescent of lightning into its side.

The copy staggered toward me. I didn't give it the chance to recover.

Shadow Step—chain—dagger. One fluid motion. The links bound it mid-lunge, and my dagger sank to the hilt into the core. Silver light flooded the chain, racing up my arm until my vision blurred. The thing writhed, then shattered in an explosion of motes that rained down like ash.

The chamber went quiet.

But not for long.

The motes didn't fade this time. They drifted toward the remaining copy, drawn as if by gravity. The moment they touched, the body swelled with light—so bright it threw our shadows across the walls in jagged, dancing shapes.

Eliza's voice was sharp. "That's it. The original."

It didn't blur this time. Didn't split. It just came at us—straight, fast, and unstoppable.

Tarn met it head-on, shield raised, the edge wreathed in burning gold. The impact rattled my bones from across the room. The two locked in place, light and silver grinding against each other, neither giving.

I circled, chain coiling at my wrist, waiting for my opening. The glow in its chest pulsed like a heartbeat, and every time it did, the floor's reflection warped, threatening to swallow us whole.

Vaelen struck for its back, but it twisted without losing pressure on Tarn, catching the Arcblade mid-swing and hurling him aside like nothing.

Eliza threw a bolt of raw force into its flank; the blow barely rocked it. Tarn gritted his teeth and shouted something in a language I didn't know—old and heavy. Golden fire flared along his hammer, spilling heat across the room.

The thing flinched from it.

That was all I needed.

The chain shot from the reflection at its feet, winding up its torso. Tarn shoved forward, smashing the hammer into its core. Light burst—and the fight became something else entirely.

The blast of golden light from Tarn's hammer hit like a sunrise breaking through storm clouds. The chains around the creature's torso tightened, links glowing as the light bled into them.

For a heartbeat, I thought that would be enough—that we'd see the fractures spiderweb, the core shatter, and the thing collapse.

But it screamed.

Not in sound—more like the entire chamber flexed, the mirrored floor buckling, the violet runes on the walls flaring so bright my eyes burned. My chain quivered, straining like a rope pulled too tight. The heat running up my arm turned searing.

The creature didn't just resist—it pulled.

Silver light raced along the links, slamming into me like a wave. My knees buckled. I felt it inside my head for an instant—cold, prying fingers searching for something.

Tarn saw it. "Cass! Break it!"

I tried. The chain didn't want to let go. It was like holding onto a hooked fish that wanted to drag me into the water with it.

Vaelen was there, lightning flashing along his Arcblade as he slashed across the links, severing them in a burst of shadow. The recoil threw me backward. I hit the ground hard enough to see stars, the breath knocked out of me.

The thing staggered, part of its chest caved in from Tarn's last hit, the glow inside flickering wildly.

"Press it!" Tarn roared.

He surged forward again, holy fire licking along the edges of his shield. Vaelen flanked, carving wide, punishing arcs with every strike. Eliza shifted into badger form and went for its legs, her claws sparking where they met glass-flesh.

I forced myself up. The chain was still there, coiled at the edge of my thoughts, and I knew this was it. The opening we'd been waiting for.

I ran. Shadows stretched with me, wrapping my legs, my arms, until the world blurred and I was there—at its back—before it could turn.

The chain burst out, not just one coil this time but three, each lashing from a different angle—the ceiling's reflection, the wall's, the floor's—snapping tight around the thing's limbs and throat. It jerked once, twice, but the links held.

"Now!" I shouted.

Tarn's hammer came down in a blaze of gold and white, smashing into the exposed core. The light in its chest flared, then fractured into a thousand shards. Vaelen's lightning met it a half-second later, pouring raw energy into the break.

The thing convulsed. Its body shattered along every fracture, silver shards erupting outward like shrapnel before dissolving into mist.

And then it was gone.

The chains vanished. The mirrored floor rippled once, then stilled.

I stood there, chest heaving, daggers still raised, waiting for it to reform. But there was nothing—just the steady dimming of the violet runes, the sound of our breathing filling the void.

Tarn lowered his hammer slowly. "It's over."

I wanted to believe him. I almost did.

And then the amulet burned.

The cold weight at my chest flared hot, so hot I staggered back a step. The mist where the creature had died didn't fade—it twisted, coiling like smoke caught in a wind I couldn't feel. The strands streamed toward me, drawn to the pendant as if by gravity.

"Cass!" Tarn's voice was sharp, but my feet wouldn't move. I couldn't move.

The smoke hit the amulet.

The silver light from the creature's body sank into the metal, bleeding through the crescent shape in molten lines. For an instant, the whole chamber seemed to tilt around me, my ears ringing with a sound like a thousand voices speaking in a language I couldn't understand.

The heat vanished as suddenly as it came.

I stumbled, and Tarn caught me by the arm. "What happened?"

"I–" My voice came out thin. "I don't know. It just... pulled it in."

Vaelen eyed the pendant warily. "That thing was laced with aether. If the amulet absorbed it–"

"–then it's even more dangerous than we thought," Eliza finished. Her gaze flicked to me. "Does it feel different?"

I shook my head, but it wasn't true. The weight on the chain around my neck felt heavier now, like it was aware. Like it was listening.

Tarn's expression was grim. "We'll figure it out later. For now, we're leaving."

The chamber seemed to hear him. A seam split open in the far wall, stone grinding back to reveal a sloping tunnel lit with faint daylight. The air that rushed through was clean—cool without the weight of magic pressing down.

We didn't linger.

The walk out was silent. No one wanted to speak, and I didn't trust my voice to be steady if I tried. The tunnel spilled us into a narrow canyon outside the dungeon entrance, the sound of wind over stone replacing the endless hum of runes.

I turned back once. The entrance was already closing, the last sliver of darkness vanishing like it had never been there.

It was over.

But as I touched the amulet at my throat, feeling the faint thrum of whatever it had taken in, I knew the dungeon hadn't just let us go.

It had given me something.

And I wasn't sure if that was a gift... or a warning.

The canyon air hit like a drink of cold water.

For the first time in what felt like hours, I could breathe without feeling the dungeon pressing back. The wind carried no violet glow, no low hum in the bones — just the rustle of grass and the far-off cry of some bird that didn't care what we'd just been through.

We stopped just outside the narrowing gap in the rock. Tarn leaned on his hammer for a breath, scanning each of us the way he did after a fight — checking for injuries before checking for words.

"You're bleeding," he said finally, nodding at the shallow gash on my arm where the thing's claws had caught me.

"It's nothing," I said, though the sting begged to differ.

He knelt anyway, setting the hammer down so he could press his hand lightly over the cut. His gauntlet was warm from the fight; his voice was steady when he murmured a short prayer.

Light spread from his palm, soft and golden, seeping into my skin until the raw edge of the wound dulled. The ache faded with it, leaving only a faint line of pink where the skin had closed.

I flexed my fingers. "Guess I should've asked for that after my trial."

Tarn didn't look up. "Wouldn't have helped much."

I frowned. "Why?"

He leaned back on his heels. "Paladin magic isn't the same as a priest's. I can knit skin, close shallow cuts, ease bruising — but anything deep, torn, or poisoned? I can't replace what's already lost. I can only help the body along if it still has the strength to heal itself."

The words made sense, but I still remembered the weeks I'd spent recovering from the trial, every muscle aching, every breath heavy. "So you could've taken the edge off."

His eyes flicked to mine for half a heartbeat. "I could have... but you needed rest more than a false sense of recovery. And if I'd spent what little I had healing you then, I wouldn't have had enough to keep you alive if something happened on the road."

I didn't have an answer for that. Not one I wanted to say out loud.

Vaelen broke the quiet with a half-hearted grin. "Well, I feel perfectly fine, in case anyone was wondering."

Eliza shot him a look. "Your hair's still singed."

"Occupational hazard."

Tarn rose, retrieving his hammer. "Those chains of yours are new."

I perked up, "Thank Eliza for that. She's the one that found the scroll."

"Let's move. We want to reach the main road before nightfall."

We fell into step, the canyon giving way to rolling hills ahead. I kept my eyes forward, but my hand kept straying to the amulet at my throat, its faint weight a reminder of what it had taken in.

Whatever waited for us back in town, I had the sinking feeling it wouldn't be the last time I'd feel it stir.

Chapter 19

LINGERING SHADOWS

Cass

The gates of the capital rose on the horizon just as the sun dipped low enough to stain the roofs in firelight. My legs ached from the steady march back, but none of us had argued about keeping pace. No one wanted to spend another night in the wilds if we didn't have to.

The streets were crowded, busier than I remembered. Merchants shouted prices, children darted between stalls, and the smell of frying bread cut through the air. Normal. Loud. Alive. After days of echoing stone and violet light, it almost felt wrong.

"Never thought I'd say this," Vaelen muttered at my side, "but I actually missed the smell of unwashed boots and cheap ale."

Eliza gave him a flat look. "That says more about you than the capital."

He grinned, unbothered. Tarn didn't even glance back. His gaze stayed fixed on the guild hall at the end of the square, posture rigid like he was already bracing for the questions we'd have to answer.

The guild doors boomed shut behind us once we stepped inside. Evening light filtered through the high windows, catching dust motes and painting the walls in pale orange. A handful of adventurers lingered at tables, armor still caked in dirt, mugs of ale clutched in tired hands. A few glanced up as we entered, curiosity flashing before turning back to their drinks.

The receptionist — a lean half-elf man named Derren who always looked like he'd been woken too early — blinked when he saw us. His eyes flicked from Tarn's dented armor, to Eliza's torn sleeve, to the faint cut still visible on my arm.

"You're back." The words weren't relief so much as disbelief. "Already?"

"Dungeon collapsed behind us," Tarn said simply. "We need to speak to the guildmaster."

Derren's mouth opened, shut, then opened again. "Collapsed?"

"Yes," Tarn said. "And it wasn't natural. We'll give the full report, but not here."

That was enough. Derren vanished through a side door, leaving us to wait. I sank into one of the benches, forcing my shoulders to relax. Vaelen stole a mug from a half-dozing adventurer and drained it before the man noticed. Eliza leaned against the wall, her arms crossed and her eyes distant, like her mind hadn't left the dungeon at all.

Tarn stayed standing. Always standing.

It didn't take long for Derren to return. "The guildmaster will see you."

We followed him through the hall, past doors I'd never been allowed beyond as a novice. The walls here were lined with weapons too fine to belong to any ordinary adventurer—trophies, reminders, warnings.

The guild master's office was less grand than I expected. A heavy oak desk buried under papers, a rack of maps, and a man who looked like he'd rather be on the battlefield than behind a ledger. His hair was iron-gray, cropped short, and his eyes carried the weight of someone who'd seen too many recruits not come back.

"Tarn," he said, rising to clasp wrists with him. "It's been a while."

"Veylan." Tarn inclined his head. "We need privacy."

The man's gaze swept over the rest of us before he nodded. He closed the shutters, locked the door, and gestured for us to sit. "Report."

Tarn didn't waste words. He spoke of the shifting corridors, the illusions, the creatures that bled silver light. Of the final chamber and the... thing we fought there. He didn't name it. None of us could. But even without a name, the memory pressed heavy in the room.

When Tarn mentioned the amulet, though, every gaze shifted to me.

I resisted the urge to touch it. "It reacted when we killed it," I admitted. "Pulled in... whatever it left behind. Aether, I think."

Veylan's jaw tightened. "You're sure?"

"I felt it," I said. "It wasn't a choice."

For the first time, his gaze softened—not kind, but understanding. "Artifacts like that rarely give you one."

"Do you know what it means?" Tarn asked.

"I know it means trouble," Veylan said bluntly. He leaned back, rubbing his temple. "Aether-bound monsters aren't common. Someone made that thing, and if they made one, they can make more. Whatever faction's behind it won't stop with one experiment."

Eliza shifted. "So what do we do?"

Veylan studied us for a long moment. "For now, nothing. Rest. Heal. Leave the wider worry to the guild."

"That won't be enough," Tarn said quietly.

"No," Veylan agreed. "But it's what we have."

The silence that followed was heavy, broken only by the scratch of Veylan's quill as he started writing a sealed notice. He pressed wax into it with the guild's crest before passing it to Tarn.

"Official recognition of completion," he said. "You four held your ground against something well beyond its tier. Consider yourselves lucky to walk out."

Vaelen took the seal and gave a mock bow. "Does luck come with coin? Because I'd really like it to come with coin."

Veylan's mouth twitched, almost a smile. "Payment will be in your account by morning. Dismissed."

We rose. Tarn lingered a moment longer, something unspoken hanging between him and the guildmaster, but he let it go.

Outside, the guild hall felt louder than before, every laugh and clatter sharper against the quiet weight of the office.

I touched the amulet again, half-expecting it to burn. It didn't. Just sat there, heavier than it should be, thrumming faintly against my skin.

Tarn caught me at it as we stepped into the square. His eyes flicked to the pendant, then to my face. "Don't let it define you."

My mouth went dry. "And if it already is?"

His hand brushed my shoulder, heavy and grounding. "Then we'll fight it. Together."

The capital always looked different after a job. Same streets, same lights, same noise – but the eyes I carried back weren't the ones I'd left with.

We cut across the square, the guild hall fading behind us, the sounds of the city washing over like a tide. Stalls were shutting down, lamps lit with oil and crystal humming against the dusk. Music drifted from taverns, rough and quick, accompanied by laughter that sounded too loud after what we'd just faced underground.

Vaelen stretched, rolling his shoulders. "I don't know about you lot, but I'm drinking until I forget the part where that thing had my face for a moment."

"You're buying," Eliza said flatly.

He shot her a grin. "With guild coin? Gladly."

Tarn led us down a side street I hadn't walked before, narrower, quieter. Not the main taverns where adventurers boasted loud enough to fill their purses with stories. This one was tucked between two shuttered shops, a lantern swinging over its door with the faintest creak. The kind of place you went to speak low and not be overheard.

Inside, the smell of woodsmoke and old ale hung heavy. A few locals kept their heads down over cards or cups, not sparing us a glance. Tarn picked a corner table, back to the wall. Always back to the wall.

We sat. For a long while, no one said anything. The barkeep delivered mugs without a word, and the silence stretched until Vaelen finally raised his cup.

"To surviving."

Eliza clinked her mug against his half-heartedly. I didn't echo them. My fingers curled around the handle, but my thoughts were still back in the dungeon, in the silver glow, in the way the amulet had pulled something out of that monster like it was meant to.

"You used magic back there," I said finally, breaking the quiet. "It's been a while since I've seen you do it."

Tarn looked up from his untouched drink. His expression gave nothing away, but the slight tightening of his jaw told me he'd expected the question.

"I use it when I have to," he said simply.

"Looked to me like you had to," Vaelen said, grinning over the rim of his mug. "Not that I'm complaining – that hammer hit was a thing of beauty. Thought the ceiling was going to come down on top of us."

"Paladin magic isn't something you throw around," Tarn said, calm but firm. "Every time I call on it, I feel it burn a little deeper. If I use it too often, or without need, it takes more than it gives."

That silenced even Vaelen.

Eliza adjusted her glasses, studying him. "So you ration it. Hold it back until the moment matters most."

"Exactly," Tarn said.

I thought of the way his hammer had lit up in the dungeon, the runes blazing like molten gold. The memory of it still burned behind my eyes – not frightening, not comforting, but something in between.

Vaelen raised his mug again, forcing the mood lighter. "Fine, then. I'll stick to lightning and sarcasm. That combination has never failed me yet."

Eliza rolled her eyes. "That's debatable."

Despite myself, a laugh slipped out. Short, quiet, but real.

Tarn's eyes flicked toward me at the sound. Just for a heartbeat. Then he looked away, and the silence settled again – softer now, but no less heavy.

We drank slowly after that. No boasting. No exaggeration. Just the four of us sitting in the quiet of a dim tavern, listening to the fire crackle and trying not to remember the silver glow of the dungeon.

By the time we left, the lamps along the street had burned low, smoke curling from the last of them. The capital's noise had dulled to murmurs of late trade, distant music, and boots on cobblestone.

We walked in silence. Not the oppressive silence of the dungeon – this one was gentler, though no less weighty.

My hand brushed the amulet at my chest again. The weight hadn't changed, but it felt heavier all the same. It hadn't stopped thrumming since the fight, like it was alive in some small, unwelcome way.

Tarn glanced at me but didn't say anything. For once, I was grateful.

The capital woke early. By the time the sun cleared the rooftops, the square outside the guild hall was already buzzing with merchants shouting over one another and adventurers clattering through in mismatched armor. The sound was almost comforting – normal, at least.

Inside the guild, things were no quieter. Boards along the walls were plastered with notices: bandit sightings, caravan escorts, wild beasts prowling farmland. None of it looked half as dangerous as what we'd just walked out of, though the crowd of hopefuls still jostled each other for the higher-paying contracts.

Derren spotted us as soon as we came in. He waved us toward the front, ignoring the muttered protests of adventurers who'd been waiting. A sealed pouch already sat on the counter.

"Guildmaster's orders," he said. "Payment in full, hazard bonus included."

Vaelen plucked the pouch from his hand before Tarn could reach it, weighing it with an appreciative grin. "That's a beautiful sound."

Eliza rolled her eyes. "You'll spend it all before nightfall."

"Wrong. I'll spend half before nightfall." He winked and tucked the pouch into his belt.

Tarn signed the ledger without comment, though I noticed his hand linger on the page a little longer than necessary. Names filled the columns, many crossed out. Too many.

I glanced away before I could read them.

We left the guild behind for the market. Sunlight spilled across cobblestones still slick from morning rain, painting the stalls in gold. The air was thick with the smell of baking bread, roasting meat, and spices I couldn't name.

Eliza darted between merchants with purpose, refilling our supplies: bandages, herbs, new chalk for marking passages. Tarn handled repairs, leaving his dented gauntlet and half-cracked shield rim with a smith who swore it would be reforged by week's end.

I lingered at the edge of the crowd, letting the noise wash over me. Every face seemed brighter than it should have been. Every laugh louder. It was like the city itself was flaunting how alive it was, daring the shadows to try again.

A pair of adventurers passed nearby, talking too low to be casual.

"...I swear, saw it myself," one said, a woman in scaled leather. "Something on the ridge. Not a beast, not natural either. Hollow eyes, light pouring out—"

Her companion hushed her. "Keep your voice down. Guild doesn't want panic."

They disappeared into the throng before I could catch more.

A shiver crawled down my spine.

When I rejoined the others, Vaelen was already haggling with a bowyer over string quality he didn't actually care about. Tarn caught my expression as I approached.

"What is it?" he asked.

"Probably nothing," I said, though my hand strayed to the amulet at my throat. "Just rumors."

His eyes searched mine for a moment before he nodded once, slow. "We'll keep ears open."

Eliza returned then, arms full of supplies, and the moment passed.

We spent the rest of the morning moving through the capital's veins. Shops, smiths, fletchers – places adventurers lived between the moments of life and death. Every face we passed looked untroubled. Safe.

I wondered how many would stay that way.

By midday, we ended back at the square, packs heavier and purses lighter. Vaelen stretched like a cat in the sun, clearly pleased with himself.

"Rest day?" he suggested.

Tarn gave him a look. "Rest, yes. Not day. We meet at dawn tomorrow."

"For what?" Vaelen asked.

"Training."

The groan that escaped him was so loud even Eliza cracked a smile.

I didn't complain. My body still ached from the dungeon, but the thought of sharpening my edge — of being more ready, just in case — sat like an anchor in my chest.

We split then, each drifting toward our lodgings. Tarn fell in step with me for a while, silent as ever, until we reached the inn. At the door, he paused.

"You did well in there," he said quietly. "Better than I think you realize."

I opened my mouth, but no words came. Not thanks. Not denial. Nothing.

So I just nodded.

His hand brushed my shoulder as he passed me on the way inside. A simple gesture. But steady. Grounding.

Later, alone in the small room the innkeeper had given me, I sat on the edge of the bed and pulled the amulet free of my cloak. The crescent-shaped metal gleamed faintly, no brighter than before, but when I held it in my palm, I could feel it: that faint, steady thrum.

The dungeon hadn't been the end of it. Whatever the amulet had taken in — it wasn't gone. It was waiting.

I closed my fist around it, forcing my eyes shut.

Waiting for what, I didn't know.

But I had the feeling we'd find out sooner than I wanted.

Chapter 20

THE ASHEN COVENANT

Archflame Vale

Incense curled from the braziers in disciplined threads, not to sweeten the sanctum but to mark its boundaries. Eryndor Vale stood at the long stone table and read two reports by candlelight: the first in a runner's hurried hand, the second in the tidy script of his aether-wardens.

The runner's account was simple and ugly. A patrol from the guild had blundered near one of the Sons' holding sites. Most did not return. One survivor—burned, raving, coherent in flashes—had reached the capital before dawn with enough horror to fill the guildhall twice over.

The wardens' ledger told a different tale: instruments in the cathedral's crypts had shivered all night from distant aether surge and counterflow. Not natural. Not weather. Prepared work.

Good, he thought. Let the guild have something to point to. Fear with a contour becomes useful.

The bronze doors rasped, and the Scion of the Hollow Star stepped in, his mask taking the candle's flame and breaking it into thin knives. He did not bow. He never did.

"You received the scout's testimony," the Scion said, voice soft and dry as parchment.

"I did." Eryndor set both reports down and folded his hands. "It serves us."

"You wanted surprise," the Scion murmured. "Now they will brace."

"They will *believe* they brace." Eryndor allowed himself a thin smile. "There's a difference. We have created a storm. I intend the cathedral to be the ark."

The Scion's mask turned, a dull-faced star. "You still insist on delaying."

"One day." Eryndor's tone left no seam to worry at. "Your handlers assure me stability improves across the second cycle. Take it. Let the guild scrape for men and chalk lines on their maps. Let the lords send runners and argue about gates. When the release comes, the blow will land where it breaks more than walls."

The Scion studied him through metal. "The Sons don't breed armies for pageants, Archflame. If you pull rein too tight, the beasts will tear in the traces. Then you'll have chaos without choreography."

"And yet," Eryndor said, "you prefer your spectacles. Consider this one curated."

He turned from the table and gestured toward the far arch of warded black stone. Cold bled from it in a narrow ring, the way it always did, as if the door drank heat in tiny sips.

"Tomorrow," he said, "my Ash Sentinels will drill the bells and barricades. We'll run the city through evacuation routes until the streets know the pattern by reflex. We'll move casks of water and bread into the nave, light the candles in the north transept, keep the infirmary empty and ready. When your creatures come, the people won't scatter to alleys and side doors. They will run to symbols." He set his palm on his chest. "They will run to us."

"Not to the labyrinth, then." There was a hint of amusement there.

"No," Eryndor said. "The labyrinth is not for the city."

He watched the Scion take that in without comment and continued, voice quieter. "The wards below have thinned with age. A stair in the old catacombs leads toward the lower foundation. Its seal will answer the Hollow Star if brought near under stress. During the attack there will be a tremor—only a peel of plaster and a seam in the stone. My wardens will make certain the crack shows where curious minds can find it. A priest with a lamp will claim a detour through the crypts to avoid panic at the doors. There are ways to *separate* a few from a crowd without anyone noticing they've been chosen."

"And those few are the ones who slew our mirror-construct," the Scion said, almost pleased now.

"They are." He kept his tone even, refusing to show the interest that had been needling him since the dungeon report. "They carry something that answers aether. They move toward doors other men pretend not to see. I want to know where those instincts break."

"If they do not descend?" the Scion asked.

"Then the priest with the lamp finds a different route. Or a barricade 'accidentally' collapses. Or a Sentinel points the wrong way with great sincerity." Eryndor lifted one shoulder. "In confusion, guidance feels like grace."

The Scion's sleeves whispered as his hands changed position out of sight. "And afterward?"

"Afterward, the cathedral stands with its doors open and its altars bright," Eryndor said. "The guild will be bloodied and grateful for an authority that can still count and feed. The nobles will sign whatever paper stops their courtyards from filling with refugees. We will convene a public council and 'temporarily coordinate' the city's defenses. The word *temporary* will evolve the way all temporary measures do."

He let that settle between them. The Scion had no love for pulpits—he was a man of glass and knives—but even the Sons appreciated architecture that could shelter their work. A ruin fed no one; a city on its knees fed everyone with teeth.

"You choose dominion over spectacle," the Scion said at last.

"I choose *usefulness*," Eryndor replied. "Your horde is a lever. I mean to pry with it, not smash the fulcrum."

Silence gathered. Above them, somewhere in the galleries, a bell clanged twice in a drill pattern then stilled. The sound traveled down the columns like a pulse.

"Very well," the Scion said. "One day. At last bell the day after, the vats open. The glass-wolves for the fields and roads, the heavier work for the bridges, the phaselights for the aqueduct mouth. We'll leave your granaries untouched and your cathedral as a lantern."

"And the guildhall?" Eryndor asked.

"Not first." A tilt of the head. "You insisted."

"I want the guild alive to be seen failing," Eryndor said. "A corpse cannot be contrasted with a savior."

The Scion's mask showed him himself for a heartbeat—a man in red and gold carved into a dozen thin reflections—and then the image slipped. "Then we are agreed. One day. We tune the vats and calm the handlers. You rehearse your Sentinels. And when your chosen few wander downward like moths to a seam of light, we will see what your labyrinth does to curiosity."

Eryndor did not answer the taunt. He offered the Scion a bishop's nod—polite, cool, impossible to mistake for deference. The emissary withdrew, the heavy doors kissing shut behind him.

For a long moment Eryndor remained where he was, listening to the sanctum's old stones hum with the passing bell. Then he crossed to the balcony that overlooked the cathedral's southern court. The capital sprawled beyond: roofs and chimneys, signal-lamps at the watchtowers, the market tents folded for night like tired birds. It was not a city to be burned. It was a city to be *tuned*.

He pictured the pattern as he had drawn it: Ash Sentinels at each choke point in polished mail, guiding lines of frightened citizens into aisles guarded by icons and law; guild captains barking orders with just enough authority to show onlookers how little they had left; the proclamation already drafted on his desk, naming a joint command under the Church "for the duration of the emergency."

They had one more day. One more day for rumors to ripen and the guild to stack spears at the gates, for diviners to mutter about rising lines on glass and convince themselves foresight was control. One more day for every faction to step into the positions he had set for them.

He closed the balcony shutters and turned back to the warded door below the dais. The chill around it had deepened, or perhaps he only noticed it more after thinking of stairs and lamps and seams in stone. He spoke a prayer under his breath—not piety, not really, but the habit of shaping intent with words.

"Not ruin," he said to the empty air. "Order."

The candle on the table guttered once and steadied. Eryndor snuffed it with a pinch of his fingers and left the sanctum to the dark, already speaking instructions in his head for drills, for food piles, for bells. Tomorrow would look like competence.

The night after would belong to the Church.

Chapter 21

THE CITY'S EDGE

Cass

T arn wakes me with my name, not some dry jab about me dragging my feet. That's how I know it's serious.

"Cass." His voice is low, steady, the kind that doesn't waste a word. "Up. Gear. We've been summoned."

The room is still shadowed, lantern-light hooded on the table. Tarn's already half-armored—he must've slept in it. My stomach twists, because Tarn never cuts corners. If he didn't take it off, it's because he didn't think he could afford the time.

"Summoned?" My voice is rough with sleep. "What, no breakfast first?"

"Guild." He buckles his bracer without looking at me. "Now."

Vaelen's already upright, rolling his shoulders like he'd been waiting for Tarn to say the word. His Arcblade leans against the wall within easy reach, faint etchings along the steel catching the lantern's light. He runs a hand through his hair, and just like that he looks put together—effortless. "That a general summons," he asks, "or just for us?"

"General," Tarn says.

Eliza doesn't bother asking questions. She's already moving, tightening the straps on her satchel, glasses glinting as she checks her belt for components. There's a calm efficiency in her that I envy; she's the kind who treats every summons like it matters.

I drag myself up and shove my feet into my boots. I nearly trip on the floorboards before I steady myself, pretending it was intentional. Vaelen quirks a brow but doesn't comment.

Daggers, cloak, pendant. I pat each in turn, the familiar weight grounding me.

By the time we're out the door, the city feels... off. Not empty—just different. The streets are muted, as if the usual sounds are smothered. No haggling from the markets. No dogs barking. Even the gulls circling the rooftops sound restless. People keep their heads down, shutters crack just wide enough to peek. It feels like the whole city knows something it hasn't said out loud yet.

We cut through the side alleys, Tarn setting a clipped pace. He doesn't look back to check if I'm keeping up—he doesn't need to. He just knows.

"You'd think they could've waited till daylight," Vaelen mutters as we pass a shuttered bakery. "I fight better on a full stomach."

"I thought you fought better with an audience," I say. "If you survive this, I'll clap twice for every swing you take."

"You've never clapped once."

"I'm saving it for a truly special occasion."

Eliza runs her fingers lightly along the stone wall as we move, like she's listening to something I can't hear. "Storm or predator," she murmurs.

"Both," Tarn says. The word lands heavy, final.

We pass the cathedral square, and there's already a line forming—families clutching bundles, faces drawn thin. Priests usher them inside with gestures that are meant to look gentle but come off more like herding. I keep my eyes forward. Tarn's jaw flexes once, a crack in the armor he tries to wear around anything with a flame-shaped sigil.

A pair of guards at the next corner lower their spears when they see Tarn, then step aside without question. One offers a quick, "Guild?"

"Guild," Tarn confirms.

"Gods watch you," the guard replies, but Tarn doesn't answer. He never does when people use the gods like currency.

We climb a narrow stair between two leaning tenements, the stones slick with frost. My boots bite in without slipping once.

The Guildhall rises ahead, pale stone looming through the mist. The banners hang limp, colors dulled by the hour. The plaza's crowded with adventurers—copper ranks clutching weapons too big for them, bronzes huddled in trios, a pair of silvers standing apart, faces grim. I catch sight of gear scarred from campaigns that don't make it onto the job boards. This isn't a call for coin. It's a call for survival.

Inside, the change is sharper. The boards are stripped bare, replaced by maps sprawled across easels. Charcoal lines mark city streets, small flags pinned like wounds. Apprentices carry bundles of bolts and bandages, faces tight with focus. Somewhere, someone is hammering braces together, the ring of iron and wood replacing the usual cheer of sparring.

My chest knots. This isn't another job. This is the city bracing itself.

A runner barrels past, sash half-tied, nearly colliding with me. "Sorry!" He straightens when he recognizes Tarn. "Great hall— Guildmaster says all ranks."

"All ranks," Vaelen mutters under his breath. "That's either generous or terrifying."

"Both," I answer, quieter.

Eliza adjusts her satchel and says softly, "We're ready." Not *we'll be fine.* Just *ready.* It's a distinction I notice.

The great hall is already crowded when we file in. The pillars stretch like ribs, the space between them packed with armor, weapons, and too many faces. The heat of bodies and low murmur of voices press down like storm air. There's no bragging here, no loud boasts—only quiet exchanges, people calculating odds and pretending not to.

At the far end, the dais waits. No trophies this time, no bored clerks handing out tokens. Just a covered crate and a knife driven point-first into a stand beside it. Two assistants move briskly, checking lists, muttering counts.

Tarn leads us along the left wall where the crush is thinner. People move aside without realizing they are. He doesn't need charisma; he has presence, and right now, it's enough to make him feel like a fixed star in a sky about to fracture. I stay close, watching his pauldron shift as he moves, and let myself breathe with his pace.

A woman with a longbow nods at me as we pass. "You're the one with the basilisk boots?"

"Depends," I say. "If you want to buy them, they're priceless. If you want to steal them, they're cursed."

That earns me the smallest smirk before she faces forward again.

The side door opens. A man in leathers steps out and calls, "Make way. Guildmaster."

The room quiets—not all at once, but like a tide drawing back.

The Guildmaster enters, red cloak thrown over chainmail, hair pulled tight. His stride is brisk, practiced. He doesn't climb the dais. He doesn't need the height. Authority clings to him like another layer of armor.

His eyes sweep the room, cataloguing. They pause on Tarn just long enough to make my pulse jump, then move on.

My hand finds the arc of my pendant. The stone rests quiet. Thank the stars.

"Listen up," the Guildmaster says, voice carrying without effort.

And just like that, the hum of voices dies.

Whatever comes next will split this day into a before and after.

"A scout returned in the middle of the night," he says, voice cutting through the air like the crack of a hammer on an anvil. "Barely breathing when he staggered through the gates. He spoke only long enough to tell us what he saw before he passed."

The great hall is silent. I can feel the words tightening around the crowd like a noose.

"He saw creatures," the Guildmaster continues, each syllable deliberate, "moving as one. Dozens, maybe hundreds. A warband of monstrosities, all Aether-twisted. They are marching toward us. By tomorrow, they'll be at our gates."

A ripple runs through the crowd—boots shifting, armor creaking, whispered curses. Someone swears loud enough to be heard before clamping their mouth shut.

I grip the strap across my chest. Aether-twisted. Like the creatures we faced in the dungeon—things that should not have existed, warped into horrors by stone and spell. If dozens of those are coming... my throat goes dry.

The Guildmaster raises a hand and the murmurs die. "This city will not fall while we breathe. The Guild will lead its defense."

He gestures to the maps behind him, assistants flipping them upright so the whole hall can see. Charcoal streets and walls marked with sigils, little wooden flags stuck in neat lines.

"We divide our strength here," he points with a gloved hand, stabbing at the map. "The north wall is our priority. Scouts say the horde is approaching from the forest road. Every copper and bronze squad will reinforce the barricades. Archers and spellcasters to the rooftops. Gold and silver will hold the gates. The cathedral has agreed to shelter the people. Anyone not carrying a blade will be inside its walls."

The word cathedral makes my jaw tighten. I glance sideways and catch Tarn's expression harden like cooling steel. He doesn't speak, but I can read the line of his mouth well enough: he doesn't trust them to keep anyone safe.

"Supplies are already being moved," the Guildmaster goes on. "Barricades reinforced, traps laid at the outer roads. This city will not be taken by beasts."

Eliza leans slightly toward me, voice low but steady. "They're organized. More than they want to admit."

I nod faintly. If the Guild is dragging even fresh coppers into this, it means they expect a wall of teeth.

The Guildmaster plants both hands on the table. "This is not a choice. This is survival. Every blade, every spell, every shield. Do your duty and we will endure."

A silence follows, heavy and suffocating. Then boots begin to shift. Swords rasp from scabbards. A bronze-ranked captain slaps his men on the shoulders, muttering orders. The great hall transforms, in the space of heartbeats, into a hive of motion.

I catch Vaelen's grin—quick, almost reckless—as he adjusts his gauntlet. "Nothing like a bit of morning doom to get the blood moving."

"You're impossible," I mutter.

"Confident," he corrects, Arcblade sparking faintly as if answering to his mood. "That's different."

Eliza's eyes flick toward the cathedral's spire through the narrow window slits. Her expression is unreadable, but her grip on her satchel strap is tight.

Tarn doesn't move right away. He stands with his arms folded, gaze fixed on the maps, as if memorizing every street, every marker. When his eyes finally cut to me, they're steady, anchored. "Stay close when they assign posts," he says simply.

My heart lurches once, traitorous, but I nod.

Around us, adventurers flood into motion. Some rush to the walls. Others grab supplies from the assistants at the crate—bolts, rope, spikes. A runner shouts orders at a cluster of bronzes, her voice cracking as she pushes them toward the courtyard. The building hums with urgency.

And under it all, in the hollow of my chest, a thought gnaws: they're preparing, yes. But the last time I saw an Aether-twisted creature, it had taken everything we had to bring it down.

What happens when hundreds come at once?

The Guildmaster's gaze sweeps the hall one more time, sharp as a drawn blade. His voice cuts through the din of preparations.

"One more thing."

The noise dims, boots stilling, armor falling quiet. Even the Gold-ranks glance his way with something like caution.

He scans the crowd, but when his eyes land on Tarn—and by extension, on me, Vaelen, and Eliza—they don't move on.

"You four. Step forward."

My stomach knots. Dozens of eyes track us as Tarn pushes through the press without hesitation. Vaelen follows with a faint grin, Eliza with her calm focus. I have to force my feet to move, because suddenly the weight of every stare feels like it could pin me to the wall.

"You've fought them before," the Guildmaster says, no room for question in the words. "In the dungeon."

The silence that follows is thick. Adventurers shift, whisper. I feel the burn of their attention. Most of them have never seen an Aether-twisted up close. They've heard rumors, sure, but standing here, they're realizing some of those stories came from us.

"Yes," Tarn says simply.

The Guildmaster's jaw works once, like he doesn't enjoy giving ground to anyone. "Then you know what we face better than the rest of us. Which means I'm not chaining you to a wall or a gate. You'll move where you're needed most. Reinforce the weak points, plug the gaps, cut down anything that breaks through." His gaze sharpens. "You will be the city's edge."

The words land heavier than a hammer. A mobile squad. No fallback point. No fixed orders. Go where it's worst, and keep it from collapsing.

For a heartbeat, the hall is quiet, then the murmurs return, sharper this time. I catch the flicker of fear, envy, even relief in other adventurers' eyes. They're glad it isn't them.

"Do you understand?" the Guildmaster asks.

Tarn dips his head. "We do."

That's it. No protest, no hesitation. Just calm acceptance. And suddenly every eye on us feels sharper, measuring, wondering why Tarn sounds so certain.

The Guildmaster turns back to the room at large. "You all know your orders. Move."

The hall erupts. Boots thunder. Voices snap orders. The crowd becomes a living current, rushing for exits, for supplies, for the walls.

I draw a breath I didn't realize I'd been holding. Vaelen nudges me with his elbow, grin in place like he thrives on this kind of pressure. "Mobile defenders. Not bad, eh?"

"Depends what we're defending against," I mutter.

Eliza adjusts her glasses, eyes distant. "It's smart. They don't know how these things fight. We do."

Her words land like a stone in my chest. She's right. We've bled for that knowledge, and now the Guild wants to spend it like coin.

Tarn doesn't linger. He gestures for us to move, and we fall in behind him as the Guildhall empties into the square. The air outside is colder, harsher, as if the city itself knows what's coming.

The rest of the day blurs into work. Barricades rise across streets. Carts are overturned, nailed into place. Smiths hammer spikes into beams. The smell of pitch thickens the air as barrels are rolled toward the walls.

We're everywhere—hauling timber, checking lines, running messages. Vaelen takes to shouting orders when green recruits freeze, his voice carrying like he's done it all his life. Eliza lends hands to the healers, chalking sigils that will flare when pressed. Tarn moves like he was born for this—steady, tireless, his presence alone enough to calm the rookies around him.

I climb rooftops, test lines, plant blades where shadows will be when night falls. Every time someone stumbles or hesitates, Tarn sends me or Vaelen to stiffen them up. Mobile already, even before the first horn sounds.

By the time the sun sinks, the city looks different. Streets are narrowed into choke points. Wooden spikes bristle from alleys. Lanterns are posted high, their glass hooded for when night comes. The cathedral bells toll, summoning the last civilians inside. Each peal reverberates in my ribs.

And then—just as the final rim of sun kisses the horizon—shouts rise from the northern wall.

I scramble up onto a rooftop with Tarn, Vaelen, and Eliza close behind. We're not the only ones; archers and lookouts line the parapets, eyes straining toward the forest road.

I see them first.

Dark shapes on the treeline. Too many to count. They move wrong—joints bending where they shouldn't, bodies too broad or too thin, silhouettes twitching and lurching in rhythms no living thing should have. The distance makes them hazy, but I don't need details. I recognize the wrongness. The same I saw in the dungeon.

The crowd of adventurers hushes, the quiet creeping out across the wall. Someone whispers a prayer. Someone else curses.

My throat tightens, and my hand finds the amulet at my chest. The stone is warm now. Not humming—yet—but aware. Watching.

The horde steps clear of the trees.

Dozens. Scores. Maybe more. A sea of twisted bodies, their movement a grotesque reflection of an army's march.

Beside me, Tarn's voice is steady, unflinching. "It begins."

Chapter 22

ASH AND THUNDER

Cass

T he first horn hadn't even faded when the horde struck.

From the rooftops, the city looked like it was bracing against a storm – and then the storm arrived, made of claws and teeth and limbs that bent wrong. They surged out of the treeline in a tide of black and grey, their bodies stitched with glowing fissures of violet Aether, pulsing like wounds that never closed.

The first of them hit the barricades with the sound of a mountain falling. Wooden spikes shattered. Iron braces screamed and snapped. The line buckled before anyone even had a chance to shout.

"Hold the wall!" the Guildmaster's voice boomed from somewhere near the gate, but even he sounded small against the roar of the horde.

I was already moving. Shadows curled at my heels as I leapt from a rooftop, landing behind the front rank where copper and bronze adventurers tried—and failed—to hold their ground. One of the things had shoved its way over the barricade, a wolf-shaped body stretched too tall, its ribcage cracked open and glowing like a furnace.

I lunged in, chains flashing into existence at a flick of my wrist. Umbral Chains shot forward, spectral links wrapping around the creature's leg mid-stride. It bellowed, more like a furnace venting steam than any sound an animal should make. I yanked hard, the chains tightening, dragging it to the ground.

"Now!" I shouted, and three bronze-ranked fighters piled on with spears. The creature thrashed, snapping one of the men in half with a swipe of its claws even as Tarn barreled in from the flank. His hammer crushed the beast's skull into the cobblestones, violet light spraying like fireflies as it died.

For half a heartbeat, the wall held.

Then the next wave slammed into us.

They climbed each other, bodies folding unnaturally, bones cracking and reshaping as they pulled themselves up and over. A half-dozen spilled onto the rooftops ahead of me, bounding across tiles like grotesque hounds. Archers loosed arrows that sank into twisted hides but didn't slow them.

"Cass!" Vaelen's voice cut sharp through the chaos. Lightning crackled as his Arcblade cleaved one beast in two, the air stinking of ozone and burning flesh. "Left flank!"

I Shadow Stepped without thinking. One moment I was at the barricade, the next I slipped through Tarn's shadow, reappearing behind the rooftop pack. My daggers tore through tendon and throat before they knew I was there.

Another beast spun toward me, jaws unhinging wider than its skull should allow. I stepped again—once, twice, three times in rapid succession—until I was behind it, driving a blade up under its ribs. The familiar rush hit me... but the drain didn't. My breath wasn't ragged, my limbs weren't lead.

I froze.

That should've been it. Three uses. Spent. But the shadows still curled around me, alive and ready.

The Mirror Stalker. I'd absorbed it. Its gift hadn't just added to me—it had erased the limit.

I could step again. And again. And again.

I didn't have time to dwell. Another monster was already lunging, and I vanished into shadow before it landed.

The rooftop collapsed under the weight of bodies, dragging three adventurers down with it. Their screams cut short as claws ripped them apart.

Eliza shifted mid-leap, fur rippling across her form as she hit the cobblestones as a bear. Her claws gouged deep, tearing one of the twisted creatures off a fallen fighter. Her roar rattled windows, but the beast still clung, raking its talons until Tarn waded in and pulped its spine with his hammer.

Everywhere, the wall was failing. Copper ranks died in clusters, Bronze squads scattered. Golds and Silvers fought like legends, each kill an epic, but even they were being dragged down by sheer numbers. The air was a storm of ash, blood, and the crack of breaking stone.

I blinked across the field again and again, cutting chains through the horde, tripping them, dragging them back from comrades who would've been gutted otherwise. My daggers found throats, my chains bound limbs, and the shadows never faltered. It should have terrified me. Instead, a grim exhilaration burned under my skin.

But no matter how many we cut down, more came. The street was drowning in them. The north wall was a graveyard waiting to happen.

And this was only the first clash.

The north wall was breaking.

You could hear it in the rhythm of the fight—the way barricades groaned, the way squads came back thinner each time. The cobblestones ran slick, and still the horde pressed in.

A Gold-rank swordswoman was dragged screaming from the barricade, her blade flashing until the mass of claws buried her from sight. Another squad folded in the side street as a hulking shape tore through them. The line was splintering everywhere at once.

"Back to the line!" Tarn's voice cut through the chaos. His hammer struck down, the blow cracking into the cobblestones with a burst of radiant force that threw creatures back. His shield flared, symbols searing across its surface before dimming again.

My chest tightened. Tarn never used his magic unless there was no other choice. Every spark of it was precious, rationed like water. But now, with the defense buckling, he wielded it without hesitation. Holy fire trailed from his hammer, each impact carrying the weight of something more than steel.

"Hold here!" he barked, voice steady even as the street shook.

I cut down a lunging beast, shadows carrying me behind its neck before its jaws could snap shut. My daggers slid deep, and before its body even hit the ground, I was gone again, slipping from shadow to shadow, striking wherever the line faltered. The movements came as easily as breathing, the rush unbroken.

A roar split the air, not from the horde—but from Vaelen.

He planted his Arcblade into the cobblestones with both hands. Lightning raced across the ground, jagged veins of light splitting stone. His eyes burned like stormfire as he whispered a word I didn't know.

"Skybreaker"

The world split.

A column of lightning tore upward, wider than a city street, blasting into the sky with a thunderclap that rattled my bones. The creatures caught in it didn't fall—they disintegrated, their bodies ripped apart in flashes of white-blue light. The shockwave knocked adventurers off their feet, cracked walls, and turned the nearest stones molten.

For a heartbeat, the street was silent. The horde closest to us was gone, reduced to ash.

Vaelen staggered, gripping his sword with white knuckles. Blood streamed from his nose and ears, his arm scorched and trembling. Still, he managed a crooked grin.

"That'll... hold 'em," he rasped, before dropping to one knee.

Eliza was at his side instantly, pressing her glowing hand to his shoulder. "Idiot. You could've killed yourself."

"Better me than all of us," he said, his voice thin but steady.

The reprieve was already ending. The roar of the horde surged back as fresh ranks poured into the breach.

Tarn's shield flared again, runes blazing as he raised it high. A wave of force rippled outward, searing into the front line. His shoulders sagged from the effort, sweat running beneath his helm, but he didn't yield.

"Cass," he called, never looking away. "Chains. Funnel them."

I snapped my wrist, and Umbral Chains shot across the street, anchoring to broken beams and stone. Shadows coiled into barriers, forcing the creatures into a narrow choke point. Tarn and

Eliza slammed into the gap, Vaelen dragging himself upright beside them despite the tremor in his arm.

We held, the four of us, while the rest of the wall collapsed around us.

But even as I fought, stepping through shadow after shadow, I could see it. Tarn saw it too—the same grim truth written in his eyes. The defense was unraveling. The Guild was losing.

And the city was about to fall.

The signal came as a single, piercing hornblast from the Guildmaster. Not the call to hold. Not the call to push. The one every adventurer knew meant only one thing.

Retreat.

The north wall gave way in the same breath. Barricades splintered, stone cracked, and the gate itself buckled under the weight of the horde. Adventurers who had stood shoulder to shoulder that morning were trampled into red ruin as the monsters poured through.

"Fall back!" Tarn roared, swinging his hammer in wide arcs to cover the bronzes scattering down the street. He stood in the breach as long as he could, shield braced, hammer blazing with one last flare of divine fire that split a charging beast's skull. Then even he was forced to give ground, his boots dragging furrows in the blood-slick street as I darted to his side.

"Cass!" His voice snapped me sharp. "Rear guard. We hold them long enough for the others to reach the cathedral."

I nodded once, the weight of it cold in my chest.

The streets turned to chaos. Civilians screamed as they spilled from doorways and cellars, clutching children and bundles, herded by adventurers into a panicked tide toward the cathedral square.

The cathedral's bells clanged, harsh and urgent, their echoes almost drowned by the howling behind us.

"Move them!" Vaelen bellowed at a cluster of bronzes frozen in place. His Arcblade carved a path clear with a burst of lightning, the air filling with the stink of burnt flesh. His arm shook from the effort, but he didn't stop, forcing the younger adventurers into motion.

Eliza shifted from bear to badger in a flash, darting under carts and knocking them into the street to block side alleys. Her chants twisted the air, roots bursting from cracks in the cobblestones to trip anything that came too close.

And me—I became a shadow.

I blinked across rooftops, down alleys, into gaps where civilians stumbled. My daggers tore, my chains dragged creatures off their feet, giving the weakest a chance to run. The shadows never slowed me. Never stopped answering. For every monster I cut down, two more poured over the walls, but I wasn't keeping score anymore. I was buying seconds, heartbeats, lives.

The horde pressed closer, their shrieks echoing off stone. I Shadow Stepped to a rooftop just in time to see one of the silvers dragged down in the square below, her screams cut off in a blossom of violet light. My stomach lurched, but I forced myself onward.

"Cass!" Tarn's voice again, closer this time. He and Vaelen were holding the mouth of the street leading to the square, bodies piled around them in grotesque heaps. Tarn's shield was cracked, glowing with fading light, and Vaelen's arm trembled as his Arcblade spat weak sparks.

"Go!" Tarn shouted at me. "Get them moving!"

I snapped my chains into a barricade of shadow across the street, buying them a moment, and then I was in the crowd, shoving terrified faces toward the cathedral steps. Priests pulled them inside with pale hands, doors slamming shut behind every group.

The tide of refugees slowed, but the monsters didn't.

A bellow split the night as something massive shouldered through the breach—a monstrosity taller than the walls themselves, its body hunched and split with glowing seams, each step shaking the ground. The sight of it broke what little order remained. People screamed, bolting in every direction.

"Fall back!" Tarn roared again, hammer blazing as he slammed it into the ground. Radiant fire flared, buying us one last instant of cover. His eyes met mine, hard and steady. "Cass. Now."

I grabbed Eliza's arm as she shifted back, dragging her toward the square. Vaelen stumbled beside us, his grin gone, his face bloodied and pale but his blade still clenched in white knuckles. Tarn followed last, his shield raised to cover our retreat.

We crossed into the cathedral square just as the bells tolled again. The priests were chanting, their voices rising in desperate waves as they pulled civilians through the doors. Adventurers formed a ragged line before the steps, weapons shaking in their hands, too few of them left standing.

I turned with the others, daggers slick in my grip, shadows already curling at my feet.

The horde was coming. The walls were gone. The city was burning.

And now, all that stood between the people and the abyss was us.

Chapter 23

THE DOOR IN THE RUINS

Cass

T he Ash Sentinels arrived like a verdict.

Grey cloaks and steel helms, they moved in perfect rhythm, shields locking into a ring around the cathedral square. Pikes angled outward, crossbows cocked in silent readiness. They didn't shout or posture; they simply *were*, and the chaos bent around them. Adventurers too shaken to breathe straightened at their presence. Civilians huddled tighter, eyes following the faceless helms as if salvation had just walked in.

Across the square, the priests of the First Flame set their circle. Braziers flared, smoke curling into the air as chalk glyphs brightened beneath the firelight. Heat rippled, the ground shivering as the runes linked. Then the barrier rose—a dome of translucent light arcing over the cathedral steps, script sliding across its curve until it locked with a hum that thrummed in my teeth.

Outside the dome, the city screamed and burned. Inside, the sounds dulled to a muffled rumble. For the first time all night, people stopped running. Some collapsed. Some prayed. Some only stared at the glowing shell, as if afraid to believe it would hold.

A priestess knelt by Vaelen, who had finally sunk onto the steps. His skin was bloodied and scorched raw where the lightning had ripped through him. He tried to grin, but it looked more like a grimace.

"Hold still," she said, setting two fingers to his throat. A soft glow pooled beneath her palm, sinking into him in steady waves. Not Tarn's clean golden fire—this ran hotter, richer, almost too much. Color bled back into his face with unnatural speed.

"Feels like being plugged into the storm again," Vaelen muttered, voice shaky. His pupils were blown wide.

"You nearly killed yourself," she answered flatly. "Next time, you will."

But when she pulled her hand away, his arm steadied. He flexed his fingers on the hilt of his Arcblade, and the tremor was gone.

Eliza watched with folded arms, lips pressed thin. Tarn stood nearby, silent, but the weight in his eyes said enough: he didn't trust the way the priestess's magic left Vaelen *better* than before.

A smith shouldered his way through with a travel anvil and tools clattering at his belt. He pointed at Tarn's shield. "Up."

Tarn laid it across the iron face. Up close, the damage was worse: a crack splitting the boss, the rim warped, the leather straps shredded. The smith stripped away what he couldn't save and hammered new bands across the break, each strike throwing sparks into the night. "Won't be pretty," he said over the ringing blows. "But it'll hold."

"It only needs to," Tarn answered.

When the last rivet cooled, Tarn slid his arm through the grips and tested the balance. It sat differently now—heavier, imperfect. His mouth tightened, but he gave the smith a curt nod.

The Sentinels continued their patrol, checking the barrier where it pressed into stone. A few adventurers sat slumped near the fountain, hollow-eyed, whispering to each other as if sound alone could anchor them.

I let myself breathe, but quiet only gave me room to think. Too many faces from the wall flashed behind my eyes. Too many weren't coming back.

"Laina..." Tarn's voice a whisper, barely audible. He wasn't looking at me. His eyes were fixed on the far side of the square, where the barrier curved over a collapsed section of the cathedral's undercroft. Fallen stone and shattered beams formed a mound of rubble against the glow. For a heartbeat, I swore his face changed—stiffened, as if he'd seen something more than wreckage.

He stepped down from the cathedral steps without a word. I fell in beside him automatically, Eliza close behind, Vaelen trailing with a tired but wary look.

"Talk to me," I said low.

"Nothing," Tarn replied. Too quickly.

We followed the dome's edge to the ruined undercroft. The barrier was stretched thin here, its hum louder, the glow warped over the broken ground. Tarn crouched, one hand braced on the stone, staring through the shimmer. His jaw tightened.

"What is it?" I asked.

He shook his head once, eyes still locked forward. "I thought I saw—" He stopped himself, lips pressing flat. "Just a shadow."

He doesn't see shadows that aren't there. Not Tarn.

I ducked beside him. The rubble sloped downward, ash drifted into the cracks. Beneath the collapse, partly hidden, I caught the sharp edge of a stair, worn but deliberate, leading down. My stomach turned cold.

"Looks like more than shadows," I murmured.

Tarn didn't answer. His hand lingered against the stone as if it might give him back what he thought he'd seen.

The rubble shifted underfoot as we worked our way down. Dust spilled in curtains, ash clung to sweat and blood, turning everything grey. Eliza crouched near the broken stone, fingertips brushing along the edges of a fractured block.

"This isn't fresh," she murmured. "The ground gave way because something beneath it was already hollow." Her eyes tracked the break like she was mapping it in her head.

She was right. The ruin had cracked open like a wound, exposing a narrow stair twisting down into dark, half-swallowed by debris.

Vaelen gave a low whistle. "Perfect place for nightmares. Naturally we're going first."

"Quiet," Tarn said. He moved ahead, shield raised, testing each step before putting weight down.

The air cooled as we descended. The roar of the city dulled behind us until only the hum of the priests' barrier bled faintly through the stone. Shadows pressed closer, curling thick against the walls. I let them—no need to resent what already belonged to me.

At the bottom, the stair ended in a short passage, half-collapsed. Stone fractured in long, jagged lines, rubble piled high to either side. And there, set into the wall, stood a door.

It wasn't wood or iron but solid stone fitted into stone, seamless, as though it had always been part of the wall. Dust lay thick across its face, but as Tarn brushed his gauntlet over it, faint carving revealed itself.

A star. Eight points crossing at the center. The Hollow Star.

My throat tightened. "That's—"

"I know," Tarn said, voice flat, though the weight in his eyes betrayed him.

Eliza leaned closer, glasses catching the faint gleam of my pendant as she peered at the lines. "Not recent. The carving's old. Worn." She glanced at Tarn. "But it was meant to last."

Tarn didn't answer. His hand went to the pouch at his belt, drawing out the key we'd carried since the basilisk hunt—the one stamped with the same star. Its surface caught the dim light, a perfect match to the sigil carved in the stone.

The wall shivered faintly, dust drifting as though the carving itself had stirred.

"Of course," Vaelen muttered, forcing a grin. "Of course the creepy buried door takes the creepy star key."

I tightened my grip on my daggers. "We don't have to open it. Not with everything else going on out there."

Tarn's eyes never left the carving. "We don't get to choose when it's already waiting."

He stepped forward, the key in his hand. The sigil seemed to pull toward it, faint ripples spreading across the stone. Tarn slid the key into the central groove. It fit perfectly, locking into place with a sound closer to a heartbeat than a click.

Light bled out along the Hollow Star's lines, crawling into the cracks until the whole pattern glowed with a sickly violet fire. The floor thrummed beneath our boots. The barrier's hum above faltered, as if two magics recognized each other across stone.

The door groaned, lines widening, dust raining down as a seam split open. Cold air exhaled from the gap, sharp with earth and metal.

Tarn lifted his shield, hammer steady. "Stay close."

Eliza's hand hovered over the fur pouch at her belt, ready to shift in a breath. Vaelen rolled his shoulders, Arcblade spitting faint sparks, his grin thinner now.

And me—my pendant pulsed once, a single throb against my skin. Listening. Waiting.

The stone parted wider, opening into a mouth of shadows.

I looked back one last time—the barrier glowing faint over the cathedral square, priests chanting, Sentinels unmoving, survivors huddled like lost sheep.

Then Tarn stepped through, and we followed him into the dark.

The door split wider, shadows spilling out like a tide. We crossed the threshold knowing only this: there would be no turning back.

Chapter 24

INTO THE DARK

Cass

The door yawned open, stone grinding against stone, and shadows poured through the widening seam. No torchlight reached beyond. No sound. Just a silence so deep it pressed at my ears, like the hush before a scream.

I hesitated at the threshold, daggers tight in my grip. The others waited too—Eliza stiff beside me, Vaelen with his Arcblade resting against his shoulder, Tarn at the front with shield raised.

But he didn't step forward right away. Instead, he turned, the glow of the barrier behind us reflecting faintly in his eyes. His gauntleted hand went to his belt, and when he withdrew it, something silver glinted between his fingers.

A bracelet.

He held it out to me. "Here. Wear this."

I frowned, caught off guard. "That old thing? Thought you said it was just some scrap from the dungeon."

Tarn's mouth twitched like he almost smiled, but didn't. "Maybe. Maybe not. Call it a charm. I'd feel better if you had it on."

I opened my mouth to argue, but his expression left no room for it. He wasn't joking. For a man who treated superstition like a stain on armor, Tarn looked damn serious.

"Fine," I muttered, sliding one dagger back into its sheath so I could take it. The metal was cool against my palm, tarnished in places, simple in design—but there was a weight to it that made me uneasy.

Tarn didn't let me fumble with it. He took it back, fastened it around my wrist himself. His fingers brushed the inside of my arm, callused and careful. The clasp clicked, snug.

"There," he said softly. "Now we're ready."

I looked away before he could see how my face heated. It was ridiculous. We were about to walk into whatever hell waited beyond that door, and my heart was tripping because Tarn had fastened a trinket on me.

Vaelen gave a low whistle. "Sweet. If we all die in here, at least you two had a moment."

"Shut it," I snapped, but my voice didn't carry much bite. Eliza smothered a laugh.

Tarn ignored them both, already stepping into the dark.

The shadows swallowed him whole, the glow of the barrier snuffing out the moment he crossed the threshold. He didn't vanish completely—I could still see the gleam of his armor—but the black pressed close, resentful of the intrusion.

I followed, one hand brushing the new weight on my wrist, the other on my dagger. The air inside was colder than it should have been. Heavier.

The moment my boots touched the stone floor, I felt it: a faint vibration beneath, steady, like the beat of a buried heart.

"Eliza?" I asked, though I wasn't sure what I expected her to say.

She shook her head, eyes narrowed. "The stone's wrong. It feels like it wants to move under us."

Vaelen clicked his tongue. "Lovely. A giant tomb that doesn't want us in it."

Tarn only lifted his shield higher. "Stay close."

We moved forward, and the darkness sealed behind us. The door that had opened so heavy and loud was now silent, and when I risked a glance over my shoulder, the seam was gone. Just unbroken stone.

A cold prickle slid down my spine.

I shifted, letting shadows coil at my heels, ready to carry me if I needed to slip. They came easily—too easily. The place's darkness was thicker, richer, as though it welcomed me. It clung to my skin, whispered against my ears.

The silver bracelet at my wrist hummed faintly. Just for a heartbeat. Then still.

I swallowed hard and didn't mention it.

We pressed deeper, the silence absolute except for our steps. The corridor bent, bent again, then returned us to the same cracked pillar we'd passed minutes ago.

"A loop," Eliza murmured.

Vaelen tapped the stone with his Arcblade, sparks spitting. "Not possible. We didn't double back."

"We did," Tarn said grimly. "The path moved around us."

The words sat in my chest like lead. This wasn't just a ruin. It was something alive.

The corridor bent a third time before spilling into a chamber. The air was colder here, metallic on the tongue, the shadows pressed even closer than before.

Something moved.

At first it looked like stone breaking loose from the wall—cracks splintering outward, dust sifting down. Then it peeled itself away entirely. A figure, human-shaped but stretched too long in the limbs, its skin marbled with veins of dull violet. Its face had no features except a hollow slit where a mouth should be.

Eliza's hand twitched toward her pouch. Vaelen swore under his breath.

"It was waiting," Tarn said quietly, his hammer already raised.

The thing tilted its head at us, its limbs swaying like it dangled on strings. One step stretched too far, the next too short, movements out of rhythm with the world around it.

Then it lunged.

I vanished into shadow before it struck, the air shivering as I stepped past its charge. Its clawed hand carved sparks into the stone where I'd been. Tarn met its second swipe with his shield, the impact ringing down the corridor like a bell.

The sound rattled my teeth.

Vaelen swung his Arcblade in a wide arc, lightning biting down into the creature's side. The jolt staggered it but didn't slow it enough. Eliza shifted, her body blurring into the stocky frame of a badger, and slammed into its legs, knocking it half-off balance.

I reappeared behind it, my daggers flashing. One strike to the back of the knee, another to its side. The flesh tore but no blood spilled—only a hiss of steam that burned my nose.

The thing shrieked without a mouth. A sound scraped raw from stone itself.

We pressed it hard, cornering it against the wall. Tarn's hammer struck down with brutal force, shattering its spine with a crunch. It writhed once, then collapsed in on itself, its body dissolving into smoke.

For a moment, the only sound was our breathing.

Then the silence returned. Heavy. Watching.

I realized my amulet was cool against my chest. Still. The blue stone lay quiet, no glow, no hum.

"That's different," I said.

Tarn glanced at me. His brow furrowed. "The Stalker... it reacted then, didn't it?"

"Yeah." I touched the pendant. "Nothing this time."

Vaelen gave a dry laugh. "So it's picky? Needs the right flavor of monster to chew on?"

Eliza shifted back to herself, brushing ash from her arms. Her glasses caught the dim light, sharp. "Or there are conditions we don't understand. This one wasn't... complete."

"Didn't feel complete," I muttered, remembering the way its limbs swung wrong, like someone else pulled the strings. "Like it was built broken."

Tarn nodded once, his jaw set. "Whatever the reason, it's better this way. We don't know what absorbing more of them would do to you."

I wanted to argue, but the weight of the bracelet on my wrist and the quiet amulet at my chest stopped me.

We didn't linger. None of us wanted to.

We pressed on, deeper into the shifting dark, the memory of the creature clinging like smoke to the backs of our throats.

And I couldn't shake the thought: if that was the flawed attempt... what would a perfected one look like?

We tried chalk first.

Vaelen marked the wall with a quick slash as we took the right-hand passage. It bit cleanly into the stone, a white scar cutting the grey. We counted steps—twenty-seven to the turn, forty to the next fork, back again to the mark that should've waited where we left it.

It wasn't there.

Instead, the chalk had slid two stones over and down, like the wall had shuffled its skin while we looked away.

"Funny," Vaelen said, but his grin didn't reach his eyes. He scored a second mark deeper, then dragged the point across the floor for a span of paces. We followed the line until it stuttered, wavered, and ended three feet up the opposite wall, as if the ground had tilted when none of us were watching.

Eliza touched her fingertips to the seam between blocks. "It's not only moving. It's choosing how."

"Choosing what?" I asked.

"Paths," she said. "Us."

Tarn glanced back at me, and I knew what he was measuring—my pace, my breathing, the little tells I hide when I don't want anyone to ask if I'm all right. I rolled a shoulder and looked ahead before he could speak.

We pressed on.

The corridor narrowed without warning, stone crowding into our shoulders; then an opening yawned, a chamber the size of a market square, empty as a snuffed stage. Columns rose in a spiral here, bone-pale and smooth, the spaces between them too even to be natural. When we got closer, the columns were not columns at all but ribs of some architectural animal, each band carved with the same neat script we'd seen on the cathedral barrier. Not jagged, not wild—orderly. Practiced. The runes were unlit, and that somehow made them worse.

We crossed beneath them like trespassers. My shadow tangled with the ribs' shadows and didn't untangle as quickly as it should have, as if the dark remembered me and was reluctant to let me go.

On the far side of the ribbed hall the floor turned to salt-slick stone, damp and faintly gleaming. Our footsteps made no sound. Every scuff died as soon as it happened, swallowed whole. My skin crawled. Sound should go somewhere. Here it fell flat and was gone.

"Every sound falls short," Eliza said quietly, almost to herself. "Like it's being taken."

"By what?" Vaelen asked.

She didn't answer.

We kept to the straightest line we could find and still hit a curve. The curve turned to a stair; the stair spiraled downward, then decided against it and flattened out into a corridor that had not been there a blink earlier. The air cooled again, the kind of cold that makes metal ring sharper and skin go numb.

"Left," Tarn said at the next fork.

We went left.

The corridor doubled back of its own accord, and we found a mark of chalk I hadn't seen Vaelen make: a small sunburst scraped low near the floor. The sight of it made my shoulders tense. Had the wall taken our mark and given it back in a different shape? Or had we done it and forgotten?

"Not funny anymore," Vaelen muttered.

The next section changed under our feet, tiles shifting in a way you didn't feel so much as notice—squares becoming diamonds becoming a pattern like overlapping scales. My boots gripped fine; someone else's didn't. We passed a scuffed skid where someone had gone down hard, smeared across three patterns of stone, but there were no bodies. No blood. Whatever had fallen here had been collected afterward.

We took a straight path and ended up standing where we'd started anyway. Tarn drew a simple map on a scrap; when we tried to use it, the lines made less sense than the corridors. He flipped the scrap over, folded it, unfolded it. The drawing had shifted with the fold.

"Not possible," Vaelen said.

"It doesn't care what we think is possible," Tarn answered.

I hated that he was right.

The next chamber was a garden of pillars, each carved with a vertical groove that caught the faintest light. When we walked between them, the grooves seemed to deepen, swallowing whatever brightness we carried and returning it thinner. Not enough to matter. Not enough to spend. The shadows along the floor crept forward like tidewater, slow and patient. None of us spoke until we were out of it.

"Maze," I said. Saying it didn't help, but it was better than pretending we'd wandered into anything honest. "It's a maze."

Tarn nodded once. "A deliberate one."

"Built to test or trap," Eliza said. Her eyes kept moving, measuring, as if she could listen with her skin to the stone's intentions. "Maybe both."

We tried thread next—Vaelen knotted a line to a broken bracket and let it spool behind us through a T-junction, a curve, a stair. When he turned to check it, the line had gone taut in the wrong direction, pulled through a crack in the wall we hadn't noticed. He tugged it once; it tugged back, gentle, like something on the other side was reminding us who held it.

He cut the thread cleanly. The line on the near side fell, limp as dead grass. The line beyond the crack reeled itself away, vanishing, as if the wall had eaten it.

I didn't say what we were all thinking. I didn't have to.

We kept moving.

The maze answered. Stone turned to iron lattice for a dozen paces, the bars etched with frost that didn't melt against warm skin. Then came a low tunnel of black brick that didn't reflect light at all, our lanterns dulling to a wounded glow. The brick gave way to a ramp with a shallow pitch; we climbed for longer than the ramp's height allowed and came out on a landing level with the corridor we'd left. I looked over the edge and saw nothing but dark. The ramp was gone behind us, replaced by a wall.

"Enough," Vaelen said, voice too bright. "If this thing shifts one more piece of floor under me, I'm—"

A whisper answered from nowhere. A whisper in his exact tone, repeating his last sentence with a sliver of delay. Then another, in mine, echoing something I'd said three turns ago. Not quite sound. More like memory thrown back at us out of order.

"Keep walking," Tarn said, quiet and even. He didn't speed up, didn't slow. We matched him.

By the time the iron smell returned, the maze had worn us down without taking a single drop of blood. That felt like the point.

"Do you feel it?" Eliza asked. "The pull? Not toward the surface. Not toward safety. Toward the center."

I felt it. I hated it. "Yes."

Tarn's hand brushed the edge of his shield. "Then we go where it wants us to go. And we make that our advantage."

"How?" Vaelen asked.

"We plan for a meeting," Tarn said.

"With who?" I asked, though I already knew.

He didn't answer.

We took the next opening.

The corridors stopped pretending to be corridors and became a procession. The walls widened into arches, the arches into halls, the halls into something like a nave—vaulted ceiling, ribs rising into darkness, a floor laid in long panels that sucked up the sound of our boots. Ahead, a slit of brighter dark—no light, but a difference in quality, like a room that remembered fire.

We stepped through and the maze opened into a vast chamber.

It was not a sanctum. It wanted to look like one—symmetry, raised platforms, a dais—but everything holy had been stripped and replaced with function. Tables stood in orderly rows, iron-framed and bolted, their surfaces a chaos of lenses, glass tubes, and instruments that throbbed faintly where Aether pulsed through capillaries of crystal. Racks along the walls held canisters with things suspended in them that might once have been animals. Or people. The liquid glowed a tired violet, the same tired violet we'd seen in the streets—flawed, hungry, wrong.

The smell hit second: oil and old fire, metal and a sweetness at the back of the tongue that meant decay had been convinced to wait its turn.

"Laboratory," Eliza said softly. No judgment in the word. Only recognition.

We moved along the balcony that ringed the chamber's upper third, keeping to the shadow of the balustrade. Tarn raised two fingers: slow. Quiet.

246

Below, at the heart of the room, a circle had been carved into the stone—clean lines, precise. It matched the runes we'd followed through holy places and hated ones. The circle was a wound that had learned to hold shape.

A man stood at its edge.

His robes fell like water, undisturbed by the drafts that wandered the room. He held his hands behind his back as if he were admiring a sculpture, not a device for ruining lives. His hair was iron-grey; his posture had the unbent certainty of a man who'd never been told no and believed it meant he was right. He did not look up to find us. He did not have to. This was his room, and in his room, things came to him.

"Vale," Tarn said under his breath. It wasn't a curse. It was a naming.

Two figures flanked the Archflame a pace behind.

The first wore a hood so deep it made a habit of the face beneath it, a shadow that swallowed expression. The figure stood too still to be a guard and too close to be a stranger.

Then the iron collar at her throat pulsed with violet light. Just for a moment. Enough to peel back the hood's shadow and show her face.

Tarn stiffened. His breath caught sharp, like the air had betrayed him. "Laina."

The name struck harder than any weapon.

Her face was the same, though paler now, her eyes dim under the collar's glow. The iron band crawled with living veins of violet that seemed to choke the warmth from her expression.

Laina.

Alive.

The second figure stood to Vale's right. Taller than I remembered a person being. Too narrow through the torso, as if ribs had been cinched to fit a pattern drawn by someone who'd never seen a chest. Wings gathered tight along the back, not feathers but panes of something like glass and fire, edges serrated, light trapped inside like a storm in a lantern. The head was turned away, profile thin and beautiful as a statue until the light found it and showed the seams.

Recognition hit me sharp and cold. I'd seen that face before—smiling, whole—in the photo I'd found tucked in Tarn's armor. The priestess standing proud beside him, young and alive, before everything went wrong.

Selara.

Now she was stretched thin over something else entirely, a body warped into the idea of an angel and corrupted in the making.

My stomach knotted. "That's her," I whispered. "The priestess. Selara."

Eliza's hand found the rail. Vaelen's jaw set.

Vale spoke to neither of them. He addressed the circle instead, murmuring something that woke the runes and sent a filament of violet light skimming from one mark to the next. The whole chamber answered with a subtle shift, like a held note changing pitch. The figure with the hood did not turn. The winged thing did, a fraction, enough for me to see a mouth that remembered how to smile and had forgotten why.

Tarn's knuckles whitened on his shield strap. One step forward and the balcony would announce us with a groan. One more and we'd be in it, early, no plan, no advantage.

He didn't move.

"Plan for a meeting," he'd said. He was keeping his own counsel from himself now, holding still by will alone.

"What's the call?" Vaelen breathed.

Tarn's answer was a single word, shaped without sound. Wait.

Below, the Archflame finished his circle and let the light settle. He didn't turn. He didn't need to. He knew we would have to come to him, through whatever the maze chose to be next, through whatever he chose to leave between us and the hooded figure at his side.

The winged woman lifted her head, angling it toward the high dark where we hid. Not seeing us. Sensing. The panes along her wings brightened a shade, like coals caught by a draft.

"We have to move," Eliza whispered.

"Not yet," Tarn said, so quiet it was almost a thought. His gaze fixed on the collar at the hooded throat, the faint vein of violet crawling through iron. He didn't look away.

My hand went to the silver band at my wrist—not because it was familiar, but because he'd put it there. It lay cool against my skin, a reminder of his steadiness even now. What he'd called a charm. I didn't know why that hurt.

Vale lifted his chin a fraction and smiled at nothing. Or at the room itself. Or at the certainty that his maze would bring us to his feet on his terms.

The laboratory hummed. The runes around the circle exhaled their tired light. Somewhere a chain tapped against a glass wall, a patient sound. The maze had led us, as designed, to its center.

"Ready?" Tarn asked, the single word an iron bar across the space between fear and action.

I nodded once. Vaelen rolled his shoulder. Eliza set her stance, eyes on the far stairs that would take us down.

We moved, low and quiet, along the balcony toward the steps, the three of us in Tarn's shadow. And below, the Archflame waited with two figures: Laina—alive—and the priestess I'd only known from a photo, now unrecognizable, broken into wings and seams.

I couldn't tear my eyes away from her face. The seams, the glasslike wings, the thing she had become—and yet I saw her smile in that faded picture, standing at Tarn's side, whole and alive.

I tried to imagine the woman she had been.

And for a moment, the memory wasn't mine at all.

Chapter 25

THE SERAPHIM'S PROMISE

Selara

T he stew was burning again.

Brannick hunched over the pot, trying to stir it into something edible, though the smell made my stomach twist. He was laughing, the kind of easy, booming laugh that made you want to believe everything was fine. He always did that—covered the edges of danger with noise. Tarn grunted something in response, too soft for me to catch, but Brannick roared like it had been a clever joke.

Laina laughed too. Of course she did. She was always quick to match his levity, her bow lying discarded at her side as though she had never needed it. She leaned against Tarn, shoulder pressing his like they had been made to fit together. Tarn didn't move away. Didn't stiffen. He just let her linger there, his eyes on the flames, mouth drawn in that unreadable line that gave away nothing but didn't forbid her either.

It made my jaw ache. Not from jealousy. I told myself that again and again. It was not jealousy. It was the wrongness of it.

A paladin and an archer, tangled like common lovers. It went against everything we had been taught. Our vows were not suggestions—they were commandments. The Flame was meant to burn away distractions, to strip us down to obedience, service, and purity. And yet here they were, bold in their defiance, their closeness dressed up as comfort.

I turned my eyes away before the heat in my chest betrayed me.

"Selara," Brannick called, spoon dripping blackened broth, "your turn to taste test. Fair warning, might be the best thing you ever put in your holy mouth."

Laina giggled, smothering it behind her hand. Tarn's lips twitched.

"I'll pass," I said flatly.

Brannick shrugged and slurped noisily from the spoon. He winced and then forced another grin. "See? Perfect. Needs just a little more salt."

He tossed a handful in, unmeasured, reckless as always.

I folded my hands in my lap, letting the warmth of the fire wash over me. Their laughter blurred into the background, a rhythm I had learned to endure. They didn't notice I wasn't smiling. They never did.

It should have been enough to serve with them. Tarn with his shield and hammer, Brannick's sword like an extension of his arm, Laina's arrows always finding their mark. And me, whispering prayers, binding wounds, holding them together. That was what the Flame demanded of me. To serve. To guide. To keep them true.

But I could feel it slipping. Tarn's faith dimming, his smiles reserved for her. Laina drawing him farther and farther from the path. Even Brannick—always reckless, always indulgent—seemed to be drawn in by her warmth.

And I? I was a shadow at the edge of their light. Necessary but unseen. Faithful but forgotten.

That was when I rose. None of them noticed. Tarn's gaze was on the fire. Brannick was still trying to make Laina laugh. And Laina—her head rested against Tarn's shoulder, content as though she had never sworn to anything greater than herself.

The disgust tightened in my chest until I couldn't bear to sit with them. I walked away. No one asked where I was going.

The forest was alive with sound. Crickets, owls, the low sigh of wind through branches. I followed the path until their laughter was swallowed whole by the dark. Until I was alone with the night.

A part of me longed to stop there, to fall to my knees and pray until the doubt burned out of me. But the Flame had been silent too long. My prayers had gone unanswered. My warnings ignored. Tarn did not listen. Laina would not stop.

So I went where I had been told.

And they were waiting.

The clearing looked like any other. Moss, moonlight, the smell of damp earth. But the two figures standing there made it sacred in its own way.

One wore the crimson and gold of the Church, his cowl shadowing his features but his posture proud, unshakable. Authority clung to him like a mantle.

The other stood half in shadow, draped in dark leathers, a star-shaped pendant glinting at his throat—split neatly down the middle. Even at a glance, I knew what it was.

The Sons of the Hollow Star.

"You came," the priest said. His voice carried no surprise. He had known I would.

"I said I would," I replied, though my mouth was dry.

The Son tilted his head, his eyes gleaming in the dim light. "Tarn trusts you. The others too. That trust is... useful. You've done well."

I bristled. "I haven't lied to them."

"No," the priest said smoothly. "You've been faithful. That's why you're here. Because you see what they will not."

He stepped closer, and his voice dropped lower. "You see that Tarn has drifted. That Laina has led him astray."

The words landed like stones. I didn't argue. Couldn't.

"She was meant to be his handler," the priest continued. "Chosen to watch him, to temper him, to ensure his obedience. But she's failed. Instead of holding him to the Flame, she comforts him. She weakens him. Her heart is his now, when it should have been the Flame's."

"She breaks her vows," I whispered, the words tasting bitter and right all at once.

The Son smiled faintly. "She breaks more than vows. She breaks his destiny. Tarn was meant to serve. Instead, he rebels. And rebellion cannot be tolerated."

The forest seemed to press closer around us, heavy with the weight of his words.

The priest's eyes gleamed as he studied me, like he was waiting to see if I would balk. But I didn't. I couldn't. Every word he spoke rang true, a truth I had already whispered to myself in the dark when no one could hear.

"She weakens him," I said again, steadier this time.

The Son stepped closer. His pendant caught a thin sliver of moonlight, its jagged split casting a crooked reflection on his chest.

"And when he falters, he'll take the rest of you with him. Brannick is too blind to see it. You, though—you still remember your vows."

The priest inclined his head as though in benediction. "The Flame rewards those who are faithful. Those who keep their vows, even when others forget. You've been chosen, Selara. You will be rewarded for your obedience."

The promise curled around me like firelight, equal parts warmth and burn. "Rewarded how?" My voice came softer than I intended, betraying the hunger beneath the words.

The priest's lips curved in something between a smile and a sneer. "The Church has ways of raising its truest servants. Higher forms. Winged forms. Do you understand?"

Seraphim. The word bloomed unspoken in the air between us. My heart stuttered.

Ever since I was a girl, sitting in the pews, I had gazed up at the tapestries of the Seraphim—beings of holy fire, winged and radiant, set above all others as chosen vessels of the Flame. Untouchable. Perfect.

"I..." I tried to shape the word, but my throat constricted.

"You doubt yourself," the Son said smoothly, "because you are still mired in the mortal way of thinking. But your faith is not unnoticed. You came here. That is proof enough."

The priest stepped forward, placing a gloved hand lightly on my shoulder. "Serve faithfully, Selara. And when the time comes, you will be remade. You will transcend what they are—what she is." His tone hardened on that last word. "While Laina is punished for her betrayal, you will ascend."

My heart thundered. For a moment I imagined it—the wings, the fire, the certainty that I was right, and more than that, chosen.

"But Tarn..." The name slipped from me before I could stop it.

The priest's expression didn't shift. "Tarn will meet his fate. He was never meant to stray from the path. His failure is his own. He cannot be saved."

"Then why send us against that creature tomorrow?" I asked, the words rushing out. "Why order us into a tomb crawling with—whatever it is?"

The Son chuckled. The sound was quiet, but it raised the hairs on my arms. "Because the Flame requires it. Tarn has already failed in his duties, and the Embersworn cannot afford weakness. His path ends in that tomb. Yours does not."

It all snapped into place, terrible and clear. Tarn wasn't meant to survive. Brannick, perhaps, if his strength carried him. But Tarn and Laina? No. They were being led to slaughter, punished for their disobedience.

And I... I was being spared.

"You won't let them kill me?" My voice came smaller than I liked.

The priest shook his head. "No harm will come to you. Not from the Flame. When the battle begins, stay near. The agents of the Church will ensure you are preserved. You need only let fate run its course."

"And Laina?" I asked before I could stop myself.

"She will be dealt with," the priest said coldly. "Alive, if possible. The Flame has punishments worse than death for those who betray their vows."

A shiver coursed through me, half horror, half vindication.

The Son leaned forward, his voice a blade. "Do not let her weakness become yours. When you see Tarn fall, when you see her stripped of everything—remember what we promised. Remember what you will become."

His eyes glowed faintly in the dark, or maybe it was only my imagination. "Seraphim," he whispered, the word coiling like smoke around my ears.

The fire in my chest burned hotter, searing away the last of my hesitation. I bowed my head.

"I'll do as I'm told," I said.

The priest's hand squeezed my shoulder once before letting go. "Good. The Flame sees your faith. Soon, you will see its reward."

The Son stepped back into the shadow of the trees, his pendant catching the moon one last time. "Go back now. They must not know. Tomorrow will prove your loyalty."

I stood alone for a long moment, listening to the silence. The forest felt changed somehow, heavier. My knees trembled, but it wasn't fear anymore. It was anticipation.

When I turned back, the path seemed longer than it should have been. My steps dragged, though the voices of my companions carried faintly through the trees. Brannick laughing. Laina humming as she fletched arrows. Tarn's low murmur, steady and calm.

The sound of them should have comforted me. Instead, it pressed against my ears like weight. They were blind, all of them. Tarn, leading with quiet certainty but no obedience. Laina, breaking vows for love. Brannick, too loyal to question.

And me.

The only one who still remembered what we swore.

I stepped into the clearing. The fire burned low, shadows playing across their faces. None of them looked at me, not right away. Laina leaned closer to Tarn, whispering something that made Brannick laugh again. Tarn's expression barely moved, but I saw the faintest flicker of warmth in his eyes when he looked at her.

It should have hurt. Instead, it only hardened my resolve. Tomorrow, it would end. Tomorrow, the Flame would cleanse what was weak.

I folded my hands in my lap and lowered my gaze, letting the firelight lick across my face, hiding the storm beneath. They thought I was one of them still. They thought we were four against the world.

They were wrong.

When morning came, the Flame would take what it was owed.

And I... I would rise.

Chapter 26

THE BROKEN ANGEL

Cass

We slid along the balcony toward the far stair, keeping low behind the stone rail. The laboratory breathed its awful rhythm—pumps, valves, the faint pulse of Aether through crystal capillaries—while the Archflame studied his circle as though it might applaud.

Vale didn't look up. He didn't need to.

"You can stop skulking," he said, voice carrying cleanly to the rafters. "Shadows don't make you smaller. Only harder to measure."

We froze. Tarn's hand tightened on his shield grip. Eliza went very still beside me. Vaelen's jaw set, a small click as he thumbed the Arcblade's activator.

Vale turned at last, not to us but slightly, as if addressing the room and thereby everything in it. His eyes were unremarkable, which somehow made them worse.

"Silver paladin," he said mildly. "Your talent for arriving late to the necessary lesson persists."

Tarn didn't answer.

Vale's gaze slipped across our hiding place and moved on. He gestured to the hooded figure at his left. The iron collar at her throat gave a faint pulse, violet threading through the metal like veins waking.

"Come," he murmured, and the woman—Laina—stood obediently at his side without lifting her head.

The word lodged under my ribs. Laina. Alive. Tuned to someone else's will.

Vale smoothed a sleeve as if we weren't there at all and then inclined his head toward the winged figure on his right.

"Seraphim," he said, with a warmth that made the title colder. "Attend to the uninvited."

The woman turned her face toward us—no, not a woman any longer, not exactly—and the balcony's shadow seemed to fold a fraction under the attention. Wings unlatched from her back in a slow, deliberate arc, panes of glass and light sliding against one another with a sound like thin crystal singing. Fractured radiance webbed through each vane, violet veins laced with paler fire. Where the edges passed air, hair-fine lines drew themselves there and vanished—cuts too small to bleed.

Selara.

I'd seen her smile in a photograph tucked in Tarn's armor. Whole. Human. Standing at his side like a promise. Now the seams showed where that face had been fitted to something else. Her eyes held too much shine to be natural; her cheekbones were glass-smooth; fissures of light traced the hollows at her temples. Her voice, when it came, was two notes at once—hers and the echo of something that had learned speech from a mirror.

"Tarn," she said.

It wasn't a greeting. It was a variable in an equation.

For a fraction of a heartbeat he swayed. Then the shield lifted another inch. "Selara."

Vale's mouth curved. "I leave you in capable hands." He touched the collar at Laina's neck; it flared and settled. "We have farther to walk, my dear. The heart will not wait."

He turned his back on us and stepped off the dais. The circle's runes dimmed on cue. Laina followed, not because she chose to but because the collar chose for her. A segment of wall unsealed into an arch at their approach, stone retracting like water parting. Vale and Laina passed through. The arch refroze, seamless.

"Stop him," Vaelen hissed.

"After," Tarn said, and that was all—decision hammered flat and set to cool—but his eyes never left the winged thing between us and the door.

Selara moved.

She didn't leap or run. She simply crossed the distance at a pace the body shouldn't have, a skater sliding from one footprint of light to the next. Shards shed from her wings as she came, feather-thin slivers that kissed stone and left white lines smoking.

"Down!" I snapped, and we dropped as the first volley scythed overhead, featherlets stitching the balustrade into lace. Stone powdered my hair. Vaelen flung his arm up; two shards rang off the Arcblàde's guard and bit sparks from the floor.

We hit the stair as the second volley came in tight. Tarn met it head-on. Feathers screamed across his shield, scoring bright furrows in the steel; the last one clipped the shield rim and shaved a clean notch out of the step beside my foot.

I slid under the rail, shadows pooling fast and eager around my ankles. The darkness here liked me too much; it came as if called and didn't argue. One step and the world twisted around the hinge of a column's shadow; I came up behind her, daggers ready, driving for the seam where wing joined back—

She wasn't there.

Light flared, a pane of wing flicking like a blade to meet empty air, and the next instant she stood three paces to my left, head tilted, listening to the place I'd been. The afterimage of my movement hung a breath too long, like she could see the echo trail.

She turned to follow it and I stabbed sideways into the brighter seam at her ribs. The dagger bit—glass and flesh together—and heat crawled up the blade, violet-white and hungry. I wrenched free before it could climb to my fingers. No blood. No steam. Just light leaking like thin syrup, then sealing as if the wound regretted itself.

She lifted a hand and flicked two fingers. Feathers wrote themselves out of her wing with the movement, curving toward me with terrible grace.

Shadow, step, twist. The last one still clipped my shoulder. It burned like polished ice. I hit the floor in a crouch, teeth bared, left sleeve smoking.

"Eliza!" Tarn's shout cut a clean path through the din.

The Animist was already moving, a string of low syllables under her breath. She stamped, palms to stone, and the floor answered like muscle. Ridges heaved up and rolled, a breaking wave of earth and grit that boomed into Selara's legs.

For a heartbeat, the Seraphim stumbled. The glass vanes flared to catch her balance, light feathering the air like frost. Tarn took the opening and drove, shield-first; the impact rang through my teeth. He pushed her back three steps, hammer grazing her shoulder with a blow that would have smashed an ogre's collarbone.

She didn't break. She didn't even grunt. The wing snapped around, hard as a gate, and hammered Tarn across the exposed side. The blow wasn't weight alone—it carried a shove of Aether that slid under the armor and tried to tear him off his feet. He skidded, boots carving bright arcs in the dust, and righted before the second strike could take his head.

Vaelen flashed past me, Arcblade flaring. He took a two-hand grip and carved a diagonal that should have been impossible to block. Selara didn't block. She slipped and turned the cut into a clot of lightning caught in the lattice of her wing, then threw it back with a twitch of her wrist. The bolt screamed by Vaelen's cheek and tore a strip out of the balcony rail that hadn't been there a second ago.

"New rule," he said through his teeth. "No giving the glass angel free power."

"Working on it," I snapped, and dragged the shadows up like a cloak.

I set a foot, picked a seam along the floor's edge, and stepped through to her flank—again, again—fast enough to make the edges of the room wobble. She tracked me in partials, correcting half a fraction too late each time, a predatory tilt to her head that said she was saving the true speed for when it mattered.

I threw Umbral Chains.

The first length cleared my palm with a soft sound, dark links knitting out of my own shadow. They coiled for her ankles and— caught. For a heartbeat. The binding bit like tar hardening in cold. The wings flared, panes brightening until my eyes watered, and the chains snapped with a sound like frozen iron breaking.

She looked at me then, fully, as if she'd been attending to homework and finally found the interesting part of the lesson.

"Little mirror-thief," she said, that doubled voice ringing exactly wrong. "You should not have taken what isn't yours."

My daggers were already moving, point down now, and I met her look with my own. "Come take it back."

She obliged.

The wing cut down and I met it with crossed steel. The impact was worse than weight—resonance shivering through the blades and rattling my elbows bone-deep. I slid with it, turned the force past me, and felt the edge kiss a braid of hair instead of my throat.

Tarn was there in the notch left by my sidestep, shield punching forward, hammer overhand. The strike landed—hard—and cracked something under the chest-seam. Lines ran from the fracture, light leaking through like water through a split bowl.

For an instant her face was only human. Just Selara, caught between pain and rage, mouth parted on a small, honest sound. Tarn faltered a finger's width. Then the light surged, bright as a kiln, sealing the crack and scalding the rim of his hammer-hand.

"Move!" I shouted, and jerked him aside as three feathers hit where he'd been. They pinned a hole in the floor the size of a bucket, edges fused to glass. Heat rolled off them in waves.

Eliza's voice rose, sharper now, teeth bared. Roots tore up through stone as if the floor had always been a thin skin over a forest. They wound for Selara's calves and knitted fast, bark blackening where Aether burned it but holding.

Vaelen lunged, blade humming. He laid a perfect cut across the bright seam of her sternum. Light geysered out—too bright—and licked up his forearm through the guard. He shouted and ripped free, smoke coiling from leather.

Selara's wings arced wide.

Every vane lit end to end, a false halo snapping into shape. The air tilted. The nearest glassware across the lab blew out in a rush of glittering dust. Shards whispered down like ash.

She rose, not with a leap but with a patient, inevitable lift, feathers vibrating at a pitch that set my molars aching. Violet-white motes rolled off her and drifted to the floor, each one eating a clean pit into the stone before fading.

Vaelen spat, wiped his mouth with the back of his hand, and glared up. "I really hate flying things."

"Keep her grounded," Tarn said.

"How would you like me to−"

I didn't hear the rest. Feather-light slashes pursued the sound of his voice, and he had to dive behind a bolted table to avoid being stitched to it. I Shadow Stepped to the table's far side, reappeared behind a crate, then into the stair's hollow−three moves in less than a blink, no drag, no limit tugging at my ribs. The world lurched like it disapproved.

"Left wing hinge," I called. "The seam that cracked−hit it again."

Tarn grunted acknowledgment. His shield took another volley; the rim was a ruined smile now. He tossed it from the burned hand to the other without ceremony and went forward anyway.

Selara descended like a verdict.

The first touch of her foot to stone sent a ring of heat skating out in all directions. The second touch turned it into a grid. Eliza had to leap the lines; the places they crossed fused to glass. Tarn slid through the only gap clean enough to bear weight and slammed the shield into her knee. It wasn't enough. She barely dipped.

Fine. If she wouldn't drop for weight, we'd make her slip.

265

I hurled the last of my chains, not at her legs but at the wing nearest the lab's broken glass. The links bit and dragged the pane across a glitter-drift, scoring it with a thousand tiny scratches. The next time she snapped that wing, the cut pane screamed and faltered for a fraction. Tarn used the breath-width and planted his hammer in the hinge.

The crack jumped again. Wider.

Light poured through the fault in sheeting radiance—and then flared hotter, trying to weld itself shut.

"Vaelen!" I yelled.

"On it!"

He came in from the blind side, Arcblade a clean line. The cut hit the same hinge. The wing's lattice fractured. Fragments rang away like bells.

Selara screamed.

Not a roar. Not an animal's sound. Glass breaking in a long, drawn-out note that seemed to come from everywhere at once. I flinched as hairline lines raced along the laboratory's viewing panes, spiderwebbing the world.

She folded inward, one knee dropping, wing hitching at a wrong angle.

"Press!" Tarn roared.

We did.

And that's when a voice drifted from beyond the sealed arch, mild and far too pleased: "Steady now, Seraphim. Their lesson is not yet complete."

The voice carried like smoke, sliding through stone as though the walls wanted to bear it for him. Vale. Calm. Certain.

Selara's head jerked toward the sound. Whatever human softness had flickered through the crack in her form was gone. Her eyes blazed glass-bright, and the broken wing unfurled again with a surge of light that nearly blinded me. She wasn't faltering—she was burning hotter, fueled by his command.

"Eliza, brace!" Tarn barked, throwing his shield up just in time.

The Seraphim slammed her wings together, and the impact birthed a shockwave. The entire balcony shuddered. Dust and shards of broken glass cascaded down around us. Eliza dug her hands into the stone, chanting low and furious—roots and thornvines burst from cracks, curling up to anchor the platform before it could collapse. Vaelen caught my arm, dragging me back from the edge as another section of railing disintegrated under the pressure.

"She's ramping up!" I shouted, covering my ears as the wing-shards keened through the air.

"No kidding," Vaelen snapped, his Arcblade flaring to life again.

Selara lunged for Tarn. Faster than before. Too fast. Her glass feathers carved streaks of violet fire through the air, each swipe coming with a precision that should have been impossible for a body still bound by bone and flesh. Tarn met her strike with his shield—but the force of it blasted him sideways into a rib-column. The crack of impact echoed, and his shield bent almost double.

"Tarn!" My throat tore on the cry.

He staggered upright, shaking the ruined shield from his arm. The hand beneath it was bloody, blistered. He didn't even glance down at it—just shifted his hammer to his good grip and braced for another rush.

She didn't give him the chance.

Selara turned on me.

The wings folded forward like blades of a guillotine. I Shadow Stepped on instinct, reappearing behind her, daggers flashing for another strike. This time I aimed high, slashing for her throat seam. The steel skittered against something harder than glass. The vibration rattled my bones.

She spun with me, too fast again, the fractured wing trailing sparks and shards. I ducked low, rolled, and felt the air shear above my scalp. If I'd hesitated a breath longer, my head would've been gone.

"Cass!" Eliza's voice cut through, urgent. "Keep her busy!"

Easy for her to say.

I Shadow Stepped again, zig-zagging between her attacks, every dodge a hair's breadth from disaster. She anticipated the rhythm, forcing me to burn each teleport faster and faster until my lungs felt hollow, until my skin prickled with the overuse.

Selara raised both wings.

The light surged brighter than ever before. I realized too late what she was doing.

"Tarn!" I screamed. "Cover–"

The wings snapped outward, and a storm of razor shards detonated in every direction.

The air filled with a thousand knives.

Tarn dove in front of me, hammer raised, the glow of his magic blazing hotter than it had any right to. The storm screamed against him, shards hissing away from the barrier of light he forced into being. His teeth were gritted, sweat pouring down his face.

The cost of that spell hit me like a punch. He was burning his strength just to keep me alive.

"Don't–" I grabbed his arm. "Don't waste it on me!"

He didn't look at me. Didn't answer. Just held.

The shards slowed, the storm thinning into a rain of glitter and ash. Tarn collapsed to one knee as the glow guttered out, his chest heaving. His armor smoked at the seams.

Selara landed, graceful even with the cracked wing dragging faintly at her side. Her glasslike eyes fixed on Tarn. Not pity. Not mercy. Just inevitability.

"Get up," she said, voice doubled and warped. "You were meant to rise higher. Why do you crawl?"

Something in Tarn's jaw clenched, but he didn't rise.

Vaelen barreled in then, Arcblade raised high. "Don't touch him!"

Lightning flared, striking across her torso in a shower of sparks. She reeled—finally reeled—back a half-step. Eliza followed, hands raised, chanting louder. The earth beneath Selara buckled and split, vines lashing her ankles, trying to pin her in place.

"Cass!" Vaelen shouted over the roar. "Take Tarn and GO!"

"What?" My daggers trembled in my grip. "We can't leave you—"

Eliza's voice cut like steel. "Vale's getting away with Laina! This is your fight, not ours! We'll hold her!"

My throat closed. The sight of Selara's wings tearing free of Eliza's vines, shards shredding the air around Vaelen—leaving them here felt like abandoning them to die.

"Cass!" Vaelen barked again. His eyes found mine, steady despite the lightning leaping around him. "Trust us."

Tarn struggled up beside me, his face pale but his eyes fierce. His hand clamped down on my shoulder. "He's right."

"But—"

"No buts. We go." His gaze locked on mine, unyielding. "They can handle her. Vale can't get farther. Not with Laina."

My heart hammered against my ribs. Selara's screech split the air behind us, glass and fire and rage. Eliza transformed in a flash of light, fur sprouting, badger-form slamming low into Selara's shins to stagger her just long enough for Vaelen's blade to crash down again.

"GO!" they both shouted in unison.

Tarn didn't give me time to argue. His good hand seized mine, and together we sprinted for the arch Vale had vanished through. The stone shivered, but Tarn's hammer struck it hard enough to break the seam back open.

Light flared. Beyond the arch, shadows twisted, beckoning us deeper.

I threw one last look over my shoulder.

Eliza, half-shifted, claws digging furrows into stone as she wrestled Selara's arm aside. Vaelen, lightning arcing from his blade, eyes locked on me for a single heartbeat before he swung.

Then the stone sealed behind us.

And Tarn and I were alone, plunging after Vale.

Chapter 27

WHERE SHADOWS BREAK

Cass

The arch sealed behind us with a grinding finality, stone swallowing the last echoes of the battle. For a heartbeat, I swore I could still hear them—Vaelen's voice shouting something sharp, Eliza's magic cracking like thunder. Then nothing but the labyrinth's silence.

I wanted to look back. To believe the others were right there behind us. But the arch was already gone, replaced by unbroken wall. No going back.

Only forward.

The corridor ahead pulsed faintly with violet veins that crawled like roots through the stone. The air pressed damp and heavy, close to the skin. Tarn walked a step in front, hammer low, every line of him set. He carried no shield now—Selara had shattered it, reduced iron and faith alike to useless fragments.

Without it, he seemed both smaller and larger at once. No barrier to hide behind, no wall to interpose. Just Tarn. Flesh, bone, and stubborn resolve.

He didn't speak right away. The weight of silence stretched, broken only by our footsteps.

Finally he said, voice even, "They can handle her."

It wasn't for me. It was for himself.

I swallowed, my throat raw. "You don't know that."

"I do." He didn't slow, didn't look back. "They're strong. Together, stronger still. Selara... she was never meant to be fought alone."

The way he said her name twisted something deep in my chest. Not longing, not tenderness. Grief.

I brushed my thumb against the bracelet on my wrist. Cold. Always cold. I hated the weight of it, the reminder that he'd pressed it into my hand before we stepped through. A charm, he'd said. But Tarn wasn't a man who believed in charms.

The corridor widened into a chamber. No ornament, just function: high ribs of stone, floor inlaid with crude channels that glowed faintly violet, funneling light toward the arch ahead. The air tasted metallic, sharp at the back of my tongue.

Tarn stopped at the threshold, staring through the archway. I came up beside him.

Vale waited within.

The Archflame stood at the center of the chamber beyond, hands folded behind his back like he was greeting guests, not intruders. His robes draped flawless, his hair catching the glow with silver edges. He didn't move as we appeared. Didn't need to. The space was his, and he knew it.

At his side, Laina.

Her hood was gone now. Her bow lowered but ready, the iron collar at her throat pulsing with a steady violet beat. Her eyes were empty things—once bright, now smothered. She stood too still, like a puppet waiting for a tug.

My stomach twisted.

Beside me, Tarn inhaled sharp, then held it. His gauntleted fist tightened around the hammer's grip until the leather creaked.

Vale's smile was measured. "Ah. The prodigal knight. And the shadow he keeps at his heel."

His voice slid across the chamber, smooth as oil. Tarn didn't answer. Didn't raise his hammer.

And I realized—he had nothing to raise. No shield. No barrier. Just himself, bare against everything that waited in this room.

For the first time, I wondered if we'd made a mistake stepping through that arch.

But Tarn took a step forward.

So I did too.

Vale didn't rush to meet us. He just stood there, calm as a priest at a sermon, as though he'd been expecting this exact moment all along.

"You survived Selara," he said, voice rich with satisfaction. "Impressive. Few mortals could have withstood her rebirth."

I clenched my jaw. "She wasn't reborn. She was broken. Twisted into something she never chose."

The words slipped out before I thought them through. Vale's gaze slid toward me, sharp and amused. "Ah. The rogue finds her tongue. Tell me, girl—do you think choice matters? Every saint, every martyr, every godling—none of them ever chose their path. They were shaped by need. By faith. By fire. Selara only embraced what she was always meant to become."

"Meant?" I spat. "By who? You?"

Tarn's hand rose slightly—not to silence me, but to steady. His posture was iron, but I saw the way his eyes burned. He hadn't looked at Vale once, not really. His gaze kept flicking back to Laina.

She stood beside the Archflame like an empty vessel, bow clutched loosely in her fingers. The violet veins across her collar pulsed in time with the glow in the stone channels at her feet. Like she was tied into the room itself.

Tarn finally spoke, low and steady: "Let her go."

Vale chuckled. "Always so direct. So noble. Tell me, Tarn—did you ever tire of carrying the weight of others' choices on your shoulders? You couldn't save your party in the tomb. You couldn't save your village. You couldn't even save your rank. And now you demand that I—"

"Let her go," Tarn repeated.

Something cracked in his voice, just barely. I felt it in my chest like a bruise.

Vale's smile didn't falter. He lifted a hand, and the collar around Laina's neck flared brighter, violet light spilling across her skin. Her head jerked slightly, like the command had tightened its leash. She raised the bow in one fluid motion, arrow already nocked.

I froze.

Tarn didn't. He stepped forward, hammer raised—not high, not wild, but low, ready. No shield to block the arrow if she loosed. No protection but himself.

"Tarn," I whispered, panic clawing up my throat. "She's not in control."

"I know," he said. His voice didn't shake. "Which means she's not the enemy."

Vale's voice dropped, oily and smug. "But she is your executioner."

The bowstring drew taut, the arrow's tip glowing faintly violet. My pulse slammed in my ears. Every instinct screamed to Shadow Step, to vanish, to *do something*. But Tarn only planted his feet, steady as stone, and stared straight at her.

"Laina," he said softly.

Her hands trembled. Just once. The collar's light surged brighter, forcing her still.

Vale turned his head slightly, studying Tarn as though he were a particularly fascinating insect. "You see her hesitation? Even now she struggles. Do you know what that means, knight?"

Tarn's grip tightened on his hammer. He said nothing.

Vale's smile spread wider. "It means she still remembers you. That's what makes this beautiful."

My hands shook around my daggers. I wanted to scream. To leap across the room and drive steel through Vale's throat. But Tarn didn't move. He stood there without a shield, without a prayer, staring at the woman he once loved as she raised an arrow to his heart.

And I realized this wasn't about power anymore. Not Vale's, not Laina's, not even Tarn's. It was about choice.

I took one step closer to Tarn's side, heart hammering. "Then let's give her one," I whispered.

Laina's bow sang as another arrow split the air. I Shadow Stepped, reappearing at her side, my dagger flashing. The strike clipped her bow, sparks skittering, the shot veering wide into the stone.

She whirled, her movements too sharp, too perfect—every strike driven by the collar's thrumming glow. She didn't fire again immediately; instead, she wielded the bow like a staff, battering me back step by step. The wood cracked against my dagger, each blow rattling up my arm.

"Laina!" I shouted, breath tearing at my throat. "Fight it! This isn't you!"

But her face was empty, her eyes glassy with violet light. She swung, faster than I could dodge cleanly. I rolled under the arc, slashing at her leg. My blade bit, shallow, just enough to stagger her. And for a heartbeat, I saw it—a flicker of something human in her eyes. Pain. Recognition.

Then Vale's voice cut through the chamber, silk turned to steel.

"Enough games. End it."

The collar flared, searing bright. Laina's head snapped toward me, bowstring drawing in one smooth, flawless motion.

"Shit—" I dove sideways. The arrow burned past, scorching the skin of my arm where it grazed me. The smell of singed leather filled my nose. I hit the ground hard, rolled, came up with another dagger in hand.

She was already nocking another arrow, her movements too fast, too certain.

Vale stood behind her, hands folded as if he were presiding over a play instead of a fight. "Do you see now, little rogue? The power of obedience. Even love bends beneath the right hand when it is guided."

"Go to hell," I spat, launching my dagger.

Laina twisted unnaturally, the blade grazing her shoulder instead of striking true. The bowstring thrummed again, and I barely Shadow Stepped in time, the arrow splitting the air where my chest had been.

She pressed harder, driving me toward the far wall. My lungs burned. My thigh screamed with every dodge. Shadows rippled at my heels, answering me, but even they felt stretched thin against her relentless pace.

Another arrow hissed past. I skidded behind a pillar, chest heaving.

I risked a glance—and froze. Tarn.

He was still across the chamber, hammer in hand, gaze locked on Laina. He hadn't moved.

"Cass!" His voice rang like an order, cutting through the chaos.

I staggered back into the open. Laina's eyes tracked me instantly, bowstring pulled taut, arrow veined in violet fire. She had me dead to rights.

Vale's smile sharpened, cruel and hungry. "Now, Laina. Strike true."

The air split with a crack of sound and light—too fast to scream, too late to dodge. The arrow shone like a shard of starlight, veined in aether, its trail bending the air behind it. My eyes locked onto it—on the way it burned, on the way it *hungered*—and I knew I wouldn't move in time.

Then Tarn was there.

He didn't shout. Didn't hesitate.

Just *moved*.

One hand raised. A shimmer of golden magic flared across his shoulders, a familiar shield spell I'd seen only once before—against the basilisk. Only this time, it cracked on impact.

The arrow pierced his chest with a sound I'll never forget.

I screamed.

Tarn stumbled forward, his knees striking stone, breath torn from him like pages ripped from a book. The glow around the impact pulsed once... then dimmed.

"No," I gasped, catching him before he could fall. "No, no, no—Tarn—!"

He leaned into me, his weight a dead thing in my arms. Blood warmed the inside of his breastplate. His hand found mine—callused and shaking, but steady where it mattered.

Behind us, the archflame said something I didn't hear. Laina stood motionless on the steps, bow lowered, eyes blank and distant. Aether glowed faintly around her collar.

"I told you not to be reckless," I choked out, pressing my hand to the wound, as if I could keep him here. "You *idiot*, why would you do that?"

His lips twitched into a tired smile. "I'm not losing the woman I love... *twice*."

My throat closed. The world blurred. I couldn't breathe.

"You—" My voice cracked. "You love me?"

"I do," he whispered, brushing his fingers along my wrist where the silver bracelet sat—tarnished from the dungeon, still warm from my skin. "I lied when I gave you this. Said it was a luck charm."

"What is it?"

His magic sparked, faint and flickering, as he pressed his palm to the charm. "An escape ward. One-use. Keyed to your soulprint. It only works on the wearer."

"No." My hands clenched around his. "Tarn, don't. We can still—"

"It's too late for me," he said, voice steady now. "But not for you."

The bracelet began to glow, threads of silver weaving upward like smoke caught in moonlight.

"I should've told you sooner," I whispered, trembling. "I... I love you too. I—"

But the magic took hold before the words finished.

A sudden pull yanked through me, not from the outside, but from the very *core* of me. Light and heat wrapped around my senses, and the world collapsed into a tunnel of rushing stars and sound.

The last thing I saw was Tarn's eyes—calm, resolute, *burning* with love.

Then I was gone.

The sky changed. The wind changed. The scent of blood and ash vanished.

I hit my knees on cold stone.

My breath caught as I looked up—staring at the high walls of the cathedral. Alone.

The bracelet dimmed.

And Tarn wasn't with me.

A NOTE TO THE READER

Thank you for walking beside Cass and Tarn through the shadows. Stories like this live only as long as they're shared, and every reader who turns these pages becomes part of that journey.

If *Where Shadows Break* moved you, I would be deeply grateful if you left a review. Even a few words make a world of difference – helping other readers discover the book and keeping Cass's story alive.

The adventure doesn't end here. Cass's path is only beginning, and the world of *Aetherbound* still holds countless secrets waiting to be uncovered.

Until then–thank you for reading.

– J. L. Athey